PRAISE FOR MARY LYDON SIMONSEN

"Using her creative license, Simonsen
Austen's beloved characters... giv

"Ms. Simonsen is an accomplished and skillful writer... she does have a clever way with satire and irony which I feel Ms. Austen herself would have admired."

—*Historical Novel Review*

"I found the writing absolutely alluring. It's witty and full of character... A wonderful sense of adventure and intrigue."

—*Literary Litter*

"With a fast-reading, engaging style, [Simonsen] brings a new and enjoyable immediacy to Jane Austen's most popular novel."

—*Linda Banche Romance Author*

"Fresh and different... Mary Lydon Simonsen has taken a beloved classic and made it a new historical romance."

—*Romance Fiction on Suite101*

"Simonsen always brings a new perspective and humor to the stories we already love."

—*Books Like Breathing*

"Fun, fresh, and enormously entertaining."

—*Luxury Reading*

Mr Darcy's Bite

MARY LYDON SIMONSEN

sourcebooks
landmark

Published by Sourcebooks Landmark, an imprint of Sourcebooks, Inc.
P.O. Box 4410, Naperville, Illinois 60567-4410
(630) 961-3900
FAX: (630) 961-2168
www.sourcebooks.com

Library of Congress Cataloging-in-Publication Data

Simonsen, Mary Lydon.
  Mr. Darcy's bite / by Mary Lydon Simonsen.
     p. cm.
  1. Darcy, Fitzwilliam (Fictitious character)—Fiction. 2. Bennet, Elizabeth
(Fictitious character)—Fiction. 3. Werewolves—Fiction. 4. England—
Fiction. I. Austen, Jane, 1775-1817. Pride and prejudice. II. Title.
  PS3619.I56287M7 2011
  813'.6—dc23
                        2011022412

Printed and bound in the United States of America
VP 10 9 8 7 6 5 4 3 2 1

To all my Jane Austen fan fiction friends for reading
my tale and for providing valuable comments
and insights that enriched this story

PROLOGUE

The Black Forest, Grand Duchy of Baden
Summer of 1798

M R. DARCY, IT WILL be necessary to remove all the baggage in order to lighten the load," Metcalf, the Darcy driver, explained. "The wheels are about six inches deep into the mud. Fortunately, we have a full moon, and, eventually, we will be able to free the carriage."

"Since we have no other choice, we must do what is required so that we may continue on our journey," Mr. Darcy said, looking at the mired wheels. "Herr Beck tells me that they have had a very wet autumn in the Schwarzwald. I believe they have had more rain here than we did in England. Hopefully, Mrs. Darcy and Miss Darcy are enjoying more favorable weather in Baden than William and I did in Stuttgart. By the way, where is William?"

"I don't think the meal we had at the inn agreed with him, sir. Herr Beck went down the road with him so that he might relieve himself."

"Again? My poor son. His mother and I have always thought of William as having a cast-iron stomach, but it seems that German food does not agree with the boy."

There was no doubt that German food did not agree with thirteen-year-old Fitzwilliam Darcy. This was the third time he had found it necessary to go into the woods, and it was a source of embarrassment for the young man. Although everyone had eaten the same food at the inn, he was the only one who was experiencing any discomfort. Herr Beck, the man whom they had hired in Stuttgart as a guide and translator, had found the situation amusing and had been teasing him about it. However, William was not amused, and when he felt another cramp, he walked farther down the road to get away from his tormentor and went into the woods alone.

Having performed the unpleasant task several times, the young Darcy was now an expert on the best position, and he used a large tree to support his back. He had been there a few minutes when he felt something brush against him. Believing it to be the foliage, he reached out to push it out of the way, and in doing so, felt something scratch him near his hip. He quickly looked about him, and what he saw terrified him. A wolf, with blazing blue eyes, was standing less than three feet away from the crouching boy.

Every instinct told William not to move or to call out, as either might cause the animal to lunge, and since he had removed his heavy overcoat, he had nothing to protect himself from any bite. But no defensive action was necessary. The wolf lay down and started to whimper before turning on her back to expose her belly. At Pemberley, the Darcy estate, there were easily a dozen dogs, and he was familiar with this behavior. A canine only did this when it was being overpowered by a more aggressive dog or if it had done something wrong. Because William was hidden by the tree, the wolf had not seen him, and the scratch had been accidental. It almost seemed as if she were apologizing for their encounter.

William retreated. But from a distance, the wolf followed him. With his heart pounding in his chest, he finally reached the road and could see the men working on the carriage. Before going in search of his father, he took one last look down the road and saw the wolf standing in plain view. Because of the full moon, the road was lit up as if it were daytime, leaving the female lupine completely exposed. Without thinking, William waved to her, and it was only then that she returned to the woods. The only conclusion he could draw was that she wanted to make sure that he was safe. But what kind of wolf did that?

CHAPTER 1

ELIZABETH WAS IN HER room reading when Mrs. Hill came upstairs to announce that Mr. Darcy was in the parlor and would like to see her. This news generated little excitement. Mr. Darcy had been in her parlor on many occasions, always with the same request: "May I ask that you join me for a walk in the garden?"

The first dozen times, Lizzy had been truly excited because it was obvious that Mr. Darcy liked her very much. The next few times, she was equally flattered by his requests because she was convinced that all of this attention, paid over the course of the six months since Jane and Charles had married, was leading to a request that they begin a formal courtship. But then some urgent business would call him back to Pemberley, and he would be gone for a week or, as had happened in June, for the entire month. When he returned, he would be back in the Bennet parlor as happy as a puppy to see his mistress. But she had tired of this routine, and today she was going to tell him so.

Lizzy went into the parlor and found Mr. Darcy standing in front of the window. The outside light served to create a silhouette of the master of Pemberley, and it was a very flattering one: tall, with wavy hair, a strong chin, broad chest, narrow waist, muscular thighs, and excellent calves. My goodness, he was a handsome man—and an excited one.

He nearly sprinted across the room to greet her. If the room had been as large as the parlor at Pemberley, she thought that he might have leapt over the tea table to get to her. There was never a lack of enthusiasm on his part when he did come calling, making his behavior all the more puzzling.

Mrs. Bennet, Kitty, and Mary remained in the parlor with Lizzy while Mr. Darcy, who was staying with the Bingleys, shared the latest news about Jane and Charles, including their decision to renew the lease on Netherfield Park. Without embarrassment, an unusual circumstance for a man discussing an expectant mother, he also shared that Jane was looking hale and hearty, and not showing any discomfort in carrying "her lone offspring." This news was well received, earning smiles all around, and after some additional small talk, the superfluous Bennets rose and departed.

As on every other occasion, Mrs. Bennet was convinced that "today was the day" when Mr. Darcy would ask Lizzy to be his wife, and she gave her daughter a knowing smile on her way out. With the door left slightly ajar, Lizzy listened for the retreating footsteps of her mother and sisters. After she was sure that Mama was not eavesdropping, she turned to Mr. Darcy. "You said Jane was experiencing no difficulty in carrying 'her lone offspring.' That is a very peculiar way of phrasing it. One child is the rule, not the exception, Mr. Darcy."

"I imagine that did sound odd," he said, fidgeting. "Our Newfoundland recently had a litter. I guess that was in the back of my mind when I made that comment."

Lizzy nodded, but asked no questions about the furry arrivals at Pemberley. Although she usually took the lead in their conversations, she was of no mind to do so today. When the gentleman asked if they might go for a walk in the park, Lizzy stated that she preferred to remain indoors.

"But the weather is absolutely perfect for a brisk walk."

"Mr. Darcy, we have been fortunate on your many visits to have had good weather. However, I am not inclined to walk today. Maybe on your next visit or the one after that or the one after that, we may go for a walk."

"Elizabeth, you are out of sorts with me, and I do not blame you. I know my coming and going has been an irritant to you."

Yes, an irritant and inexplicable. Your excuses for your frequent absences never satisfy.

"But my purpose today is to invite you to Pemberley. My cousin, Anne de Bourgh, is coming with my sister from London, so that we might all go together." Mr. Darcy came and sat next to Lizzy on the sofa and took her hands in his. "If your parents approve, I would like to set out as soon as possible because there is something I would like to share with you, but I must do it at Pemberley."

Lizzy's mood altered immediately, and she was so bold as to kiss him on the cheek. But Mr. Darcy was even bolder, and he put his hand on her neck and brought her toward him. Her kiss was as wonderful as he had imagined it would be, and he could feel the heat rising. Reluctantly, he let her go, but whispered. "Everything will be decided at Pemberley. Will you come?" Lizzy went to the library to get her father's permission to go to Derbyshire with Mr. Darcy.

❧

Lizzy had already made the acquaintance of Anne de Bourgh during her visit with Charlotte Collins in Kent in the spring. After Mr. Darcy's departure from Rosings Park following his awful marriage proposal, Anne had called on Lizzy at the parsonage. She had made no attempt to defend the words her cousin had uttered on that dreadful afternoon but was very keen for Lizzy to hear about the Fitzwilliam Darcy she knew and loved. After listening to her recitation of Mr. Darcy's many virtues and kindnesses to Miss Darcy, Her Ladyship, and herself, Lizzy could feel the bulwark of her prejudices crumbling, and she immediately developed a fondness for the daughter of the insufferable Lady Catherine de Bourgh.

Lizzy's first meeting with Georgiana Darcy was at Jane and Charles's wedding. With her black hair and gray-green eyes, she was as beautiful as her brother was handsome. She stood a head taller than Lizzy, and her height accentuated her long elegant line. But there was much more to this lovely young woman than good looks and beautiful clothes. There was a graciousness in her manner and a kindness in her addresses that immediately drew the approval of all who met her, and Lizzy was very pleased that Mr. Darcy was eager to bring them together again and expressed his hope that they would become the best of friends. In that one statement, he revealed that he wanted to renew those attentions he had been paying to her during her visit to Pemberley before the sordid affair between Lydia and Wickham necessitated their separation.

Although complete opposites, Georgiana and Anne were very close—more friends than cousins. Anne loved Georgiana's enthusiasm for just about everything, while the young Miss Darcy admired her cousin's composure and grace. But the fragile Miss de Bourgh and the exuberant Georgiana did have one thing in common: They loved Fitzwilliam Darcy, and both had hinted that a union between William and Elizabeth would please them greatly.

On the journey to Derbyshire, their opinion of Elizabeth increased with each passing mile. From the couple's playful exchanges, it was obvious to Anne and Georgiana how well suited they were to each other. Lizzy frequently teased William and invited the two ladies to join in. He finally held his arms up in mock surrender.

"I don't have a chance," he said with the half smile Lizzy so loved. "Three against one and with nowhere to go," he said, looking out the carriage window at the passing countryside. "But be careful, ladies, when we stop at the inn, I might run into the woods to get away from you." He turned and winked at his sister and cousin, and they returned the wink with knowing smiles.

When Lizzy got out of the carriage at Pemberley, a brilliant harvest moon was rising in the east. It was a fantastic shade of orange, and the face of the man in the moon was clearly visible.

"We shall have a full moon tomorrow night, Mr. Darcy," Lizzy said, looking at the lunar wonder.

"No, the full moon will actually be the following night. I have an interest in such things, and I keep charts and a telescope in an attic room."

"Well, I won't disagree with you, but I must say that there are few who would recognize such a subtle difference."

"Yes, but I am one of them."

⁂

Of all the places in England that Lizzy had ever visited, none gave her as much pleasure as the landscape of Pemberley. An English garden and great expanses of lawn gave way to wooded paths with centuries old oaks and chestnuts paralleling them, and at the higher elevations, great towering pines claimed the ground. On her previous visit to Derbyshire, Mr. Darcy had taken Lizzy for a ride in a phaeton and had pointed out all the different types of fauna on the estate. From the humble field mice to red deer with huge antlers, Mr. Darcy knew so much about them, their habitats, and how much meat you could get from each.

"Surely, you are not implying that you would eat a field mouse?" Lizzy had asked. Mr. Darcy did not answer her question directly, but rather he explained how his interest in such things had come about.

"As a boy, I read Defoe's *Robinson Crusoe*, and I wanted to think that if I was ever stranded on an island or found myself lost in the wilderness that I would survive. When you look at it like that, then everything becomes food—field mice, voles, woodland birds. They are all meat. But you have to know their habits and where they nest and how to flush them out or you will starve. Of course, if you run with a pack, you can go after the bigger game, such as the red deer who graze in such numbers on the estate. But your timing has to be perfect, and then you are only likely to bring down a fawn or possibly a doe."

"But the only animals that hunt in packs are wolves, and there haven't been wolves in England for at least a century. They may exist on the islands off of Scotland or in Ireland, but they no longer roam the English countryside."

"As I said, it was a boy who found interest in such things, but there is something about a wolf that inspires awe. They are powerful and resourceful animals, work well in a hierarchy, and mate for life. There is much to admire there."

"Wolves mate for life? I did not know that." Lizzy inched closer to Mr. Darcy, but she could not explain why she had done so.

The following day was most agreeably spent. After breakfast, Anne, Georgiana, and Lizzy went through a maze that was the focal point of the lower gardens. It had been reconfigured the previous season, and even Georgiana found herself getting lost. The fact that they were giggling all the time did not help their efforts to find the exit.

After lawn bowls and a light repast, Mr. Darcy drove the ladies into the nearby Peak District, a favorite of Anne's. The rugged landscape was so different from anything she could see at Rosings, and Mr. Darcy would stop frequently so that Anne and Elizabeth might get out and view the great open expanses that went on for miles before disappearing into the horizon. He commented on how easy it would be for hunting dogs to trap any animal caught out in the open in such terrain. "They wouldn't stand a chance," and he smiled as if he had accomplished such a feat himself.

Georgiana and Elizabeth provided the evening's entertainment. While Miss Darcy played the pianoforte, Lizzy sang some of her favorite ballads, and at one point, Mr. Darcy asked his cousin to dance. Because she had such weak lungs, this was something Anne rarely did, but with no one other than her loved ones about to make comment, she stepped lively—or as lively as one as frail as Anne could.

The day had been perfect, except for one thing. Whatever Mr. Darcy had wanted to share with her remained a secret, and Lizzy hoped that this would not prove to be the Pemberley equivalent of one of the gentleman's parlor visits to Longbourn.

CHAPTER 2

W HEN LIZZY WENT DOWN for breakfast, the relaxed atmosphere of the previous evening was gone. Mr. Darcy fairly sprang out of his chair to greet her, and there was a nervous intensity in his manner that reminded her of Magic, the family terrier, who jumped up and down in front of the door whenever she wanted to go outside. On the other hand, Georgiana and Anne looked anxious. What was the reason for such a change?

After pleasantries were exchanged and the previous night's entertainments commented upon, both ladies excused themselves, stating that they "hoped" to see Lizzy later in the day.

"What a curious thing to say. Why would I not see them?" Lizzy asked Mr. Darcy. "Surely, they will be here when we return. After all, we are only going for a walk in the gardens."

"I think they meant to say that they *hope* you will want to see them after our walk. So shall we go?"

Lizzy found that statement to be even odder. What could possibly happen during a stroll in the park that would make Lizzy not want to be in Georgiana and Anne's company, and she felt a queasiness growing in her stomach.

The pair did not walk alone. David and Goliath, Mr. Darcy's whippets, were at their master's heels. They were as lively a pair as Lizzy had ever seen, and they loved to run just for the pure joy of the exercise. It was truly a sight to behold when they went all out.

"You like dogs, don't you, Elizabeth?" Darcy asked, following her gaze.

"I am very fond of dogs. At one time, we had as many as five of them in the house, but after each one died, Papa asked that they not be replaced. Since he now requires the use of his spectacles, he found that he was always tripping over them. The only one remaining is Magic, our little Scottie."

"Do you know that dogs are descendants of wolves?"

"Yes, I did know that, but it is hard to imagine Magic running with a pack."

"Yes, that would be hard to imagine because pack animals are not selfish. But it is true that dogs are domesticated wolves."

Lizzy decided to let the comment about Magic pass. It would be difficult to defend the Scottie's behavior considering that she basically ran the household and listened to no one, except Mr. Darcy, even though he spent so little time with her.

"You seem to have a real interest in wolves, sir. Is this another scenario you imagined as a boy—running with a pack of wolves?"

"Not a large pack—more on the order of one or two other wolves—or werewolves."

"Werewolves!" Lizzy started to laugh. "Surely, you do not believe in such legends. Vampires and werewolves. They are stories made up to scare children into behaving themselves."

"I agree with you that stories about vampires are utter nonsense and are believed only by the simpleminded, but a lot of legends have their roots in fact."

"That is true of some things, but not werewolves."

Darcy stopped and turned to Lizzy, and she looked into

his eyes. They were a beautiful gray-green and one of the first things she had admired about him. But he had never looked at her with such intensity, and a sense of foreboding came over her.

"I love you, Elizabeth Bennet. Whenever I see you, I am filled with joy." After stepping away from her, he continued. "I actually never thought I would fall in love for reasons I shall shortly explain. However, I *am* in love—deeply and profoundly in love—and if after I share my secret you have not run back to Pemberley, I shall have a question to ask you."

"Mr. Darcy, you are making me nervous. What secret could you possibly have that would cause me to run away from you?"

"That is a good question, and my answer begins with an event that happened fourteen years ago when my father and I were traveling in the Black Forest in Germany. Our carriage became mired in mud, and while the men tried to dig it out, I went into the woods. Not very deep, but Nature called. This next bit is rather embarrassing, but it is necessary for you to understand what happened. Nature required that I have my pants down, and just at that moment, a wolf walked by. She had not seen me, and because I had startled her, she scratched me with her fang. I know that it was an accident because she began to cower and whimper."

"Mr. Darcy," Lizzy said, interrupting, "are you saying that you were bitten by a wolf in the forest and that this wild animal was trying to apologize for biting you?"

"That is close to what I am saying, but I need to add one other detail. It was not a wolf who bit me, but a werewolf."

Lizzy now burst out laughing. "Shame on you, Mr. Darcy, for going on in such a way. Is this what I have to look forward to? Scary stories on the night of a full moon?"

Lizzy waited for Mr. Darcy to break out into his wonderful smile—to let her know that he had been teasing her—but he did not.

"Mr. Darcy, please tell me you are in jest."

"I wish I could, but that would be a lie, and I promise that I shall never lie to you," he said, and Lizzy could hear the tension in his voice. "Elizabeth, as a result of that bite, I became a werewolf."

Darcy recounted for an ashen-faced Elizabeth the sequence of events that followed his being bitten in the Black Forest.

"As soon as I got back to the carriage, I told my father what had happened and showed him the bite mark. When he saw it, he was greatly relieved. 'A mere scratch,' he kept saying over and over as if to convince himself that it was impossible for his son to have ever been in danger of being harmed by a wild animal. But Herr Beck, our translator, was alarmed by the she wolf's actions, insisting, quite correctly, that no true wolf would have acted in such a manner and informed my father that it was known that there were werewolves in the Black Forest. 'Werewolves? Those are stories invented for the amusement of the uneducated,' Papa insisted. Everything Herr Beck said was met with the same dismissive attitude by my father.

"When we arrived in Baden, Papa told me that nothing should be said to my mother. The reason we were in Baden was so that Mama might take the waters. Two years earlier, she suffered a miscarriage and had been in poor health since that time. We were traveling around Europe looking for a cure for her malaise and had been told that the waters at Baden were very beneficial for women who had weakened constitutions, and she did improve. Unfortunately, she died three years later after giving birth to a stillborn child.

"My father was deeply unsettled by what happened in the forest, and even though Herr Beck advised against it, Papa immediately began to make arrangements for our return to England. Although he had been hired for the purpose of serving as a guide and interpreter and not as a guardian of my person, my father accused Herr Beck of neglect, and he was dismissed. Despite being discharged, he continued to press my father about the bite. He provided him with the name of a doctor in Baden who was known to have treated wolf bites. It was only at my request that Papa finally agreed to visit with Dr. Philipp because the wound was not healing.

"As soon as the doctor heard my story, he told my father that there was no doubt that I had been bitten by a were-wolf, and he knew exactly what would happen to me in the coming months. During the full moon of the first month, I would run a high fever, and my dreams would be overtaken by visions of running through forests and hunting game. At the time of the second full moon, some of the physical char-acteristics of the wolf would emerge, and a full transforma-tion would take place with the arrival of the third full moon.

"After returning to England, everything happened exactly as Dr. Philipp said it would, and so before the third month, Papa and I went to a hunting lodge in the north of England, and that is where my first full transformation took place. I was not yet fourteen years old."

Lizzy looked around for some place to sit down, but there was none, and she was afraid that if she moved, her knees would buckle underneath her. This was insane. There were no such things as werewolves. Had she fallen in love with a man who was given to flights of fantasy?

"Elizabeth, it is not as bad as you think. It wasn't so much a bite as a scratch, and that does make a difference. You see,

I only transform into a werewolf for two days, and then I am back to being Mr. Darcy."

"You keep using that word, 'transform.' What does it mean?"

"It means I become a wolf. A big, black, wolf. Somewhat above average in size for a werewolf and with a very nice coat. You might prefer to think of me as a large dog rather than a werewolf," he said, smiling weakly.

Lizzy was horrified by his story and started to walk backwards away from Mr. Darcy, moving in the direction of Pemberley, but Mr. Darcy reached out to stop her.

"That is the reason I had to leave Hertfordshire so often, the reason I must leave you now. This is where I need to be during my transformation, and tonight is a full moon. At dusk, the change will begin. I am sure, at this moment, you are thinking about how quickly you can leave Pemberley, but I would ask that you stay. While I am gone, Georgie and Anne will be with you to explain everything. We have arranged a signal. If you want to see me as a werewolf, they will light the candle in the window in a front bedroom, and I will come and introduce myself.

"If, however, there is no candle, I will remain in the woods, and I promise I will never see you again. You can go on with your life acting as if none of this happened. Whether or not we are together is now in your hands." Mr. Darcy looked up into the sky. "Tonight is the eve of All Saints' Day. At this time of year, the days are very short, and the sun will soon sink behind the hills. I must go."

Mr. Darcy extended his arm, but as the pair walked to the manor house, not a word was exchanged between them.

CHAPTER 3

M<small>R. D</small>ARCY WALKED WITH Lizzy as far as the house,
but then excused himself and went off in the direction of the stables. When she entered the foyer, Georgiana
and Anne were waiting for her, and both ladies could tell that
Darcy's revelation had completely shattered her composure.
With all color drained from her face, Elizabeth looked as if she
had just had the fright of her life, and she might very well have.

Georgiana looked to her twenty-five-year-old cousin, hoping that she would know what to say, but Lizzy spoke first.

"I just want to go to my room, so if you will excuse me."
She swept past them and went up the stairs.

Georgiana thought that they should go after her, but
Anne discouraged her. "She needs time to think about what
she has just learned. If we speak to her now, we might only
make matters worse."

"From the look on her face, I don't think that is possible," Georgiana said, and she felt tears welling up in her eyes.
"Will loves her so much. If she rejects him, it will break his
heart," she said as the tears spilled down her cheeks.

"This is far from over," Anne said with an optimism she
did not feel, but for William's sake, as well as Georgiana's,
she had to hope for a better outcome than one could reasonably expect at the moment.

Lizzy's room was on the north side of the house, and

although it was early afternoon, the room was already growing dark. She went to the bed and removed the ties holding
the curtains open and climbed in as if she were crawling into
a cave. She did not want to see anything that reminded her
that she was in the home of Fitzwilliam Darcy, master of
Pemberley, country gentleman, and werewolf.

She curled up into a tight ball and lay there as if paralyzed,
and she felt as if her brain was frozen as well because she
could not take in what she just heard. Mr. Darcy, a werewolf? But werewolves only existed in fright tales, such as
those published by the Grimm brothers, and she only knew
of their existence because Charlotte's brothers loved to tell
such stories and derived great pleasure from scaring the living
daylights out of the Bennet sisters.

Lizzy lay in that position all afternoon, and when she heard
Ellie, the maid, come into the room to ask if she planned to
come down for supper, she pretended to be asleep. When
she heard the door open again, she assumed it was Ellie. She
had no idea how much time had elapsed, nor did she care.

"Elizabeth, it is Anne. May I please speak to you?" When
Lizzy did not answer, Anne told her that she would sit quietly in a chair near the fireplace until she was ready to talk, but
Lizzy desperately needed to use the chamber pot and asked
Anne to come back in fifteen minutes. Maybe, possibly, in
that span of time, she could compose herself enough to talk
to Mr. Darcy's cousin.

When Anne returned, she was carrying a candle, but Lizzy
asked her to put it out. "I do not want any misunderstandings."

At first Anne was confused by her response, but then she
realized that Elizabeth was afraid that William would see the
candle and interpret it as a sign that all was well.

"Do not worry about the candle," Anne reassured her.

"The arrangement William and I agreed upon was that a candle would be lit in a specific room on the south side of the house. A light in any other room would have no significance."

Anne looked at Lizzy who was sitting in a chair with her legs pulled up underneath her and with her head resting on the arm of the chair. Because she had not bothered to undress, her frock was wrinkled from her having slept in it, and her hair had broken free of its ties and was an uncombed mess.

"Would you like for me to send for some tea?" Anne asked.

"No. I do not want anything." But then she sat up. "Actually, I do want something. I want to return to Longbourn as soon as possible. I will say nothing of what I have learned here, but I cannot remain at Pemberley."

"I understand, and I will speak to Mr. Jackson immediately to make the arrangements."

After several minutes of silence, Lizzy finally spoke. "He is out there right now, isn't he?"

"Yes, he will be gone tonight and tomorrow night. But as soon as the sun rises the day after tomorrow, he will return to human form, and it will be as if nothing had happened."

"As if nothing happened? How is that possible?"

"Because he was bitten fourteen years ago, nearly half of his lifetime. He is quite used to it."

"But to be all alone, roaming the countryside."

"Oh, but he is not alone. He runs with a she wolf from a nearby estate."

"What?" It was hard to believe that such a thing as a werewolf existed. Now, she was being told that there were at least two in England, and one of them was a female. Lizzy felt something stir within her. Mr. Darcy was out there loping through the countryside with another woman. No that wasn't right. Another she wolf.

Anne explained that William and the neighbor were far from being the only persons living in the country who had been bitten by a werewolf.

"It is ironic that it happens almost exclusively to people from the higher echelons of society or their servants because they are the ones who have the money to travel and who can hire private carriages. People who travel by coach are much safer because a wolf will not go near so large a party. But if a carriage breaks down in the woods with only a few passengers, then a wolf might be bold enough to go near it, or in William's case, not even be aware that he was there. That is what happened to Nell as well."

"And who is Nell?"

"I would rather not use her real name without her permission, but she is the daughter of a peer who lives on a nearby estate. Her family was traveling in Ireland when their carriage broke down. Nell told me that she went into the woods to relieve herself and was bitten on the leg. The werewolf remained nearby until someone responded to her calls for help, which, of course, was very dangerous for her to do. If she had been caught, she would have been…"

"Please, do not say it. I couldn't bear to think that something might…"

"Yes, I understand your feelings, but William is quite safe here. While Nell and he are transformed, they remain on the Pemberley estate where there is plenty of food for them to eat, and both are expert hunters."

"Of course, he hunts. That explains why he knows so much about all of the animals hereabouts. He said it was a matter of survival."

"He was referring to werewolves in general, and for some, it truly is a matter of survival. When a wolf is hungry, he is more inclined to take risks and to come out into the open, but William and Nell do not have such concerns."

"I am happy to hear that he is not alone. How old is Nell?"

"I believe she is just shy of her twenty-first birthday."

"But if Nell is of a marriageable age, why does Mr. Darcy not marry her? He would be marrying one of his own kind."

Anne was careful in formulating a response. She did not want to say anything that would further distress Elizabeth, but Miss Bennet was in need of correction.

"In order for William to marry 'one of his own kind,' as you put it, he would need to marry a human as he was born a human and that is the form he takes for all but two days in every month."

Lizzy could see that her question had stung, but was it possible to be both human and animal?

"What I meant to say was that if he married Nell there would be no misunderstandings. Both would come to the marriage knowing each other's altered state, and his chances of being happy would be much greater."

"That is true that there would be no secrets between them. But there is a problem. William is not in love with Nell; he is in love with you."

Lizzy fell back into the chair. She felt as if someone had reached into her chest and pulled out her heart. Yes, Mr. Darcy was in love with her, and she was in love with him. She had come to Pemberley with such high hopes, only to find that her handsome gentleman turned into a furry Mr. Darcy with every full moon.

At that moment, there was a mournful howling very close to the manor house, and Anne looked alarmed.

"William is nearby. I do not understand. He never comes this close to the house. It is not wise." Anne went to the window, but before she could unlatch the door leading to the balcony, Georgiana came running into the room.

"Anne, did you hear Will calling? He is too close. A servant or one of the grooms might see him."

"Yes, dear, I know. But William has a cool head on his shoulders, and he will soon depart." But no sooner had that statement been uttered than another heartbreaking howl was heard.

"Oh, God, Anne. He knows. That is why he is nearby." Georgiana fell to the floor in a heap, her body wracked with great heaving sobs, and then she looked up at Lizzy, her face a picture of the anguish she was feeling for her brother. "He knows that there will be no candle in the window, and he cries out in his grief."

CHAPTER 4

GEORGIANA WAS INCONSOLABLE. NOTHING Lizzy said or did calmed Mr. Darcy's sobbing sister, and Anne only succeeded in getting Georgiana off the floor and into a chair. When she was finally calm enough to talk, she began a litany of praise for her brother. "He is the best landlord and best master that ever lived. He is generous to a fault, and Mr. Keller, our vicar, would praise him all day long for his attention to the poor of the parish. All of his tenants and servants will give him a good name," Georgiana said, while making little chirping sounds brought on by all her crying, "and whatever can give me pleasure is sure to be done. There is nothing he will not do for me."

"I am sure he is kindness itself," Lizzy said, fully believing that he was, but he was also a werewolf.

"Then you will light the candle?"

When Lizzy said nothing, Georgiana renewed her crying.

"Please, Georgiana, I would ask that you give me time to think. Anne tells me that you have no memory of your brother when he was not a werewolf. You must give some consideration to how I feel now that I have learned that your brother is not fully human. Until yesterday, I was not aware of the remarkable transformation he undergoes during a full moon." *And I certainly did not know he chased mice or that he howled.*

"Then you will stay so that you might have more time to think about Will's offer?"

Lizzy looked to Anne, and although she said nothing, there was such pleading in her eyes that she agreed. "Yes, I will stay for another day or two."

"The day after tomorrow, when you wake up, my brother will be back in human form, and he will be able to address all of your concerns."

Lizzy's commitment to remain at Pemberley satisfied Georgiana, and she went to her room with Anne. As soon as her young cousin fell asleep, Anne returned to Lizzy, who was staring out the window looking up at the moon. She would never look at that celestial orb in the same way again.

"I hope you do not think less of Georgiana for her emotional display. She does have a flair for the dramatic, but then she is only eighteen and her exposure to the real world is so limited. She knows little beyond her own family and friends."

"On the contrary, her love for her brother is laudable— and quite touching."

"That is very kind of you. However, if you still wish to leave in the morning, I will release you from your promise to Georgiana as it was made under duress. You have every right to go home if that is what you wish to do."

"No, a promise is a promise. Besides, it would be wrong of me to leave without saying good-bye to Mr. Darcy, as I came to Pemberley at his invitation, and he deserves the courtesy of a proper withdrawal."

"Very well. I shall leave you now, but if in the morning you have any questions, I will be happy to answer them. Good night, Elizabeth. Sleep well."

☙

But Lizzy did not sleep at all. Although totally spent by all the emotional turmoil caused by Mr. Darcy's revelation and Georgiana's hysteria, her mind would not settle. Finally, she decided that she needed to go outside into the night air in order to clear her head, and after donning a cloak, she made her way to the terrace that overlooked a great expanse of lawn.

Because of the lateness of the season, the chairs were all covered, and so Lizzy sat down on the stone steps. It was unseasonably warm for late October. The mild temperatures had been a favorite topic of conversation at Longbourn and in Meryton because it had allowed all the villagers and those who lived on the neighboring farms to have more time to visit out-of-doors. The Americans had a term for it: Indian summer.

Lizzy looked up at the moon, and from its light, she could easily make out the lawn that led to a wooded area. Mr. Darcy must have been in that patch of woods when she had heard him howling, and she shuddered at the memory. Was he really crying out in grief as Georgiana had suggested? She did not want to think so because that would mean that he had fallen into despair. But he was with Nell, and perhaps she had a strong shoulder for him to lean on. She knew that when Magic, her terrier, thought someone was sad, she would come and lie next to that person as a way of comforting her. She hoped that Nell would do the same for Mr. Darcy.

And why had he placed himself in such peril by coming so close to the house. She doubted that he was at risk of discovery from the senior servants. They had been on the staff of Pemberley for so many years that they would have to have known him before he had been bitten. What role did the servants play with regard to Mr. Darcy being a werewolf? Did such a creature require a special diet and were such things discussed with Mrs. Bradshaw, the cook? "Mr. Darcy, may

I suggest wood mice sautéed in a burgundy sauce and served with a side of lambs' ears or voles on a skewer? Of course, I can always prepare your favorite, steak tartare."

And what of dear Mrs. Reynolds, the faithful housekeeper? Lizzy actually smiled as she thought of Georgiana's praise for her brother. It was taken almost verbatim from what Mrs. Reynolds had said to Lizzy and the Gardiners on their tour of Pemberley. The housekeeper was obviously in the habit of saying the same thing to everyone who toured the estate, and over the years, Georgiana had memorized her speech.

It would be impossible for his manservant not to know his secret, and she wondered if Mercer had to sweep up tufts of fur like the Bennet girls did for Magic. And what clothes did Mercer lay out for his master on those nights when he knew he would shortly be transformed? Or did he just wear a great coat with nothing underneath? Lizzy understood that these ridiculous notions were a result of her being physically and emotionally exhausted, and she wondered who else might be privy to this dreadful secret.

Of course, Mr. Jackson, the butler, must be among the select few. Surely, he had the most challenging job because he would need to make sure that none of the junior servants learned of their master's condition. If such news got out, it would spread like wildfire, and Lizzy thought about the possible repercussions. A vision of torches and a mob marching to the manor house shouting, "Kill the beast!" appeared before her, and Lizzy pulled her knees up to her chin and closed her eyes to blot out any scenario in which Mr. Darcy might be in danger.

Although her eyes were closed tightly, Lizzy had the feeling that she was being watched, and when she looked up, she saw a shadow moving along the treeline and then a pair of gray-green eyes. Slowly, the animal crept closer, one studied step at a time, so as not to frighten her. But she wasn't frightened; she was mesmerized. The form coming toward her was a wolf, a magnificent animal with a lustrous black coat and a well-muscled form. Mr. Darcy had come calling.

She could not take her eyes off of him, but then she heard laughter coming from the stables, and fearing that one of the grooms might walk their way, she stood up and tried to shoo him away.

"Go. You should not be here. Run away." She waved her hands in an attempt to get him to move in the direction of the woods, and then she saw a second pair of eyes. Nell was nearby in case she was needed, but from her uneasy movements, Lizzy knew that Mr. Darcy's friend was uncomfortable with him being so close to the manor house.

"Nell has more sense than you do. Please, go now. You might be discovered." But the wolf continued toward her, and without thinking, she extended her hand, palm up, to let him know that it was safe to come to her. He closed the short distance between them, and while she was thinking what she should do next, he pushed her with his nose, and pushed her again, so that she was forced to take a step back toward the French doors. And then again and again. He wanted her to go into the house.

"You may push me all you want, Mr. Darcy, but I will go inside when I am ready and not before." Then he nudged her again. "Stop that. You are not going to force me to do something I do not want to do." But he ignored her complaints and continued pushing her with his nose until he had backed her up to the doors.

"You are not a werewolf at all. You are a stubborn mule or worse, a bully, who is used to having his own way. Don't you need to go chase some rabbits?"

But then Lizzy looked around, and she realized that with the light of a full moon shining down on the landscape, he was completely exposed, and if anyone were to walk between the house and the stables, they would see him. Nell confirmed this by inching closer to the manor while making whimpering sounds to warn Darcy that he had gone too far and needed to retreat.

"All right," Lizzy said exasperated. "I will go into the house as soon as I see you and Nell safely back into the woods." Darcy ran circles around her to show his approval for her decision before sprinting toward Nell. But then he came to an abrupt halt, turned around, and ran toward her at full speed. Just before he reached the terrace, he leapt so high into the air that he was almost vertical, and then he made a dash for the treeline.

"I don't believe this!" Lizzy said with her mouth hanging open at the spectacle she had just witnessed. "I am being courted by a werewolf!"

CHAPTER 5

I T WAS NEARLY NOON before Lizzy came down to breakfast. Her face was gaunt with dark circles under her eyes,
and she felt a listlessness that she had never experienced outside of the sickroom. She poked her head into the breakfast
room and found Anne waiting for her.

"All the dishes have been cleared away, but I can have
Mrs. Bradshaw make something for you if you would like."

"No, thank you. I am really not hungry." The events of
the previous day had completely unsettled her, and the very
thought of eating made her queasy. "It seems that I have slept
half the day away, and you should have done the same. You
look very tired." But Lizzy understood that Anne would not
rest until her cousin had returned to his human form.

"Do not worry about me. I intend to have a very quiet
evening, and if it makes you feel any better, Georgiana is still
in bed. On an average day, she can easily sleep ten hours, and
since it was so late when she finally fell asleep, I do not expect
to see her until after two o'clock. But her absence will provide an opportunity for you and me to visit. I imagine that
you have a great many questions for me."

"After last night, I have even more." Lizzy related the
scene on the terrace with her nocturnal visitor.

"Forgive me for laughing," Anne said, "but there is
something quite funny about William putting on such an

exhibition, although I should not be completely surprised. You may find this odd, but until a few years ago, my cousin was fairly content to be a werewolf for those two days each month. Because he is one of England's most eligible bachelors, mothers and fathers are always seeking him out on behalf of their daughters, but because of his unique situation, he can show no emotion, as it would be interpreted as a sign of interest in one of the ladies. And, of course, that cannot happen. So you can imagine what a release it must be for the staid Mr. Darcy to run wild and free."

"Mr. Darcy is content to be a werewolf? Are you in jest?" Lizzy could hardly imagine such a thing.

"Why wouldn't he be? When he is a wolf, he is free of all societal restraints. For twenty-six days of the year, he becomes a part of Nature with no responsibilities other than to his pack."

"You said he was content to undergo this transformation 'until a few years ago.'" She turned around to see if anyone was listening. "What has caused him to change his mind?"

"He wanted to find a mate and have pups." Anne said, repeating a phrase that her cousin found amusing, but Lizzy's expression showed that she did not.

A mate? Pups? Lizzy swallowed hard, and there was that queasiness again.

"I know that sounds awful to the ears of someone who is fully human, but no matter the words, what William is saying is that he wants to get married and have children."

Lizzy felt her heart sink. Children? She had not given any thought as to what the offspring of Mr. Darcy would be like because she was still dealing with the idea of what it would be like to be his "mate."

Anne could see from the expression on Elizabeth's face that she believed that as Mr. Darcy's wife, she would give birth to a litter of pups, but she explained that that would be impossible.

"A werewolf can only sire human children, and they can never become werewolves themselves. In the womb, they develop an immunity to whatever transmits the characteristics of the werewolf."

"How do you know this? How can you be so sure of such a thing?"

"Because there is a medical doctor in Edinburgh who has been married to a she wolf for thirty years and has spent many hours researching his wife's condition. All the werewolves have a gathering at an estate in Scotland every July, and all of this information is shared."

For the next hour, Anne shared with Lizzy all that she knew about werewolves. Lizzy learned that they had the ability to recognize one another on sight, a trait that allowed them to assist members of their community in moving safely about the country and beyond, and that the length of their transformation depended on how deep the initial wound had been. For some, the change lasted as long as five days, but never less than two.

"If I understand you correctly, the wife of the werewolf would not have any such immunity, and if bitten, she would become a werewolf as well."

"That is correct, and because of that, William is rarely in the house during his transformation. It is only in the worst weather that he remains indoors in a room accessible through a hidden panel off the study. During that time, he has no contact with anyone other than Mercer and Mr. Jackson, and it is only when he is in his altered state that there is any danger to a human from a bite. But rather than discussing William, why don't we go see him. Mr. Ferguson, the gardener, has cleared an area high on the ridge where he and Nell romp during the day."

"Mr. Darcy romps?" But then a picture of an enthusiastic Mr. Darcy nearly jumping over the tea table at Longbourn came to mind, and Lizzy decided that it was possible that Mr. Darcy actually did romp.

"Then that settles it. We must go up to the clearing, and I shall speak with Mr. Jackson immediately. We shall take the phaeton, and, yes, I do know how to drive one. So, my dear, go change into your traveling clothes. We are going on an adventure."

❧

"How appropriate that Mr. Darcy was transformed on the eve of All Saints' Day," Lizzy said to Anne as they traveled up toward the clearing. "That is when ghosts, goblins, and witches come out."

"Surely, you do not believe in such irrational drivel," Anne said.

"Until yesterday, I did not believe in werewolves either."

Anne looked at Lizzy with the most quizzical expression. It was as if she was saying, "How absurd for you to believe in such superstitious nonsense."

"As far as ghosts are concerned, the dead cannot rise without the assistance of a higher power," Anne began, "and there are no such creatures as witches and goblins. They have been invented by people who use them to explain that which is not easily understood. On the other hand, werewolves are a combination of two living beings."

Before continuing, Anne shortened the reins as the road grew steeper and more rugged. "Have you read about Mary Anning, the young girl in Lyme, who discovered a crocodile-like skeleton unlike anything known in our time? What happened to these creatures? The answer is that they became something else."

"How silly of me to put werewolves in the same category as ghosts and goblins," Lizzy answered, and she placed her hand on Anne's. "If everyone had such devoted friends, the world would be a better place."

They soon came to an area where the phaeton would be obscured from any travelers by a boulder and huge trees with moss hanging from their branches, creating the perfect hiding place for the conveyance. After giving each of the horses a bucket of oats, Anne led Lizzy over fallen trees and past stone formations to a narrow path that cut through the thick vegetation. Without a guide, it would have been impossible to find the path.

Once clear of the thickets and other obstacles, they looked down upon a large open area where two wolves were playing lupine tag, and Nell was "it." If Lizzy expected Mr. Darcy to be a gentleman, or a gentle wolf, and let Nell win, she was in for a surprise.

"He is not being very gracious to Nell," Lizzy finally said after watching Mr. Darcy run Nell ragged.

"He never is. He is the alpha male, and he makes everyone in his pack work hard."

"Everyone? There are others?"

"Yes. There are two werewolves who live on the property, but they are currently in Scotland. One is a groom on the estate who always demonstrates exemplary behavior, while the other is here by a special arrangement made with a titled family." Anne's disapproval for the visiting werewolf was apparent in her tone of voice. "But all must follow William's lead or risk being disciplined."

Lizzy's attention returned to Mr. Darcy and Nell. For a man who doted on his sister and saw to her every need, he was doing an excellent job of roughing up his female hunting partner. He pounced, wrestled, broadsided, and flipped her over, but she seemed none the worse for it. In fact, there was something teasing about her actions—a bit of the coquette.

"I do believe Nell is flirting with him."

"Possibly. She may be practicing the art of courtship as she will soon be going to Devon to pay a visit to a werewolf she met in Scotland during the rendezvous. If all goes according to plan, Nell and that special someone will be tying the knot next spring." Or so Anne hoped. "No need for you to be concerned."

Lizzy looked at Anne. "I was not concerned," she said as she watched Nell sidle up next to Mr. Darcy, swishing her hips all the while. "When does she leave for Devon?"

"I think I heard that she is to go sometime after the new year," a pleased Anne answered. There was no doubt that Lizzy was experiencing a tinge of jealousy. What Lizzy did not know was that Darcy was aware that he was being watched. The whole thing was a staged performance so that Elizabeth could see what a fine animal he was. When combined with his attractive physical qualities when he was in his human form, it was hard for Anne to believe that Elizabeth would be able to walk away from him.

❧

As soon as the phaeton pulled up in front of the manor house, Georgiana was out the door. She had been standing by the window for the past thirty minutes waiting for the travelers to return.

"I am positive you went up to the clearing. Oh, Elizabeth,

isn't my brother magnificent when he is at play? I could watch him for hours. And the way he and Nell get on. Well, it's comical, isn't it?"

"Georgiana, you are not allowing Elizabeth to answer, and may we please go in?" Anne said in a tone that was meant to tamp down some of her cousin's excessive enthusiasm. Elizabeth still had a ways to go before she was of a mind to consider an offer of marriage from a werewolf.

The ladies went into the drawing room where Georgiana continued to prattle on and on. In her mind, Elizabeth had gone to the clearing because she had come to terms with Darcy's unique situation and would agree to become his wife. Anne was hopeful, but it was by no means a foregone conclusion.

"Georgiana, do you know what Mrs. Bradshaw is serving for dinner? Since Elizabeth hasn't eaten today, I think it would be helpful to know what she has planned. Our guest must have nourishment."

Georgiana agreed to speak with the cook, and as soon as she had gone, Anne turned to Elizabeth.

"I sent Georgiana away because I need to speak with you. I think you can discern from Georgiana's attitude that she believes you have made a decision in favor of her brother, but I would like to hear it from your lips."

Lizzy looked away from Anne. She had thought of little else since Mr. Darcy had revealed that he was a werewolf. She had run the whole thing through her mind over and over again. Could she marry a man who would disappear for two days every month and run about the countryside? Would she be able to lie by his side and forget that he was part wolf? And what of their children? Granted, they would not be werewolves themselves, but what would such young minds think about their father howling and hunting rabbits?

"Anne, I care very much for Mr. Darcy, but this matter of… of his becoming a werewolf. I do not think I would ever get to the point where I would be comfortable with such a transformation, and now that I know that there are she wolves of marriageable age, I think it would be best if he looked for a mate from among his… his peers. I am sure he would be happier in the long run."

"I certainly understand, and William will understand as well. It was a risky thing for him to do—to fall in love with someone who is fully human. But he is so in love with you that he was willing to place his heart in your hands and hope for the best. So there will be no candle in the window to-night, and when he returns tomorrow morning, you may take your leave of him and return home. I am sure you will remain friends since Mr. Bingley is one of his dearest friends and that will be of some consolation to him."

"Anne, I am truly sorry," she said, her voice cracking.

"No need to apologize. If you cannot give yourself to him completely, then you should not become his wife because William would know that your feelings did not match his own and that is a burden he should not have to bear."

CHAPTER 6

At supper, Elizabeth was engaging and conversant, but it was merely a performance. Although she thought there was an element of deceit in such false cheerfulness, she feared that if Georgiana knew she was to return to Longbourn alone and unattached, there would be a repeat of the previous night's histrionics. But she could keep up such a pretense for only so long, and she played so poorly at cards that Anne suggested to Georgiana that she perform one of the pieces she had been practicing so diligently.

While Miss Darcy played, Anne and Lizzy chatted quietly. Anne insisted that there was no need for Elizabeth to apologize for appearing to be in good spirits when she was not.

"I understand completely. I know how unsettling it was for you to see Georgiana so distraught, and you certainly would not want to have to witness such an exhibition again."

Lizzy squeezed Anne's hand, comforted by the knowledge that she understood her difficulty. "I am a mere three and a half years older than Miss Darcy, but I feel so much older than she is."

"That is because she has been protected her whole life," Anne answered, "as are most of the girls who will come into society in the spring. I think it is rather unfair actually. Because once they are out, they are expected to act as adults when they have been treated as children up to that time."

"I am sure that Mr. Darcy, in his role as Georgiana's older brother and guardian, acted in the same way as he thought his parents would have," Lizzy said.

"Exactly. He has felt the weight of being her guardian for the last five years. He has frequently said that in all decisions regarding his sister he would err on the side of caution, and so her upbringing has been very conservative. Despite what happened yesterday in your bedchamber, Georgiana is actually quite mature. But she loves the theater, and it shows."

After finishing her piece, Georgiana rejoined the two ladies and suggested that Elizabeth accompany her while she played a ballad.

"Georgiana, I shall answer for Miss Elizabeth. She is very tired, as am I, and we are going to retire early."

"Retire? It is only a quarter past nine. The evening has just begun."

"Not everyone slept most of the day, and I really must insist that the evening come to an end, as I am weary to the bone."

"All right then. I shall go to my room and read, but I can tell you that I am too excited to sleep. I shall be thinking about my brother and how he will be here by breakfast time, and I know one person who will be especially glad to see him," she said while looking at Lizzy.

"Georgiana, you are too hasty," Lizzy responded, beginning to feel cornered. "There are so many things that need to be discussed. I would not wish to give you false hope."

"Oh, I am not worried about any of that. You will be persuaded. I am sure of it."

❧

Shortly after Lizzy went to her room, Ellie appeared to help her prepare for bed. When Lizzy had first arrived at

Pemberley, she was puzzled as to how Ellie knew exactly when Lizzy required her assistance, but then she realized that Mr. Jackson had a way of signaling the staff when any of the Darcys or their guests were on the move. He anticipated everything and planned accordingly, which was probably why Mr. Darcy's transformation remained unknown after fourteen years of secrecy to all but the most trusted servants.

As her long curly hair was being brushed, Lizzy asked Ellie about her master. "Is he often at Pemberley?"

"Oh, he comes and goes quite a lot, but he's usually here at least once a month. And he's always here for May Day, which is a big thing hereabouts. The Darcys always take part in the village celebrations, and they usually supply all the meat. Mr. Darcy is a big meat eater."

"Yes, I noticed."

"And he's sure to be here for the Harvest Festival because the Darcy family is the host of it. It is the biggest event of the year. Everyone from the village and farms comes to Pemberley for a day of feasting, and I do mean feasting—what with a hog being killed and tables filled with all kinds of fruits and puddings and breads and lemonades. By the time you're finished eating, you feel like a stuffed pig. After everyone has had their fill, they push the tables out of the way, and the dancing starts. Mr. Darcy and Miss Darcy and their partners always lead off the first dance, and they can really kick up their heels."

After putting Lizzy's hair in a braid, Ellie continued, "Mr. Darcy really is the best master, and he is very kind to his servants. Before Christmas, we get gifts and some coins so that we can buy gifts for others. And the cottages for his tenants are always in good repair, and I can tell you that that is not true on a lot of the other estates. Some of them are frightful—little more than caves, and he does other things as well. People around here have lots of kids, and they need to work. So he helped to pay for the building of the potteries and a flannel manufactory." Ellie put the brush down. "I think that will do for your hair, Miss Bennet. Is there anything else you want?"

"No, Ellie, I will have no further need of you tonight, so you may retire."

"Thank you, Miss. Mr. Jackson said if we got all our work done early, we could have a story. He started reading *Robinson Crusoe* to us last night—me and all the other junior servants is what I mean. Have you read that book, miss?"

"Yes, I have. It is about a man stranded on an island, far away from any friend or family."

"That's the one. I can't wait to hear what happens next."

Lizzy wondered if such things were planned to coincide with the nights when Mr. Darcy was transformed. If Mr. Jackson was reading to the servants, all would be accounted for, and no one would be wandering about the estate. Then Lizzy thought of something else.

"Ellie, where are David and Goliath? I have not seen them all day?"

"And you won't. Not until Mr. Darcy comes back. It's the funniest thing. When the master ain't at home, the dogs disappear. No one knows where they go, but we know they're about because, in the morning, their food and water dishes are empty. And here's another funny thing, we always know when the master is coming back because the two of them are on the prowl looking for him in every nook and cranny."

Was it possible that the whippets knew what happened to their master and that they stayed away from him so as not to put him at risk of discovery? This whole thing was becoming stranger by the minute.

Before Ellie left, Lizzy told her that she would ring for her in the morning when she was needed. "I am not sure I will have breakfast tomorrow, and since the weather is still so mild, I will not require a fire."

"Yes, miss," Ellie said, and after curtseying, she left. After she heard the door close, Lizzy went to the window and stepped in front of the drapes.

"Where are you, Mr. Darcy? Are you nearby watching as you did last night?" But because of the emotional events of the last few days, a wave of fatigue descended, and she went to her bed. As she closed her eyes, she thought, *one more day and I will be on my way to Longbourn; and I shall try very hard to put all of this behind me.* But she knew that it was unlikely that she would succeed.

CHAPTER 7

Lizzy awakened, and after looking at the clock, fell back onto the pillows. It was only midnight, and she had been asleep for less than two hours—another seven hours until dawn. But there was a restlessness within her that would not allow her to remain in bed. She went to the armoire, took out her cloak, and quietly made her way down the stairs and out the French doors that led to the terrace. Hugging the wall of the manor house, she walked until she had reached a point where she could see the woods but where she would not be seen. She searched the treeline for any sign that Mr. Darcy and Nell were about, but all she saw were silhouettes of towering pines and the sound of rustling leaves stirred by a quiet breeze.

At the far end of the terrace, she pulled the draping off the long chair closest to the stone wall and positioned it in such a way that neither human nor animal could see her. After gathering the cloth cover about her to keep out the chill, she leaned back in the chair and looked at the silver moon. If there had never been such a thing as the moon, would there still be werewolves, she wondered? As much as she loved seeing this spectacular orb glowing in the night sky, she would do without it if it meant that Mr. Darcy would remain human.

There were other things that she wondered about as well. For instance, what was she doing curled up in a chair on the terrace in the wee hours of the morning? Was it because she wanted to be a part of Mr. Darcy's world and to feel some of what he was experiencing or was it because she wanted to be near him on this their last night together? And when she thought of her departure, she felt the tears welling up in her eyes. How cruel Nature could be. Because of a brief encounter on a mountain road in the Black Forest fourteen years earlier, she would never be Mrs. Fitzwilliam Darcy. She would be willing to give up everything: Pemberley, the carriages, and all the other worldly goods, if only she could have a fully human Mr. Darcy. But such a thing was not possible because becoming a werewolf was not a disease that could be cured or an affliction that could be healed. It was a state of being, and he could no more stop being a werewolf than she could cease to be a woman. Pulling up the hood of her cloak, she turned her back to the moon and eventually sleep overtook her.

Unaware of how much time had passed, Lizzy was awakened by a cold wind, and with its arrival, the last of Indian summer departed. Even if the weather had remained balmy, falling asleep on a chair had probably not been a good idea because her neck and shoulders were stiff, and with her eyes closed, she made circles with her head trying to loosen the tension in her muscles. But when she opened her eyes, she saw him, lying in the grass, no more than ten feet from her, and he had probably been there the whole time she had been sleeping.

She swung her legs over the side of the chair until she was facing him, her eyes never leaving his face. He had the most remarkable eyes, and she felt as if she was in a trance, held in his power by his piercing gaze. Under any other circumstance, she would have been uncomfortable with anyone

staring at her in such a way, but that was not the case with
Mr. Darcy. It was actually a comfort for her to know that he
had been watching over her.

"I suspect you have been there awhile, Mr. Darcy." Lizzy
shook her head and smiled at the absurdity of someone talking to a wolf. He probably did not understand her any better
than her little Scottie did, but then again, Mr. Darcy was not
a dog, but a wolf *and* a man. So it was possible that he was
able to comprehend what she was saying.

"Is Nell nearby?" Lizzy asked, and Darcy turned his head
in the direction of the woods. "Ah, so you do understand
me. And how have you been occupying your time this evening? Have you been hunting rabbits or did you flush out
some pheasants from their coveys? You are not saying. I understand. You do not want to reveal the secrets of your hunting success. All right then, shall we speak of that business
in the clearing this afternoon? I shall tell you what I think
happened. You knew I was watching you as you ran circles
around Nell. I am also of a mind to believe that you and
Anne had planned that excursion so that I might see what a
fine animal you are. Am I correct, Mr. Darcy?

"Yes, I can see that I am right. You turn your head away
from me because I have guessed correctly. You staged a bit
of theater for my benefit. Well, I shall concede that you and
Nell were quite entertaining, but I do not approve of how
you run at her. She is a girl, a lady, a female, whatever you
want to call her. You should not be so rough."

Darcy gave a low growl. "Oh, I know all about your being the alpha male and that you command total obedience,
but, sir, that is only in the wild. I imagine that it must be
very hard for you to return to your human form and find
that there are those who will not agree with you all of the

time." Darcy lifted his head as if pointing at her, and Lizzy gave a quiet laugh. "You are remembering when we first met—when I would not defer to you in all things. I believe that is what fixed your attention. I daresay you had grown tired of too much deference, and you wanted someone who showed some spirit."

Lizzy closed her eyes and, in a moment, all that had happened to bring them to this day flashed before her. Their rough beginning at the Meryton assembly, his inept attempts to make amends, his offensive proposal, his kindness in rescuing Lydia, their reconciliation, and his many visits to Longbourn. When in Hertfordshire, it was obvious how much he had wanted to ask her to be his wife, but then he had revealed the reason he had not proposed—that awful secret that would eventually be the cause of their parting. Lizzy lifted up her head in an attempt to keep her tears from spilling over, but it was impossible to hold back so much sorrow. When she looked at Mr. Darcy, he had crept closer to her, and she slid off the chair so that she was sitting next to him.

She ran her hand over his magnificent coat. It was as black as ebony, thick and curly—just like his hair, and he responded with a quick lick on her hand, but no more because, after all, it was a mere scratch that had turned him into a werewolf. Lizzy covered her mouth to keep from sobbing openly.

"If you wanted, how easily you could have your way. All it would take would be the tiniest scratch, and I would be a she wolf and would become a part of your world. But you will not do it because you truly love me." She buried her head in his coat. "Oh, Mr. Darcy, what are we to do?"

CHAPTER 8

A<small>N EXHAUSTED LIZZY HAD</small> fallen asleep next to Mr. Darcy, and she would have remained there if not for the cold nose on her cheek, and then there was a repeat of the pushing she had experienced the previous night. Even if she had possessed the energy to resist, she would have yielded because he would not have stopped his poking and prodding until she had done exactly what he wanted, and because of her fatigue, she was willing to take orders from the alpha male.

Once inside, she watched as the lone wolf made his way back to the woods, walking slowly, with as little energy as she had shown. But when he was within ten yards of the edge of the wooded area, Nell came running out to meet her friend and that caused him to pick up his pace, and Lizzy felt better because of it.

When she got to the top of the staircase, she was met by Mercer, Mr. Darcy's faithful manservant. They had become acquainted during the many months that his master had been calling on her at Longbourn. As a former post coach driver, he had wonderful stories about all the goings-on at the roadside inns, and many of the tales were about his sweethearts at the different stops along the Derby to London route. But tonight the twinkle in his eye was absent. Believing that his master's heart would be broken with the dawn, his face was drawn and tired.

"You should be in bed, Mr. Mercer. It must be at least three or four o'clock in the morning."

"It is four forty-five, miss. But the master asked me to stay close in case you needed anything. Since I knew you were outside on the terrace, I was just waiting for you to come in."

"Did you, by chance, see what happened out there?"

"Yes, miss. If I may be permitted to say so, it was a very tender scene."

Fearing that she might start tearing up again, she made no response. "What time is sunrise tomorrow, Mr. Mercer?" She knew that he would know the exact time right down to the minute, so that he would be ready for the return of his master.

"Six fifty-four. The days are getting shorter. After all, it's November 1st, the feast of All Saints' Day. May I inquire why you need to know that, miss?"

"Because I have made my decision. I have decided not to decide." When she saw Mercer's confusion, she continued, "What I mean is that I will let matters run their natural course."

This intelligence seemed to be viewed as good news by Mercer because a bit of a sparkle appeared in his eyes. He understood that Miss Elizabeth had very nearly been devastated when she had learned of Mr. Darcy's other life, and he was rightly concerned for her welfare. His master's orders had been that she was not to be by herself at any time other than when she was in her bedchamber, and because of those orders, Mercer had been a witness to the scene on the terrace. If ever there were two people in love, it was his master and Miss Elizabeth. It would be such a shame if something as inconsequential as a transformation that lasted all of two days each month kept them apart.

"Mr. Mercer, considering the circumstances, I am going to forego the usual conventions of propriety." She took a deep breath and asked, "Is it possible to arrange for a bath?"

"Yes, miss. In fact, one is already prepared for the master. All I need to do is add some hot water. I will go get Mrs. Brotherton?"

Mrs. Brotherton was Georgiana's lady's maid, a kind and thoughtful lady, who had replaced the conniving Mrs. Younge, George Wickham's accomplice in his attempted elopement. Without being overbearing, she provided her mistress with the sound advice necessary for someone who was about to step into the public arena that was London society, and Georgiana loved her dearly.

"But won't that raise questions with Mrs. Brotherton about why I need a bath at this hour?"

"No, miss. Her son is a werewolf. He's one of the grooms who works in the stables. That's how she came to be here. She met Mr. Darcy at a gathering in Scotland, and Miss Darcy was in need of a new lady's maid because the last one got booted, and rightly so."

"What if someone should see me coming out of Mr. Darcy's bedroom? What would they think?"

"That's not possible. No junior servants are allowed on this floor after the family has retired. If they even tried it, they'd be sent packing without a character and that would make it near impossible to get another job in service."

Lizzy nodded in understanding. Everything that happened at Pemberley was well thought out because any error might expose Mr. Darcy. Even though he was highly regarded by all his neighbors and tenants, no one could anticipate what another's response would be to the revelation that he was a werewolf, especially considering the horrible stories that were told about them, including ones in which they attacked humans on sight and ate recently buried corpses. According to Anne, werewolves did everything they could to avoid humans and ate only freshly or recently killed meat.

When Lizzy entered Mr. Darcy's room, she saw that Mrs. Brotherton was waiting for her and that she had brought with her everything necessary to bathe a lady. She had little time to look around the room, but what little she did see of the furnishings, she liked, including the largest bed she had ever seen. Would she ever sleep in that bed, she wondered?

Since both ladies had something in common—they both knew a werewolf—the two had a nice chat while Lizzy was bathing and having her hair washed. Knowing that there was no such thing as a "happy" werewolf story, Lizzy still found Mrs. Brotherton's son's narrative to be particularly sad.

Teddy had been serving as a groom in the London townhouse of a wealthy merchant, who had decided to sell his business so that he might live the life of a country gentleman, and this man, so new to the gentry, decided that those of the genteel class traveled. Since Napoleon's armies prevented him from going abroad, they went north to Scotland. While in the Highlands, the carriage stopped so that everyone could get out and stretch their legs and respond to calls of Nature.

"Quite suddenly, a wolf came out from behind a boulder," Mrs. Brotherton explained, "and was running right at Teddy's master, so Teddy jumped in front of the wolf to protect him and fought him off with a whip, but not before he was bitten on the hand. It took about three months for the transformation to happen, but when it did, even though my son had saved his life, his master kicked him out the house. If it hadn't been for Mr. Darcy, I do not know what we would have done."

Lizzy tried to reconcile all that she knew about Mr. Darcy with her first impression of him. To his family, he was beyond reproach, his servants and neighbors held him in the highest regard, and he had provided employment and a home for Teddy and his mother.

To all who know him, he walks on water, so why was he so rude to me? Lizzy asked herself. *According to the master of Pemberley, I was not handsome enough to tempt him to dance, I willfully misunderstood him, and I was guilty of the sin of pride in rejecting him. But now I come to Pemberley and find that he is regarded as St. Fitzwilliam Darcy of Derbyshire, patron saint of werewolves.*

Trying to dry Lizzy's thick curls was a fool's errand, and she said so to Mrs. Brotherton. Since there wasn't enough time left before dawn to get the damp out of her hair, she pulled her curls back and hoped that her tresses would not break free of the ribbon.

Then she thought: where should she meet him? After pondering the possibilities for several minutes, she remembered Anne saying that there was a secret room behind the study where her cousin would stay during the most inclement weather. It would make sense for such a room to have an outside entrance so that Mr. Darcy might return to the house without being seen. In that way, he could enter the house while still in his wolf form, dress, and emerge unseen through his study.

Lizzy let out a huge sigh. She was getting all prettied up in order to meet a man who had just spent two days in the wild running through woods and thickets and would probably have twigs stuck in his hair. Even if this was meant to be, it was still going to take some getting used to.

Because Lizzy had chosen an everyday dress that buttoned in the front, she thanked Mrs. Brotherton for her help and dismissed her, as she had no further need of her services. After a few dabs of rose water, she took one last look in the mirror and went in search of Mercer.

⋙⋘

"Everything is ready for you in the study, miss. Mr. Jackson has a good fire going, and I have lit some candles so you won't bump into the furniture. I should warn you that as soon as Mr. Darcy sees the light, he will be on his guard, fearing discovery, so you should immediately make your presence known and identify yourself."

"Thank you, Mr. Mercer. I understand, and I shall do as you advise. But did you say that Mr. Jackson made the fire?"

"Yes. The joke belowstairs is that he is the Jackson of all trades," Mercer said, chuckling. "He started here at Pemberley when he was a mere lad, hauling coal and lugging water up the stairs for Mr. Darcy's father, and there ain't nothing he can't do."

"And he is as faithful a servant to the son as he was to the father, and as for you, Mr. Mercer, Mr. Darcy could not be better served by any man in the kingdom."

Mercer acknowledged the compliment with a nod. "Miss Elizabeth, I'm forty years old, and I've met more than my share of people. I know paupers who are princes, and nobles who I wouldn't walk across the street to help if they fell on their rumps. I know quality when I see it, and it has nothing to do with the houses they live in or the carriages they drive around in town. Mr. Darcy is one of the most decent people I know, and I'm not going to let a little thing like canine teeth keep me from serving him."

Lizzy smiled at Mr. Mercer, who rarely failed to amuse. "How did you meet Mr. Darcy?"

"It was five years ago, and we sought shelter at a coaching inn during a snowstorm. Now, a man of Mr. Darcy's standing could have had a room all his own 'cause he had the coin to pay for it. Instead, he huddled up in a corner and slept on the floor so that the women and their children could have his room. As the night wore on, we got to talking. I said how I was tired of driving the mail coach, and he said he was looking for a manservant 'cause his man had taken ill and wasn't up to the job anymore.

"I knew there was something different right from the beginning, but I just kept doing my job. And over time, I came to admire him, and then to... Damn! I'm tearing up," he said, wiping his eyes with his sleeve. "I came to love him like a... like he was one of my kin. And then one night he sat me down, and we had the talk, and I told him it didn't make one bit of difference to me. I knew that the man inside was a good man and that's all I needed to know. That's the way it's been ever since."

"Mr. Mercer, I do not know what is going to happen tonight," Lizzy said, placing her hand on his arm. "I really don't. So I am going to ask your forgiveness if it does not work out the way you had hoped it would."

"There will be no need of forgiveness because I've seen how you looked at him out there," he said, pointing in the direction of the terrace. "You looked past that wolf exterior and saw the man inside, just like I did. My advice to you is to keep an open mind, and if you do that, you'll open your heart as well."

CHAPTER 9

LOOKING AROUND THE STUDY, Lizzy understood why this room would be a sanctuary for Mr. Darcy. In the corner, there were French wines and fine Madeiras next to a crystal brandy decanter and snifter glasses. Despite the wars raging on the Continent, Mr. Darcy had somehow managed to procure wine and brandy from France, or, more likely, Mercer knew someone who had bought the banned spirits from smugglers slipping into the numerous coves on the Channel coast.

Next to the sofa, there was a table reserved for *The Times* of London as well as some French newspapers. Another table had a stack of newspapers published by Cambridge University, his alma mater, and she wondered how he had managed to attend university without someone taking notice of his disappearances. She knew that he often attended cricket matches, but surely it was not possible for him to have been a regular player on the Cambridge team or someone would have noticed his fur coat.

That is not funny, Lizzy, she thought, chiding herself.

She then walked over to examine the jewel in the crown of Mr. Darcy's study: his book collection. One whole wall was floor-to-ceiling bookcases, and after picking up a candle, Lizzy scanned the titles. The collection included the complete works of Shakespeare, the *Iliad* and the *Odyssey*, Isaac

Newton's *Philosophiae Naturalis Principia Mathematica*, bound copies of *Poor Richard's Almanacs*, and the collected works of Cicero and Ovid. Sharing the shelf with the work of poets from Pindar to Cowper was the fiction of Sterne, Defoe, Richardson, and Fielding. One of Fielding's titles, *An Apology for the Life of Mrs. Shamela Andrews*, was unfamiliar to her.

Taking the first volume out of the case, Lizzy inquired of the absent Mr. Darcy, "Perhaps I could borrow this book when you are busy doing other things?" Lizzy started giggling. Her silliness was a result of nerves, fatigue, and fear of the unknown. What could she possibly say to a man returning to hearth and home after spending two nights in the woods as a werewolf?

"Maybe a glass of sherry would help to steady me." She was reaching for the bottle when she heard a noise on the far side of the room. There was a sliding sound and then another, and Mr. Darcy stepped out of the shadows. He was barefoot, his hair unkempt and his shirt open to his waist. In other words, he was magnificent.

As soon as he saw the fire and candles, he froze, and Lizzy froze as well. His eyes darted back and forth, scanning the room, and her heart went into her throat. She barely managed to croak out, "Mr. Darcy, it is Elizabeth." But rather than her voice reassuring him that he was in no danger, her presence seemed to displease him, and he told her to come into the light.

"What are you doing here?" he asked in an emotionless voice that contrasted sharply with the fire in his eyes.

"I am very sorry, sir. I have made a mistake." She started to walk backwards away from him, but before she could reach the door, he grabbed her roughly by her arm. Now she was truly frightened. "I want to go," she said, and after seeing the fear in her face, he released her.

"Please do not go. I did not mean to hurt you. It is just that it takes some time to stop being one thing and to start being another. I usually have a brandy and wait for a half hour or more before I go upstairs to bathe."

"Shall I get you a brandy before I leave?" This had been a terrible idea, she thought, as she tried to calm her racing heart. She had no idea what was involved in his transformation from wolf to human. Maybe it was exhausting or painful. Why hadn't Mercer warned her? Probably, because he did not know. He would rightly have waited for his master to come to him.

"Thank you, but I will have a brandy later. Right now, I would prefer to talk to you." He gestured for her to sit down, but she shook her head no. Understanding her nervousness, he tried to calm her. "You look very pretty. I don't think I have seen that frock before."

"It is just an everyday dress—not something that your sister would ever wear," she answered while trying not to act frightened.

"Regardless, you still look pretty in it." He looked at her sideways and stepped closer to her. "Your hair is wet."

"Yes, I took a bath. What I mean is, I took your bath— the one Mercer had prepared for you."

"Well, that is a pleasant image." Darcy could hear her take in a gulp of air. "In this flickering light, I cannot be completely sure, but I believe you are blushing."

Every inch of Lizzy was blushing. Why had she told him that she had taken a bath in his tub in his room? Not knowing how to respond, she answered, "You smell like mint."

After he stopped laughing, he explained that he always ate

mint before he returned to the house, but he did not mention the reason. It was to cover up any lingering odor from a kill. But that was not the case tonight, as his anxiety about Elizabeth had resulted in a loss of appetite, and even when Nell had offered him some of her rabbit, he had declined.

"So you look pretty, and I smell nice. Now, what shall we talk about?"

Lizzy bit her lip. What *should* she say? "On the terrace, we said that we needed to talk," she answered, looking away from him toward the fire. "Perhaps later today."

"Your memory is faulty, Elizabeth," he answered, refusing to follow her gaze. He would not be distracted. "You placed your head on the back of my neck and said, 'Mr. Darcy, what are *we* to do?' Not 'you' and not 'I,' but 'we.' So now I ask you, can you accept me for who and what I am?" Then he hesitated. "But, perhaps I already know the answer. There was no candle in the window last night, and I know that because when I was not with you, I kept that window in my view from dusk until dawn."

That statement sounded very much like an accusation, and if it was, he was being unfair. How could she possibly have signaled him that all was well when it was not?

"I still do not understand. Why me? When we first met, you found me so unappealing that you could barely tolerate my company."

"Quite the contrary," he answered, shaking his head. "I was completely taken in by you and your impertinence, and it was because of my attraction to you that I pushed you away. I did not want to fall in love and risk being turned down when you found out about my altered state. I had imagined so many times how you would look at me when you found out, and, yesterday, I saw it for myself. You were repulsed, and I cannot blame you. But you must remember that I did not choose this way of life. It is a hand I have been dealt, and I do the best I can under the circumstances."

"But your proposal at Hunsford Lodge? If you wanted me so badly, why were you so insulting?"

Darcy put his hands on both of her arms and pulled her gently toward him. "After being with you in Hertfordshire and seeing you at Rosings, I wanted you more than I have ever wanted anything in my life, and it took every ounce of my courage to go to the parsonage that day. But in the back of my mind, I knew that you would reject me because I was a werewolf, and so I went on the offensive."

"So you made that obnoxious proposal so that I *would* reject you?"

"Yes, in that way I would not have to reveal that once a month I become a creature of the night. Logic is not my strong suit."

"I should say not."

Darcy started to laugh. "You see this is why I love you. You have such spirit and independence. You will not be put down by anybody—not by me or Caroline Bingley or my aunt Catherine. You are fearless, and after love and loyalty, that is what I prize most. So now I will tell you that I love you, and I always will. But if you cannot accept this reality, then we shall say good-bye, and even though I risk losing a good friend in the bargain, I shall not call on Charles Bingley at Netherfield Park for fear that I might see you. I may be part wolf, but I am still a man with a heart, and it can be broken."

Lizzy closed her eyes and felt the stillness of the room, and in the quiet, she could feel his love filling every part of her being. And then she knew—beyond a doubt she knew—that she would stand by this man no matter what.

"There is no window in this room, Mr. Darcy, but here is the candle." She picked it up, and it illuminated them. With a shaking hand, he took the candle from her and placed it on the table, and he brought her to him. But as he felt her body against his, his passion overtook everything, and he picked her up and took her to the sofa and lay on top of her. As he moved against her, his warm lips kissed her mouth and neck, and then his fingers reached for the buttons on her dress. While he was attempting to open the tiny pearl buttons, she pushed him as hard as she could, and he fell off her and onto the floor. Although she was nearly panting from passion and exertion, she managed to sputter, "Mr. Darcy, you must not. I am a maiden."

"I know. But I don't mind." He tried to get back on the sofa, but she stopped him with her foot.

"No, it is not all right. It is my intention to leave this room in the same way I came in. And what do you mean you don't mind? You would never marry someone who is not a maiden."

"I would if the former maiden was you, and I was the reason you weren't." There was that half smile that had so charmed her—the reason she had forgiven his objectionable behavior at Hunsford and why she had allowed him to come to Longbourn time after time even though he would depart without making her an offer of marriage.

"You see, it does not matter," he said, and the fire in his eyes returned. "There are few advantages to my situation, but one of them is that I am the freest of creatures when I transform, and because of that, I see how stupid society is with its suffocating rules. In my world, I am bound only by my loyalty to my pack, that is, my family. All of this nitpicking nonsense invented by people who need something to fill their idle hours does not matter.

"In the wild you deal with the reality of the moment. There are no such things as artifice and lies, and so I speak what I feel. Right now, I want to tell you how much I love you and need you and want to make love to you. I want to taste and touch every inch of your body and…"

"Mr. Darcy, please," Lizzy said covering her ears, but placing her hand over her ears did not stop what was happening to her physically.

"Mr. Darcy!" he cried. "Mr. Darcy! There is another damnable convention—no first names are permitted," he said in extreme frustration. "Call me Fitzwilliam or William or Will, I answer to all three, but do not call me Mr. Darcy, especially when we are alone together as we are now."

"Very well. Fitzwilliam, William, and Will, I am going to bed."

When she started walking toward the door, he called after her, "Would you like to see my scar?"

That statement caused her to stop, and she turned to look at him. "Your scar? Do you mean from when you were bitten? But you said the bite was on your, um, your rump."

"Yes, it is. Do you want to see it?" And there was that devilish grin again.

Lizzy's mouth dropped open. "Certainly not."

"You are not curious?" Lizzy shook her head vigorously. "Elizabeth, before you say anything else, there is something you should know. Because I am part wolf, all of my senses are heightened, and I can tell what you are feeling and where you are feeling it."

"Oh, my God!"

"Exactly. I know that you want me as much as I want you." He started to close the distance between them.

"Yes, I would like to see your scar," she quickly said in

order to stop his advance, and when he started to open his breeches, she closed her eyes.

"You may look now. You see, it looks fresh, but if you touch it, it is smooth."

Lizzy looked at his muscled buttocks, and she felt a jolt go through her, and after looking at his smirk, she knew that he was aware of her physical response, and she tried to focus on his scar.

"There is not much to see, is there?" she said, trying to modulate her voice. The scar was bright red, and barely a half inch in length, and without thinking how inappropriate her action was, she placed her finger on it and found that it was as smooth as he had said it would be. "I do not understand. It has healed, but it looks as if it just happened."

"I know. It is a curious thing." After pulling up his breeches, he said, "Now where were we?"

"I was making good my escape," she said as she moved closer to the door. "You may not care if I remain a maiden, but I most certainly do." Lizzy scooted past him, opened the door, and practically ran across the foyer. She was halfway up the stairs, when he called after her.

"Lizzy, I have not yet proposed."

"Oh, my love," she sighed, "that is the first time you have called me Lizzy." She started to go downstairs, but then stopped because she knew what would happen.

"Will you not come back so that I may ask you properly?"

"No, I shall not. Ask me after breakfast when you have shoes on and your breeches buttoned." She blew him a kiss before running up the stairs, and Darcy fought the urge to go outside and let out one of his loudest and longest howls.

CHAPTER 10

MR. DARCY OPENED HIS pocket watch for the fifth time and held it out so that Anne and Georgiana could see that it was now eleven fifteen. The morning was nearly gone, but Elizabeth had yet to put in an appearance.

"She has changed her mind and is holed up in her room or is making good her escape. She said as much last night," Darcy said, addressing his cousin and sister, who were sitting across from him at the breakfast room table.

"William, that does not make any sense," Anne insisted. "If Elizabeth had changed her mind, she would have asked Jackson to see to the necessary arrangements so that she might return to Longbourn. She most certainly would not 'hole up' in her room like some frightened sparrow or 'make good her escape' by climbing down a trellis."

Darcy was not reassured. He had assumed that Elizabeth would be as excited as he was after their passionate time together in his study and would come downstairs as early as possible. That is exactly what he had done. Looking in the mirror, he saw that he looked like a perfect peacock. He could have attended a ball without changing his clothes.

"From what you told us this morning, I do not understand why you would think that you have not secured Elizabeth's affections. What was the last thing she said before you parted?" Anne asked, pressing her cousin.

Darcy smiled at the memory of Elizabeth standing on the staircase with her long curls flowing over her shoulders and the top two buttons on her dress undone. "She called me 'my love.'"

"Is that not proof enough of her affection?"

"It is just that I have waited so long to find a mate. I don't want anything to go wrong."

"I would suggest that you not use the word 'mate.' I made the mistake of using that term, and when I did, she blanched," Anne counseled.

It was another ten minutes before he once again produced the pocket watch. "The time is now 11:25. She has changed her mind," Darcy said and started to pace.

"Will, she may have overslept," his sister said. "She was greatly affected by your revelation, and when you consider that she spent part of last night out on the terrace and then waited for your return at dawn, it is perfectly logical to assume that she was exhausted and needed her sleep."

Georgiana had guessed correctly. When Lizzy had returned to her room, her spirits were soaring, and she was too excited to sleep. She went to the settee and replayed the events of the night in her mind, beginning with Mr. Darcy finding her on the terrace and standing watch over her, followed by that awful moment in the study when he had found her waiting for him, and she had been truly frightened. But he had quickly recovered from his surprise and had put her at ease by telling her how much he loved her. And when he had kissed her, she experienced a sensation that was so new to her. It made her want to slip her hands under his open shirt and run her fingers over his muscled chest. The same warmth that she had felt then returned now, and her eyes popped open thinking that if Mr. Darcy was nearby he would know that she was thinking of him and his member, which, when pressed against her, was as hard as her father's walnut walking stick.

There were no words to explain what she felt when he had lain on top of her fully aroused. At least, she hoped he was fully aroused. When he had first reached for the buttons on her dress, she had allowed him to open the first two before regaining her senses. If she hadn't stopped him at that moment, she would have been down to her chemise in no time at all, and with thoughts of Mr. Darcy helping her out of her undergarments, she drifted off to sleep. Flooded by warm memories and new sensations, she remained in a deep sleep and did not hear Ellie when she came into the bed chamber at 9:30, 10:15, and again at 10:45.

"*Elizabeth* was exhausted and needed her sleep?" Darcy said to his sister and cousin. "Well, excuse me. Even though I have barely closed my eyes for the past two days, I did not go to bed. It shows a lack of interest on her part." Once again he pointed to the ever-present pocket watch. "It is now 11:35. Jackson," he called to his butler, "breakfast is over. You may clear everything away and await my instructions. At present, we do not know if our guest will remain closeted in her room and will choose only to join us for supper."

Georgiana looked sympathetically at the butler. Jackson would understand that Mr. Darcy was in a fit of pique, but that it would pass. The butler had known the master of Pemberley for most of his life and had witnessed many such scenes as the gentleman he served suffered from a lack of patience.

Darcy was pacing in front of the window when Lizzy burst into the room. "My most sincere apologies, Miss Darcy, Miss de Bourgh, Mr. Darcy. I overslept. Ellie, fearing I was unwell, finally gave me a shake to see if I was still of this earth."

After spreading her hands wide and turning around, she said, smiling, "As you can see, I am." Rather than look at Mr. Darcy, who was clearly out of sorts, she turned her gaze upon Anne and Georgiana. "How is everyone this morning?"

"Splendid," Georgiana said. "It is truly a beautiful day." When her brother glanced out at the chilly gray day and made a face, she refused to follow his gaze. Instead, she glared at him. "Beauty is often a matter of opinion, and to me, it is a beautiful day."

Anne interjected herself between the two staring siblings. "It is true that it is not the prettiest of days, but it will do for a walk. Georgiana, will you accompany me?"

"No, she will not," Darcy said in a firm voice. "Anne, you are not going outside. You will catch a chill, and then your mother will have been right about how ill advised it was for you to come to Pemberley in the autumn."

"So that is your concern? Not my health, but my mother and her opinions and which of you was right? Very well, we shall remain indoors and go to the conservatory."

"You know exactly what I meant," he called after his cousin as Georgiana and she walked arm-in-arm out of the room.

Once he turned his attention to Lizzy, she asked if she should return when he was in better humor. "I see that someone got up on the wrong side of the bed this morning."

"I did not get up on any side of the bed. I never went to bed." Softening his tone, he asked, "Did you really oversleep?"

"Yes. I fell asleep on the settee and slept for three solid hours, which is the most I have slept since you shared your news with me. It was eleven o'clock when Ellie woke me, and I have been running around like a chicken without its head so that I might complete my toilette and get down here as quickly as possible. And how am I greeted? With a sour look and a sharp tongue. But I must say that you look very handsome. Are you going somewhere?"

Darcy went over and took Lizzy in his arms. "You are a saucy, impertinent girl. Even so, I love you. I was afraid that you had changed your mind."

"If I were to change my mind, it would not be for the reason you think."

"And what reason would that be?" he said with a hint of concern creeping into his voice.

"You are very bossy. You order people around with your harsh tone of voice or by pushing them about with your muzzle. You may be the master of Pemberley, but you will not be the master of me. I must be free to speak my mind."

"When have you not spoken your mind?" Darcy stepped away from her, and with his hands behind his back, he recited word for word a part of Elizabeth's refusal of his offer of marriage. "'You are mistaken if you suppose that the mode of your declaration affected me in any other way than sparing me the concern I might have felt in refusing you if you had behaved in a more gentlemanlike manner.' Need I say more?"

"No, please don't. You should not repeat what I said. A memory at such a time as this is unpardonable."

"And what time would that be, Elizabeth? Are you saying that you will accept my offer of marriage?"

"Not yet. There are things I would like to discuss."

"Then let us go into my study."

Lizzy laughed. "Absolutely not. I will not risk a repeat of last night. I suggest the first drawing room."

"The first drawing room? The one next to the foyer where all of the servants go back and forth? If we are to have no privacy, why don't we just sit on the stairs in the foyer and have everyone listen in on our conversation?"

"I think mine is the better suggestion, but whichever you prefer is fine with me, dear," she answered while trying to suppress a smile.

Darcy gestured for her to go ahead of him into the first drawing room, and so she would have her way once again, he thought. Shaking his head, he reminded himself that he had wanted to marry a lady with spirit. Well, he was about to get his wish—in spades.

CHAPTER 11

DARCY DIRECTED LIZZY TO a corner of the drawing room that was not directly in view of the foyer, but rather than sitting on the sofa, Lizzy chose one of a pair of chairs nearest to the fire. Although Darcy had surrounded himself with the most loyal of servants, there was no doubt that the lives of their master and mistress were of keen interest to those who lived belowstairs, and Lizzy's presence had prompted much speculation as to whether the master would finally take a wife, creating a palpable buzz in the house.

After moving his chair closer to hers, Darcy began by apologizing for his aggressive behavior the previous night. "It may be helpful if you understand what happens during my transformation back to human form. As soon as the sun appears over the horizon, the changes begin. The physical process lasts for about twenty minutes. However, it takes longer for the mind to adjust to the altered state. Because of this, I remain in my study until I am sure that I am thinking as a person and not as an animal. But last night, as soon as I entered the room, I knew that someone was there, and my lupine instincts took over. I am truly sorry that I frightened you."

"I *do* understand," Lizzy quickly responded. "I should have waited for you to come to me in the morning. That was really my fault, not yours."

"Thank you for that," he said and reached across the divide and took hold of her hand. He wanted to kiss it, but that would have meant bending over so that his head was almost at her knees. "Damn it! This is ridiculous," he said standing up.

"Why don't we go to the second drawing room, where we will have more privacy?" Lizzy offered.

"Thank you," he said with a sigh of relief, and the couple quickly made their way to the yellow drawing room. But they were not alone. David and Goliath had been with their master all morning, ready to spring into action if necessary. Lizzy was of the opinion that the whippets did not approve of her and that would explain why they seemed always to walk between Mr. Darcy and her. After signaling to his dogs that they were to stay put, he looked at Lizzy. "Now, where was I?"

"You were speaking of your transformation."

"Ah, yes. Well, the same thing happens when I go from human to wolf form. It is in that first hour that I must be careful, as my mind has not fully gone over to being a wolf. Lest I confuse you, you should know that there is a part of me that always remains human, which is why I understood what you were saying on the terrace, and there is a part of me that always remains a wolf, which is why I knew that…"

"Yes, I understand," Lizzy quickly interjected. "You were speaking of your transformation."

Darcy smiled, remembering Lizzy's embarrassment when she learned that he knew how she was reacting to him physically. He would never have kissed her in such a way if she had not signaled her interest with her scent.

"I realize that I quite overpowered you last night when I carried you to the sofa and…"

"William, I completely comprehend what happened last night. There is no reason to go into detail. All is forgiven." She looked away from him because the mysterious stirring had returned, and there was no way he would not know what was happening to her.

"Again, I thank you for your understanding," he said with a smile in his voice. "Now, you said that you had some questions for me." With that, his back stiffened. He could just imagine what she must be thinking and what questions she would ask. Would she be disgusted by the idea of his hunting down an animal and eating it raw? Would their children be werewolves? Why did wolves howl? But the question he feared the most was that she would want a detailed description of his transformation. She would be repulsed by a vision of a man dropping to his knees as his arms became legs, followed quickly by the thickening of his neck, an emerging muzzle, and the change in his teeth that were designed to tear an animal apart. The metamorphosis was completed when his hair became fur. She would want to know all of that, and his stomach churned at the idea of speaking of such things to the woman he loved.

Lizzy hesitated, realizing that any question would be intrusive, but there were things she needed to know. "Tell me all about Nell?"

"What?" Darcy burst out laughing, in part because he had been so wrong about what question she would ask and in part out of relief. "Nell? You want to know about Nell? Why?"

"Because you spend two whole days—and nights—together every month. I know she is attracted to you."

"Attracted? She is a friend, neighbor, and member of my pack—no more than that."

"And because she is your friend, you think she cannot be attracted to you? Haven't you noticed how she sashays when she is near you?"

"Sashays?" Darcy started to laugh again. "You know, Elizabeth, once a year, there is a werewolf gathering on an estate in Scotland, and there is a time set aside for exchanging stories and anecdotes. I now have mine. When my fellow lupines hear that Nell 'sashayed' so that she might attract me, they will truly howl—with laughter."

"Do not make fun of me. Call it what you will, but she is flirting with you."

"Yes, she is, but only to practice her skills. I have no interest in her as my mate, and let me put your mind at ease. A werewolf is more human than wolf, and as such, the males engage in the act of procreation only when we are in human form because we only sire human children. You need not be jealous of her."

"I am *not* jealous of her. I was just pointing out what is patently obvious to me." But she was not fooling him for one second. "Is she beautiful?"

"I have heard her described in such a way."

"What color is her hair? A mousy brown, perhaps?"

"Not mousy at all. She has hair as golden as Jane's and eyes as blue as a summer sky."

"I see you have a poetic side that I did not know about. How do I compare to her?"

"You are beyond comparison with any woman. If you are fishing for compliments, and I can see that you are, I shall tell you the truth. I love your dark curls that are impossible to restrain. You have an adorable nose and mouth, a firm chin, and the cutest dimple. But it is your dark eyes that draw me in, but you should know that they reveal much about you.

I can tell your mood quicker from your eyes than from what comes from your mouth. How did I do?"

"You were doing fine until that last bit, but since you said that I was beyond comparison, I shall forgive you. Shall I get to meet Nell?"

"Yes, and quite soon, as we are all to attend a reception in honor of Lady Elaine, the younger daughter of the Earl of Granyard, who is coming of age, and it would please me greatly if you would accompany me."

"I would be honored," she said, reaching out and taking his hand. "I am satisfied with your answers regarding Nell, but I do have more questions." She hesitated to say the name of the man Mr. Darcy detested more than any other. "What of Wickham?"

"Wickham? What do you mean?"

"Wickham is now my brother-in-law, and he can be dangerous. There is always the risk of discovery. I do not understand how you succeeded in keeping your altered state from him since he grew up on the Pemberley estate."

Elizabeth knew something of Wickham's personal history. He had come to Pemberley after all of his family had died in a typhoid epidemic, and the only relation the local parson could find who would care for a six-year-old boy was Mrs. Wickham, the wife of the estate's butler.

"You already know that Wickham is a liar, and he started lying at a very young age," Darcy explained. He professes to have secured my father's affection, when the truth is quite the opposite. My father recognized his true nature and enrolled him in a grammar school in Essex, and from the age of ten, he was permitted to return to Pemberley only twice a year so that he might visit with the Wickhams, who, for reasons beyond my understanding, had grown fond of him.

Apparently, in that short interval, he was able to convince my sister that a correspondence between the two would be appropriate. He told her that because he was a member of the extended Pemberley family, I need not be advised of an exchange of letters. Well, you know the rest.

"But you need not concern yourself on his account. I was truly unhappy that the successful conclusion of Lydia's escapade required that she marry that villain. Because of that, I have retained the services of a firm that employs men to follow individuals. Most of the time, it is a wayward spouse or a prodigal son who is being watched, but they do other things as well. Wickham cannot make a move without it being observed. I receive monthly reports, and I can now tell you that your sister has readily adapted to the life of an officer's wife and that she is safe and secure. Additionally, all the merchants have been made aware of Wickham's habits and his outstanding debts, and so his pay is not being squandered in the shops. The same holds true for the public houses in Newcastle. Hopefully, we will see little of him."

"You have been watching over Lydia all this time?" Lizzy leaned over and kissed Darcy's cheek, and then rested her head upon his shoulder. For a long time they sat with their fingers entwined, but there was so much Lizzy wanted to know. "How many wolves are in your pack?"

"It varies. I have had as many as seven. Nell and Teddy are permanent members, but I am occasionally asked to take on a young man who is in need of some instruction in survival techniques, such as stalking and hunting, but it is also important for any new member to understand the hierarchy of the pack and its society. For the protection and well-being of all, there is only one alpha male. Currently, I have under my aegis a young man named Rupert, who was getting into trouble because he kept straying into populated areas. I was not happy with his progress while he was here at Pemberley, so I sent him to a large estate west of Edinburgh. Conditions there are primitive. Such a stark contrast to the life of privilege he has led will, I believe, provide sufficient incentive for him to behave properly. Hopefully, he will come back and retake his position in the pack. If not, he goes back to his father."

"Poor Mrs. Brotherton. She is deprived of her son's company because of this Rupert person."

"Not really. Teddy is destined to become an alpha male, and this is excellent training for him. He was glad to have the opportunity to practice his leadership skills."

"But while Rupert was at Pemberley misbehaving, were you not at risk of discovery? What if someone saw him? A hue and cry would go up until he was tracked down and killed." Lizzy felt a chill run down her back, and Darcy, sensing her anxiety, pulled her closer to him.

"Until recently, we had a Newfoundland dog, a big, black, burly animal that scared people because of his size but that was actually as gentle as a golden retriever. If anyone reported a wolf-like animal in the area, it was assumed that it was Wolfie, the Darcy Newfoundland."

"Wolfie?"

"If anyone cried 'wolf,' we would have one to show them."

"I assume that since you said that you had Wolfie 'until recently' he has died. Why have you not replaced him?"

Darcy took his arm from around Lizzy's shoulder and seemed to be squirming, and the reason was soon revealed. "Because he was odd dog out with David and Goliath, and they were not very nice to him. After he died, the whippets asked that I not replace him because they are quite capable of securing the perimeters."

"David and Goliath *asked* you? Are you saying that you understand the language of a dog?"

"Yes, it is referred to as 'canine,' and I do speak the language. It is very close to lupine, as wolves are the ancestors of dogs. Think of it as the animal equivalent of the Romance languages. Spanish and Italian have a lot of words in common."

"I do believe you are serious that you are bilingual."

"I made it a point to learn canine because they are our cousins and can be of great help to us. When Nell, Teddy, and I are in the woods, David and Goliath are on patrol running off poachers. The whippets are vital to our safety."

"But you are putting yourself at risk because David and Goliath do not want another dog on the property. That is not how an alpha male should act. You must be firm with them."

Darcy flinched at the criticism of his leadership abilities, and knowing their master was unhappy, both whippets stood up and moved closer to him.

"Elizabeth, I would not talk if I were you. Your Scottie is the most ill-behaved dog I have ever seen. She runs circles around every Bennet, including your father."

"Why you are complaining? Magic is always on her best behavior whenever you visit." Darcy gave her a look to let her know that he was the reason for the improvement. "Oh, I see how it is. She recognized you as an alpha male, and you said something to her, didn't you?"

"I mentioned that if she were in my pack I would pick her up by the scruff of her neck and deposit her somewhere on the far side of the property, and I would wish her luck in getting back to Longbourn."

"That is so mean! How could you say such a thing to that little Scottie? She must have been terrified."

"The desired end was achieved. She no longer yaps endlessly when I arrive, and she certainly does not demand to be fed from the table. But this is totally off the topic we were discussing."

"What *is* the topic?" Lizzy said, happy to return to the reason they were sitting side by side in the drawing room.

Darcy stood up and asked, "How do you want to do this? Formal or informal? Kneeling or sitting?"

"My goodness! Aren't you romantic?"

"Well, tell me. What is your preference?" he asked kindly and with a smile.

"Sitting," she said, rolling her eyes, but inside she was delighted.

"Do you want a declaration first?"

"Mr. Darcy, I mean, William, you do not ask if you should make a declaration of your love. You just do it."

Darcy took a deep breath and launched into his proposal. "Miss Elizabeth Bennet, despite your inferior connections and the criticisms that will ensue once our betrothal is announced, I love you, and I wish..." Lizzy started to laugh and fell into his arms.

When she finally stopped laughing, she asked him to be serious. "This is a serious business," she said, chiding him.

"I shall begin again," he said, and then his tone softened. "Miss Elizabeth Bennet, from the moment I saw you, I have loved you. That may sound impossible, but I can assure you that during the assembly at Meryton, I felt an aching in every part of my being, and I knew that the only cure for my pain was to be with you—forever. There is so much to admire about you, and I am not just speaking of your physical beauty, which is considerable. More important to me is your kindness and spirit and willingness to forgive a man with so many faults. I am not the most romantic of men, and I cannot express what I feel as well as some. But no one loves more than I do, and if you could see inside of me, you would find a heart that beats only for you.

"But before you answer this most important of questions, I want you to acknowledge that you fully understand that there will be trials in our marriage unlike any other, and that you will not be able to discuss them with your family. I require your total commitment and loyalty. More than most wives, you will become bound to me because of what I am. Can you do this?"

"Yes, I can," she answered without a moment's hesitation, "and I agree to all and everything because of 'who' you are not 'what' you are. I cannot imagine my life without you."

Darcy then got down on his knee and said the words Lizzy had been waiting to hear ever since her first visit to Pemberley. "Elizabeth, I love you and ask that you consent to be my wife."

Lizzy placed her hands on both sides of his face and kissed him. "I would be honored, and I will do everything that is required to protect you from harm."

David and Goliath, who had never seen their master kiss, inched forward and kept watch, and they had to do so for quite a while.

CHAPTER 12

DARCY MADE A MENTAL note that when Elizabeth and he were married David and Goliath would not be allowed in their bedchamber. It was obvious that the dogs were wary of Elizabeth, and while he had been kissing her, they had inched closer and closer to the point where they were now at his heels. It was damned annoying, and he would have to speak to them about it. However, Lizzy was grateful for the distraction because she was quite overwhelmed by Mr. Darcy's ardor, and his annoyance at his pooches presented her with an opportunity to wiggle free of his embrace.

"William, why do we not find Anne and Georgiana and share our good news with them?"

Knowing that Darcy could sense even the most subtle changes in her, Lizzy did not want to give him the impression that liberties could be taken, that is, until they were married. After they were wed, well… and she gave him a quick glance to see if he had noticed the glint in her eye. He had.

"There is only one thing that would please me more than sharing our joy with my sister and cousin," Darcy told her, "and that is for you to agree to travel with me to Gretna Green so that we might marry immediately. The Castletons have an estate in nearby Carlisle, and we could stay at their manor house. I know that the family is in London, so we would have the place all to ourselves."

"Gretna Green? My understanding is that the wedding ceremony is performed by a blacksmith, which is why they are called 'anvil marriages.' Please tell me you are not serious."

"No, I would never ask you to do such a thing. We shall grab a parson from Carlisle and take him with us."

As far as she was concerned, going to Gretna Green was no different from the Welsh custom of jumping over a broom. They might as well go in search of a broom and save themselves an arduous journey to the Scottish border.

"My family would be very upset if they were not present when we exchanged vows," she said with great emphasis.

"Please forgive me. I am not explaining myself very well. What I meant to say is that we shall marry in Gretna Green and remarry in the village church in Meryton in view of all our friends and family."

"My love, you have not thought this through," Lizzy said, shaking her head. She knew why he was in such a hurry. While he had been kissing her, she had felt the reason for his haste pressed against her leg, but she would never consent to such an ill-advised and, to her mind, immoral plan. "Please understand that such a scheme was used by Wickham to convince Lydia to leave Brighton with him. The idea is repugnant to me."

"Of course, you are right. I was not thinking about that at all." In fact, he had done very little thinking since he had carried her to the sofa and had felt her move beneath him. It had lasted but a moment, but, oh, what a moment! But, then again, he did not want to frighten her either. "There is another solution. I shall send word to my solicitor to take all necessary steps to procure a special license as quickly as possible."

"Special licenses are very expensive."

"I have a few pounds in the bank, Elizabeth. You need not concern yourself about such matters."

"My preference would be to have our banns announced for three weeks as Charles and Jane did, and I might add, as almost everyone else does, and to have our wedding breakfast at Longbourn."

"That is not possible," he said in a tone of voice that showed he was becoming annoyed. Why wasn't she as eager to marry as he was? "That will take us right up to the full moon. As my wife, you must adapt to living by the lunar calendar."

"Which I shall do when I am your wife and have had time to learn everything that is necessary to adapt to our situation," she said in a tone matching his own. "However, marrying a week or two after the full moon will take us only to mid-December. That is not so far in the future, especially when you consider that you called on me for six months without my having any idea as to whether you would ever propose. I have waited for you; now you must wait for me."

"Do I have a choice?"

Lizzy kissed him and whispered, "Not really."

❧

Anne and Georgiana had no doubt of the outcome of Darcy's proposal and were expecting a jubilant suitor to join them in the study, but when Darcy entered the room, he was wearing a frown because he had not prevailed in his wish to marry as soon as possible. Nevertheless, as soon as he saw Georgiana's smile, he could not hold back his own, and when she ran to her brother, he picked her up and spun her around.

"You see, I was right," Georgiana said, addressing Lizzy. "I told Will months ago that you would marry him no matter what, but he kept hemming and hawing, traveling back and forth between London and Longbourn or Pemberley and Longbourn."

"But that is now behind us," Anne quickly interjected. "Are we free to share your good news with others?"

"Not yet," Lizzy answered. "I would like for William to speak with my father before any announcement is made. He will gladly give his consent, and it is merely a courtesy on William's part, but I would appreciate it if we observed this particular formality."

"Of course," Anne said. "But that does not mean that we cannot have our own celebration. I anticipated your happy news and have asked Mr. Jackson to bring us the best wine from Pemberley's cellar so that we may wish you joy. Am I correct in assuming that you will marry in six weeks after the full moon and the banns have been announced?"

Darcy made a face and looked at Anne and then back at Lizzy. "I see evidence of collusion here."

"No, you do not, sir, and I hope you are not this suspicious when we are married," Lizzy said. "Anne and I have discussed nothing about a wedding. Her statement is based on how one would proceed—logically."

"Oh, never mind. I shall not allow anything to dampen my spirits. This is the best day of my life." After taking Lizzy's hands in his, he added, "Up to this point."

CHAPTER 13

WHEN THE MANOR HOUSE of the Earl of Granyard came into view, Elizabeth could hardly believe it. Granyard Hall was actually larger than Pemberley. For the most part, the architecture was Jacobean with some later additions that, to her mind, gave the house a busy, cluttered look. She much preferred the symmetry of a Georgian manor house, and from the look on her face, Darcy correctly interpreted that her preference was for Pemberley over this rambling abode.

Elizabeth had been nervous about going to a reception for the daughter of a member of the aristocracy, but once she had been accoutered from head to toe by Georgiana and Anne, she felt more at ease. With so many prominent guests in attendance, she anticipated that once she went through the receiving line, no one would pay any attention to her.

The earl was married to his third wife and had children from each of his marriages, and it seemed as if all eight were present. His Lordship was flanked by his eldest daughter, Lady Helen, and the young lady who would shortly be coming out into society, Lady Elaine. She and Georgiana were great friends, and Georgiana had delayed her own debut so that they might be presented to the queen at the same time.

As pretty as Elaine was, it was her older sister who was garnering the lion's share of the attention. She was the most beautiful woman Lizzy had ever seen. Dressed in an exquisite mauve silk gown and weighed down with jewels, she had all the men gawking at her, that is, every man except Mr. Darcy. Lizzy found this to be most curious. Not looking at the beautiful Lady Helen was like trying to ignore the existence of the sun.

After making her way through introductions of all the siblings, Lady Elaine, and His Lordship, Lizzy was greeted by *la belle femme*, and she wondered if another Helen, Helen of Troy, whose face had launched a thousand ships, was as beautiful as she was. And although she knew that they had never met, there was something vaguely familiar about Lady Helen. Lizzy was trying to think where she might have seen her—in a portrait gallery perhaps—when the lady took her by both hands and walked with her to a nearby alcove. Lizzy looked to Mr. Darcy for guidance, but he had stayed behind so that he might converse with His Lordship.

"Oh, Elizabeth, how good it is to see you again."

"Again, Lady Helen? Forgive me, but I cannot recall our being introduced."

"Oh, we were never formally introduced. The situation was not conducive to such an exchange," she said, giggling. "However, we have been in each other's company, but from a distance. You know me as Nell."

Lizzy went wide-eyed. This was the she wolf that Mr. Darcy was running around with! The most beautiful woman in the world! And she looked over her shoulder hoping to catch his eye, but her betrothed was now talking to Viscount Wilston, the earl's heir.

"I am not surprised that Alpha did not tell you about me. He is very protective of members of his pack." She looked at Mr. Darcy and let out a little sigh. "But even though he is very strict, we get along famously." Although a lupine, she was practically purring.

"Yes, I know. I saw you running together in the glade."

"Oh, were you there? I had not realized that you were up on the hill. Alpha was very rough that day, running at me from every direction, giving me a nip here and another there, and repeatedly jumping on top of me. He is always like that with me."

"That is exactly how one would expect a brother to act," Lizzy said, smiling, and then she thought of Mr. Darcy's portrayal of their relationship. According to dear Will, Nell had no interest in him whatsoever. What did he call her overtures? Harmless flirting? Merely getting in a little practice before she became betrothed to a peer in Devon. What nonsense! According to Nell, she had not realized that she was being watched by Lizzy from atop the hill. Well, that was interesting since Lizzy had not mentioned where she had been that day. There was absolutely no doubt that Nell had set her sights on Fitzwilliam Darcy, and she was letting Lizzy know it. This situation required some redirection, and Lizzy leaned forward and whispered, "I understand that you are shortly to become engaged."

"Oh, no! Not shortly. If such a thing should come about, Lord Angelsey and I have agreed that a lengthy courtship is desirable. He is exactly my age and needs some maturing as he is most definitely not ready to take on the responsibilities of the leader of a pack. Lord Angelsey must be Alpha's equal. Otherwise, I would be marrying someone who is beneath me. Besides, men change their minds all of the time, don't they?"

"One would hope that men would be as constant in their affections as women."

"Yes, one would hope. But in reality, it is not the case at all, and life is so unpredictable."

A crowd that had been waiting for Lady Helen to return

to the line was pressing in on them, and so Lizzy excused herself and went in search of "Alpha."

❧

Now that she had met Nell, Lizzy was sorry that she had suggested their engagement not be announced until Mr. Darcy could speak to her father. As a result, Nell did not know that they were to become engaged, and she was acting on the assumption that there was still time to capture Mr. Darcy's heart before he gave it to another. To highlight their differences, Nell had referred to William not as "Mr. Darcy" but as "Alpha," making it clear that she was able to offer him something Lizzy could not: uninterrupted companionship and a complete understanding of his world.

Before arriving at Granyard Hall, Mr. Darcy had explained to Lizzy that because of Anne's health, he had asked his cousin for the first dance because it would be a minuet and, therefore, suitable for so frail a lady. Such an arrangement was perfectly understandable, but because Mr. Darcy was a Granyard family favorite, the second dance went to Lady Elaine and the third to another sister, which was also understandable. But then the amateur members of the Granyard family gave way to the professional. By careful maneuvering on her part, Nell had succeeded in getting Mr. Darcy to claim the fourth dance. Because of the number of couples, the dance would last nearly an hour, and custom dictated that those who danced the last set before supper would dine together. Darcy and Lizzy exchanged glances, and she gave him enough of a smile to let him know that she understood his dilemma.

With Darcy and Nell dining at the most lavishly adorned table and Georgiana talking happily with a handsome young man, Lizzy sought out Anne's company. She was in an anteroom, far removed from the cacophony created by a hundred voices all chattering at the same time. Anne did not like balls and would not have attended this gala but for one reason: Nell. Unlike her cousin, who was unaware of Lady Helen's plans for him, Anne was not equally deceived.

"I had hoped that Mr. Darcy, you, and I would take supper together," Elizabeth said with a sigh, "but it seems that his presence is required by another."

"I am sorry, Elizabeth. I am sure you are asking yourself, 'Why did Anne not warn me?' But, honestly, it is a performance not to be missed."

"I find it difficult to believe that Mr. Darcy does not know that the lady is actively pursuing him. She is the most outrageous flirt I have ever seen. She makes Caroline Bingley look like an amateur."

"William and I have spoken about this subject on several occasions, but he insists that he only sees her as a member of his pack. And, yes, I do believe him. Two years ago, the family was very keen to have them become engaged, but William succeeded in convincing His Lordship that it would be like marrying someone whom he regarded as a sister, and he could not do it. When it was discovered that Lord Angelsey, whose estate is in Devon, was in a similar situation, that match was promoted."

"They may promote it all they want, but she only has eyes for…"

They were interrupted by servants presenting trays full of hors d'oeuvres. Both accepted, but Lizzy did not touch hers. Watching Nell's intrigues had resulted in a loss of appetite. But a smile returned to Lizzy's face when Mr. Darcy, looking somewhat sheepish, came to talk to Anne and her.

"First, Miss Elizabeth, may I request the honor of the

next two dances?" he asked, smiling broadly, guessing that he might be in trouble.

"Gladly, Mr. Darcy, that is, if you can fit me in."

Darcy sat back in the chair and let out a sigh. "I am not happy with the way the evening is progressing, but the Granyard and Darcy families are so intertwined. We are related by marriage and are near neighbors here in Derbyshire as well as in London. His Lordship's first wife was a good friend of my mother's. We have always been close, etc., etc."

"Some members of your two clans seem to be closer than others."

"I know how it appears, but let me assure you there is nothing…"

"Mr. Darcy, excuse me for interrupting, but I can assure you that there *is* something, and that something needs to be addressed."

And then the goddess herself put in an appearance, and before she returned to the ballroom, she had succeeded in securing the last dance with Mr. Darcy.

As Lizzy watched Nell return to the ballroom, she thought, "Tonight, you may have won the battle, but it is my intention to win the war."

∽

The Darcy party did not return to Pemberley until four o'clock in the morning, and after such a long night and so many dances, Lizzy longed for her bed. But the gentleman begged a word with her before she retired. She agreed, but declined his offer to go into the drawing room. If she sat down, she would not get up—she was that tired. Instead, she went to the wrought iron staircase and took two steps up. In that way, she could look into his beautiful green eyes.

"Are you angry with me?" he asked while running his fingers along her hand.

"No, I am not, but I am amazed that you are unaware that Lady Helen is determined to have you as her husband," she answered, as she traced the outline of his chin.

"Well, after tonight, I have to admit that I can see that there is an interest there, but it does not matter. I love another," he said, moving up one step.

"Will, she is the most beautiful woman I ever saw."

"Do you think so?"

"Who do you know who is more beautiful than she, and do not say me?"

"I have seen portraits of Lady Hamilton, Lord Nelson's amour, painted by Romney. She is very pretty," he replied, while putting his hands around Lizzy's waist. "I am partial to brunettes."

"I too have seen a portrait of Lady Hamilton, but she cannot hold a candle to Nell."

"Again let me say, it does not matter. I do not love her. Besides, she is boring."

"What do you mean she is *boring*?" Lizzy asked, taking a step up and away from him.

Darcy let out a sigh. This was not the way he had envisioned the evening ending. Rather, he had pictured something more intimate involving the use of lips and hands.

"When we are in the woods together, there are only two topics of conversation with her: food and grooming. She eats every bit as much as I do, and I have twenty pounds on her. Allow me to give you an example of the enormity of her appetite. In the spring, four of us took down a deer. By the time we had finished, there was no meat left on the carcass and everyone was satisfied, except Nell. No sooner had we finished eating than she ran out and caught a rabbit, and when it comes to pheasant, she kills more than the best gun I have ever hosted at Pemberley."

That statement made Lizzy wonder. If Nell gained weight while she was a she wolf would she keep the weight on once she had regained her human form? She might end up looking like Wolfie, the Darcy Newfoundland. One could hope.

"What do you mean by grooming?"

"Tonight, you may have gathered that Nell spends a lot of money on jewels and dresses and whatnots. She devotes a lot of time to her appearance. Well, in the wild, you tend to get dirty, have grass and twigs in your coat, etc., but she will not let anyone rest until all unwanted material is removed."

"And how is it removed?"

"Thank goodness for Teddy Brotherton, as that chore usually falls to him, but since Teddy and Rupert are in Scotland, I have to do it. So I rake through her coat with my claws."

"Hmmm."

"I could do the same for you," he said, stepping closer to her. "Would you like me to help you take your hair down?"

"You are very kind, sir, but I must refuse your generous offer. However, may I suggest that we journey to Longbourn as soon as possible so that you may ask my father for his consent to our marriage? After doing so, we will share our good news with all our friends and that would include the family of the Earl of Granyard."

Darcy started to laugh. "That is fine with me. But, again, I must tell you that it does not matter what Nell wants. She cannot have me."

Lizzy leaned into him, and after placing her cheek against his, she whispered in his ear, "No, she cannot have you."

CHAPTER 14

RATHER THAN HAVE A repeat of the previous day's unfortunate speculation by Mr. Darcy as to the meaning of her coming down so late to breakfast, Lizzy was in the breakfast room by nine o'clock. Even so, she was the last one to put in an appearance. She understood the reason for Georgiana's early arrival. Mr. Darcy's sister wanted to make sure that she did not miss anything, especially any comments made about the previous night's ball. But Anne looked exhausted and should have stayed in bed.

Georgiana did most of the talking, and a good deal of her conversation concerned Mr. Albert Norwall. Although not the handsomest of men, he had a most pleasant disposition and was an excellent dancer. When Darcy was asked by Anne for his opinion of the young gentleman, he merely grunted. When pressed by Georgiana, he said, "He is too young. He has not even finished his studies at Oxford."

"Will, all I want to know at this point is, did you like him, because I most certainly did."

"I shall need to know a good deal more about him before forming an opinion," he said, looking at his sister with a furrowed brow. "I have reason to question his judgment in choosing Oxford over Cambridge, and to the best of my knowledge he neither plays cricket nor attends the matches, which makes him suspect in my book." Georgiana groaned at her brother's comments.

Between yesterday's grumbling and today's grouchy responses, Lizzy was getting the impression that Mr. Darcy was not a morning person. Another possible cause for his grumpiness might be the realization that he would soon have gentlemen asking for his permission to call on his little sister. A third reason, and the most likely for his being peckish, might have to do with Anne. Had she said something to him about his performance at the Granyard reception? She had hinted at her displeasure during the carriage ride to Pemberley, but Mr. Darcy had ignored her comments and had stared out the window, saying nothing.

"Perhaps we may all go for a walk after breakfast," Lizzy suggested. "Granted, the day is chilly, but the sun is out. And the ground is carpeted with fallen leaves that make that wonderful rustling sound."

Anne excused herself, citing fatigue, and Georgiana declined, stating that she had to practice on the pianoforte because she would be performing a particularly difficult piece at a dinner party in Berkeley Square during Yuletide.

"And what is your excuse, Mr. Darcy?" Lizzy asked.

"I have none. Nor do I want one. However, you will need to wear a heavier coat and bring your muff and scarf. If you are agreeable, I thought we might walk up to the gazebo. You can see all of the manor house and the gardens from there, but it does get windy."

As the ladies rose to leave the room, the slightest of smiles appeared on the lips of Anne and Georgiana. It had turned out exactly as they had hoped.

When they reached the top of the hill and the gazebo, there was a stiff breeze, and Lizzy stood behind Mr. Darcy to use him as a windbreak. But he had an even better idea, and he pulled her to him and held her tightly without saying a word. He just wanted to experience the joy of being able to take her in his arms knowing that it was where she wanted to be.

"After we have admired the view, we shall walk over to the copse where it will be less windy."

"As long as you hold me close, I do not mind because I love the view from here." She thought about the first time she had ever seen it. It had been two months after she had rejected Mr. Darcy's offer of marriage at Hunsford Lodge. On the occasion of her visit to Pemberley with her aunt and uncle Gardiner, he had been so gracious and forgiving, and by that time, she was in need of forgiveness because in his letter he had exposed Wickham's true character. The weight of her error in judging Mr. Darcy so harshly had crashed down upon her, and the thought of what her misjudgment had nearly cost her was something she did not wish to dwell on.

"Before you came into the breakfast room this morning, both my cousin and sister were admonishing me for neglecting you last night," Darcy said. "Their criticism is justified. I should have asked you for at least the third dance before we ever left Pemberley, but my mind was more agreeably engaged. I was thinking about how fortunate all of Lord Granyard's guests were to have an opportunity to meet my Elizabeth."

"My goodness, William, such flattery. But since you are not known for meting out excessive amounts of praise, you may continue." They both laughed, and Elizabeth assured him that his sister and cousin had judged him more harshly than she had. "If the purpose of your kind words is your way of asking for my forgiveness," Lizzy continued, "there is no need, as I was treated to an exceptional performance by Nell."

"How so?" Darcy asked, genuinely puzzled.

"Nell had the whole thing planned out. From previous balls, she knew that because of Anne's health the first dance would go to her, and of course, being a family friend, you would engage Lady Elaine, who was coming out, for the second set. And while you were dancing with Lady Millicent, Anne explained to me that the lady is a ward of His Lordship, and although she seems to be perfectly lovely, she is somewhat plain, her fortune is meager, and she is dependent upon the kindness of Lord Granyard for all her expenses, which explains the lack of dance partners. Nell correctly anticipated that if she asked you to dance with the plain Millicent, you would not refuse. After you had agreed to that request, and with Nell standing right there, what could you do but ask *her* to dance? At every turn, you were outmaneuvered by Lady Helen."

"It is exactly as you have described," Darcy said in amazement. "I am embarrassed to find that I am so easily manipulated—in human form, at least."

Darcy thought about how different he was when he was transformed. He was a fair but firm leader, and he tried to take into consideration the different personalities of those in his pack. Although he might agree to rake through Nell's coat to remove debris that did not mean he would hesitate to discipline her if the situation merited such action. Not all of his nips were playful. And then he thought about Rupert, the most recent addition to the pack.

Because of the circumstances surrounding Rupert becoming a werewolf, Darcy had been wary of taking the twenty-year-old as he was irrevocably prejudiced against him. Only an imbecile would tease an animal whose leg was caught in a trap, and his thoughtless actions had resulted in the werewolf being executed. But because of his father's rank, it would have been all but impossible to refuse the request, especially when Lord Granyard had intervened and asked Darcy to take him under his wing as a personal favor to him.

The meeting between Darcy and the Prince of Wales had gone better than Darcy would have expected from a man who took orders from no one, including his father. After making it perfectly clear to His Royal Highness that if Rupert did anything to jeopardize the safety of another werewolf he would be disciplined, the prince agreed to every condition as the son had exhausted all of his father's patience with his juvenile antics. Additionally, the prince lived in fear that a reporter from one of London's scandal-driven magazines would learn of his son's dual nature, and the story would be carried in every paper in every corner of the globe. Who knew what such a scandal would do to the royal family, which was why none of the other royals knew of Rupert's condition.

Lizzy was in such a fine mood that she had not noticed how distracted Mr. Darcy was, and she was still talking about the ball when his attention returned to their conversation.

"Lest you become conceited, William, I shall inform you that you were not the only handsome gentleman there. Viscount Wilston is a fine looking man, and he engaged me for two dances."

"I like the gentleman, as he takes good care of his sister's needs with regard to her transformation, but I have never thought of him as being particularly handsome."

"That is because you are not a woman. But speaking of Nell's transformation, it is quite a coincidence that she became a werewolf in exactly the same manner you did."

Darcy looked at her with the most quizzical expression. "Who told you that?"

"Anne did. My impression was that she received that information directly from Nell. Is it not true?"

"No, it is not. What did you and Wilston talk about during your two dances?"

"Oh, no you don't. You are not going to leave me with a simple no and expect me to be satisfied. You must tell me how Nell came to be a she wolf."

Darcy let out a sigh. Because he was uninterested in gossip, he failed to understand its attractions for others. However, it was understandable why Lizzy would want to know all about a woman who was vying for the attention of the man she loved.

"Prior to marrying His Lordship, Lady Granyard was married to Lord Boyle, an Irish peer. They have an estate near Macroom in County Cork in Ireland that is adjacent to the Gougane Barra, a wilderness area of remarkable beauty and one of the few remaining places in Ireland where there are wolves—and werewolves.

"The Granyards were visiting the Boyles, who happened to have a son close in age to Nell. Without a chaperone, the two went into this wild woodland and happened upon a wolf's den sheltering a half dozen pups. While the parents were out hunting, the den was being watched by a werewolf. It is not uncommon for werewolves to live in close proximity to a wolf pack, as it affords the werewolves additional protection because if a werewolf is sighted, it can be explained by the presence of the other wolves. Nell stupidly picked up one of the pups and was bitten by the defending she wolf. When Boyle attempted to beat her off, he was bitten as well.

"There is an organization in Britain that is simply known as the Council. It was organized thirty years ago to provide protection for werewolves and their families. Any encounter between a werewolf and a human must be reported to the Council as soon as possible. If it is determined that a human has been bitten, the Council will write a letter to the family explaining what will happen to the person in the next few months."

"But who would believe such a story?" Lizzy asked.

"Every particular of the encounter is detailed, and the purpose of the Council as a source of information is emphasized so that it will not be seen as threatening. The family is advised to stay in the area for three months until the first transformation takes place. In that way, another werewolf will be nearby to assist them. Because enough of it rings true, most do as they are instructed. After the first transformation, the family receives additional instructions as to how to make use of all the Council has to offer by way of protection and resources."

"And this is how you learned the truth about how Nell became a werewolf?"

Darcy nodded. "Of course, being her neighbor, I was contacted by the Council and advised of what had happened to her in Ireland. Teddy was already in my employ at that time, so Nell became the third member of my pack. Any other questions?"

"Actually, I do have one. You have explained that a werewolf can only sire a human child, but when you were at Longbourn, you mentioned that Jane was carrying a 'lone' child. You said that you had been thinking about the litter that your Newfoundland had just had, but Wolfie was a male and incapable of giving birth."

A cloud passed over Darcy's face, and he looked uncomfortable. When he had said that his Newfoundland had just given birth, it was a lie, pure and simple, and he detested lies. But at that time, there had been no other way to cover up his careless remark. Obviously, if Lizzy still felt it necessary to ask that question, she was in need of reassurance that it was impossible for her to give birth to a litter of lupine pups.

"When I told you that wolves are cousins to dogs, I failed to mention that werewolves are half brothers and half sisters of wolves, and when members of our family are in difficulty, we help them, just as we would provide assistance to our human relations. In June, I received a letter from a friend that a wolf on her property had given birth to six pups, but that her mate had died. They were in grave danger, and so I arranged to have them transported here, where they remained for about three weeks. Without a male to protect her and the pups, the entire family was at extreme risk. That situation prompted my 'lone offspring' remark because I had spent so much time with the pups, and they were still on my mind. You should know that since such situations occasionally arise, the services of a sea captain have been retained. The man will do anything for money, and he transported the mother and her six pups to British North America. Two people, both fully human, went with them to make sure that they were safely released into the wild near Hudson Bay."

Lizzy made no response. There was so much danger in every step taken by those who had provided assistance to the fatherless family, but from the tone of his voice, Lizzy knew that Mr. Darcy was honor bound to do no less.

"You mentioned that this happened in June. So that is the reason you did not come to Longbourn for the entire month."

"Yes, it was June, and that was the reason."

"Does such a thing happen often?"

"No. But when it does, there is an organization in place

that was formed to protect the native wolf population that responds quickly. A more common scenario would be to provide a place for wolves to stay who have made the decision to leave England, Wales, or Scotland while arrangements are made for transportation to North America."

"And the reason they are choosing to leave is because they are being hunted down. You are trying not to say it, but I believe the pups' father died because a human killed him. Am I correct?"

"Yes. The male killed a lamb and was pursued. I am told that he died ten miles from their den. He did the right thing in leading the pursuers away from his family." After taking her hand, he continued, "Lizzy, you must understand that I have a responsibility to help those in danger. The only thing that would make me hesitate to provide food and shelter for another wolf is if my immediate family was at risk. Otherwise, I must act. But is this what you want to talk about? Should we not be making plans for our wedding? I am hoping that we will marry on the first available date after the full moon."

In the past few days, Lizzy had experienced emotional highs and lows and everything in between, and what had happened to the male wolf trying to feed and protect his family could easily have reduced her to tears. But she was determined to fight off such dark thoughts, and she arose from the bench, and after stepping in front of Darcy, she pulled him up with both hands.

"Let us return to the house so that we might invite Anne and Georgiana to join in planning our wedding. I shall need all the help I can get as there is so much to think about, including when and how to tell your aunt Catherine that we are engaged."

❧

On their way back to the house, Darcy and Lizzy roughed out some of the details of their wedding breakfast. Because of the colder temperatures, it would be necessary to have the reception inside, but Darcy assured her that his staff would go to Hertfordshire to take charge of ordering and preparing everything necessary to host such a celebration.

As they entered the drive leading to the house, they had to give way to an express rider. Darcy looked puzzled. He could not imagine what message was so important that it necessitated hiring an express rider, and he wondered if it was another of his aunt Catherine's ploys to have Anne return to Kent. The last time his cousin had been away for any length of time, his aunt had written a letter stating that there had been a disaster at Rosings. When Anne returned to Kent, she found that the drains had backed up after a storm and the kitchen was flooded, which, of course, she could do nothing about. Aunt Catherine was never happy when Anne was away, and not just because of the obvious selfish reason of not wanting to be alone in that large house, but also because she genuinely feared that she would outlive her daughter. Despite her shortcomings, Darcy's aunt loved her daughter and worried more about Anne's health than anything else.

When they arrived at the entrance, Jackson was talking to the rider, and he immediately handed the letter to Mr. Darcy, who opened it as soon as he stepped into the foyer.

"Dear God!" he said as all of the color drained out of his face.

"What is the matter, Mr. Darcy? Is someone ill?" Elizabeth asked, and when he did not answer, she continued to question him. "Is there a death in the family?" What else could account for his shocked countenance?

After handing the post to Mr. Jackson, he explained, "This is a letter from Mr. Underhill. He is the manager of the Council operations on the estate in Scotland where Rupert and Teddy have been staying. Apparently, they were found running around in the woods unclothed."

Lizzy let out a sigh of relief. "Oh, that is not so very bad. They are both lads, and this can easily be explained as the antics of two foolish young men."

"I wish it were that simple, but there is more. Rupert was shot in the arm. He is not seriously injured, but the man who shot him insists that he was shooting at a wolf." Lizzy felt her heart drop into her stomach. "I must leave for Scotland immediately."

CHAPTER 15

D ARCY HAD HANDED UPHILL'S letter to Jackson because his butler would know exactly what to do, and once he had informed Mercer of events in Scotland, his manservant began packing for what would be an arduous and lengthy journey. When Darcy had banished Rupert to the wilds of Scotland, he had sent Teddy and Mercer with him. It had taken the trio six days to get there. Even if the roads were in good repair and the weather cooperated, he would be gone a minimum of three weeks. There was no time to lose because they were racing against the rising of the next full moon.

Darcy pulled off his neckcloth and threw it on the bed before quickly discarding his linen shirt, fine leather boots, and tan breeches, exchanging the clothes of a gentleman for a man who would be spending his nights at a string of coaching inns paralleling the Great North Road to Edinburgh.

After giving Mercer some final instructions, he went downstairs to find Elizabeth. What the devil was he going to say to her? She already understood some of the dangers that wolves faced, but this episode threw a harsh light on just how vulnerable they were on a daily basis. The irresponsible actions of one wolf hundreds of miles away might put others in jeopardy, including his own family. Until he knew what Rupert had said to those who had found him, he could not rest because if that idiot had panicked and blurted something out, the trail would lead directly to Pemberley. And what right did he have to ask Elizabeth to join him in sharing such a life? He should have heeded the advice of the Council to take a she wolf as a bride from among the German or French wolves who had settled in Herefordshire near the Welsh border after fleeing the Continent because of Napoleon's endless wars. But when he had set out in search of a wife, he had stopped at Netherfield Park to visit Charles Bingley at his new country estate and had been coerced into attending a local assembly, and the rest, as they say, is history.

In order to make sure that their conversation could not be overheard, when Darcy went downstairs, he gestured for Georgiana, Anne, and Elizabeth to follow him into his study, and he quickly assessed the situation. His sister had been crying, Anne looked gaunt, and Elizabeth had such a look of bewilderment on her face that it hurt to look at her. Addressing the three ladies, he summed up his plan, which was simple. He must get to the Underhill estate as quickly as possible, recover Rupert and Teddy, and return to Pemberley before the next full moon.

"After I am on the road, Jackson will send word to Lord Granyard detailing what I know of the events in Scotland and ask that he have his men keep watch for any unusual activity near Pemberley. I am not anticipating any trouble, but since we do not know what Rupert might have revealed when questioned, I will err on the side of caution."

Both ladies nodded, signaling that they understood the possible consequences of Rupert's actions, but Lizzy remained silent. It was only her eyes that revealed how alarmed she was and that she comprehended the gravity of the situation.

"Georgie and Anne, I would like to speak to Elizabeth alone." After the pair had left the study, Darcy sat on a chair across from Lizzy, but he made no effort to reach out to take her hand or to console her in any way. It was as if some fault in the earth had opened up, creating a chasm between them.

"Elizabeth, I am in a race against the lunar calendar," he explained, "so I must leave now."

Lizzy, who was trying hard to keep the fear out of her voice, asked him how long he would be gone.

"If all goes well, three weeks. We will need at least a week to get there, plus however long it takes to resolve the situation. Then, I must allow for a few days' rest before returning to Pemberley, and everything depends on road conditions and the weather."

"It seems to me that you are racing headlong into danger. Is there no one who can go to Scotland to deal with this matter who is less easily recognized?"

"No. I must take care of this myself because Teddy is a member of my pack, and it was at my direction that he went with Rupert to Scotland. I will not rest until I know that he is safe. Rupert does not have an ounce of common sense, but I am hoping that his being shot has so frightened him that he has kept his mouth shut. However, there are no guaranties, so I must go.

"As for our discussion this morning, we did not have time to put our plans into action. No announcement was made; therefore, no explanation is required. In the next few weeks, you will have ample time to reconsider, and please know that you owe me nothing. You are not bound to me. But I really must go."

After he left, Lizzy went to the window in the drawing room and watched as he made his way to the stables with David and Goliath at his heels. He never looked back.

Lizzy did not know how long she had been staring out the window when Anne came and put a shawl around her shoulders. What she saw when she turned around and gazed into the face of the daughter of Lady Catherine de Bourgh was a steely resolve. Anne would stand watch until her cousin returned and resumed his role as master of Pemberley.

"Until today, I never understood why the Darcy crest was not emblazoned on the carriages. Because it is necessary to respond to emergencies such as this, William does not want anyone to know who is in the carriage."

"Yes, William must travel anonymously. However, he does want people to know that he is a gentleman. Because of his rank, as evidenced by the quality of his conveyance, he will not be approached by strangers, and no one will ask questions."

"Where is Georgiana?" Lizzy asked.

"She is with Mrs. Brotherton. Because Teddy is a member of William's pack, Georgiana has developed an affection for him that is, to say the least, unusual between a mistress and one of her servants."

"I had forgotten that Mrs. Brotherton is Teddy's mother. How awful for her."

"She is a strong lady who believes that all will turn out all right because her son is a sensible lad."

"I know that Mr. Darcy speaks highly of him, but it is because of the actions of another that he is in trouble." Lizzy finally asked who this young man was and why such risks were being taken on his behalf.

"Of course, you would not know about Rupert. William is very cautious when it comes to sharing information about those under his protection, but let us return to the study where a fire is burning and we can be more comfortable."

Lizzy sat in the chair closest to the fire—Mr. Darcy's

chair—but it brought no comfort or warmth. She recalled his last words. "You will have ample time to reconsider. You are not bound to me." With such uncertainty, it would be impossible to go forward. She understood that he had uttered those words out of concern for her, but she was unhappy that he had anticipated that she would reconsider his offer at the first sign of trouble. Did he believe that her love for him did not match his own?

"Elizabeth, do you drink brandy?"

"No, but I am thinking about starting," she answered. In three days, she had known the depths of despair, only to have her spirits soar when she realized how much Mr. Darcy loved her and how deeply she was in love with him. But now, she was at the bottom of the well again—with only a hint of sunlight—and she reached out to take the glass from Anne.

"You asked who Rupert was, so I shall tell you. His grandfather is the king."

Lizzy gasped. "Oh, no! Not *that* Rupert. He is only twenty years old, but he is already fodder for the gossip pamphleteers."

"Yes, he is *that* Rupert."

"The newspapers have reported that he is in Ireland. If only he were."

Rupert was one of the many illegitimate children fathered by the Prince of Wales who were scattered about the country. All that was known of his mother was that she had died giving birth to him.

"With such a history, no wonder he was banished to the country. But with reporters following him everywhere he goes, is it not possible that Rupert could lead prying eyes directly to Pemberley and Mr. Darcy with disastrous consequences?"

"Rupert's coming to Pemberley was arranged by the Council, and so many precautions were taken when he was brought here. It is unfortunate that this task fell to William because he did not want to take him in. However, you can imagine how difficult it was to say no to the heir to the British throne. When he finally agreed, William made it clear that if Rupert misbehaved he would be turned over to the Council and that it was highly likely he would be banished to an area of British North America near Hudson Bay where a mixed werewolf/wolf colony lives. Because the hunting is so good, I understand that it is a wolf's dream come true, but if you are a wolf for only a few days a month, it can also be a frozen version of hell."

Lizzy could feel her anger rising. From what she had read about Rupert, a year or so in a place of endless winter might be just what was required to straighten out so misguided a youth.

"Mr. Darcy spoke briefly to me about the Council. What do you know about it?" Lizzy asked Anne.

"We have already spoken about the gathering in Scotland in July. It is at that time that a leader is chosen from all the wolves living in Britain, Scotland, and Wales. He, in turn, chooses two counselors—one a werewolf and the other fully human. For a two-year term, the three serve as judge and jury to all those werewolves who do anything that jeopardizes the wolf population. Even for those with royal blood, you are allowed only one mistake. This is Rupert's second."

"Does Mr. Darcy go to these gatherings?"

"Not every year, but he does try because he does so enjoy them. While he is at the Underhill estate, he is completely at ease. It is my understanding that there is a mix of werewolves, their families, and trusted associates. It was at such a get-together that William met the brother of a werewolf who would be attending Cambridge, and so arrangements were made for them to share a room."

"But how could Mr. Darcy go to university?"

"When he enrolled, he claimed to have asthma, a disease that restricts passage of air into the lungs, so he would leave Cambridge, feigning illness, at different times of the month, not just at the time of the full moon, so that no one would be suspicious of his comings and goings. Of all the things William has endured because of his being part wolf, it was his inability to play cricket at Cambridge that bothered him the most because he is an exceptionally talented batsman. Because of his 'illness,' William could only be an honorary member of the team, and he had to stand by and watch as those inferior to him played a game he loved. Although he was permitted to practice with them, he could never play against Cambridge's competitors, and it nearly drove him to distraction. But at these gatherings in Scotland, he does play cricket and, recently, a number of them have taken up the game of golf."

"None of this surprises me," Lizzy said, with a half smile. Although it pleased her to think of the athletic Mr. Darcy standing on a cricket pitch, it was probably something she would never see for herself because he had decided *for both of them* that marriage would be too great a burden for her to bear, and that thought brought on a wave of fatigue that completely sapped her.

"Anne, I am so tired. I can hardly think. Will you please excuse me?" She went to her bedchamber.

After untying the ties on the drapes around the bed, she climbed into her cave. Even though she had burrowed deep into a mound of quilts, she was still shivering, and she found that the only way she could get warm was to curl up into a ball, very much like a dog would—or a wolf.

Lizzy would have preferred to stay in her bedchamber for the remainder of the day, but with Mr. Darcy's sudden departure and Georgiana being closeted in her room with Mrs. Brotherton, if she did not go downstairs, it might invite comment from the servants. Besides, it seemed cowardly. If Mr. Darcy would not retreat from his responsibilities as the head of the Darcy family and the leader of his pack, she would not hide under her bedcovers, and so she rang for Ellie so that she might dress for supper.

When Lizzy went into the drawing room, she found Anne, Georgiana, and Mrs. Brotherton having a lively chat. There was no sign that this was a family in crisis. In fact, the atmosphere was definitely positive—almost cheery. What had happened while she had been resting?

"Oh, there you are, Elizabeth. You look so much better now that you have rested," Georgiana said, greeting her guest. "Mrs. Brotherton will be joining us for dinner, which should be ready within the half hour. Anne has just asked that I perform a piece that she is particularly fond of," she said as she walked to the pianoforte.

Anne gestured for Lizzy to sit on the sofa with Mrs. Brotherton. It was obvious that Georgiana's lady's maid had something to share and that Miss Darcy's playing was meant to prevent their conversation from being heard by others, but with Mr. Jackson standing nearby keeping watch, she did not see how that could happen. Obviously, everyone was exercising an abundance of caution.

"Elizabeth, I think you will be very interested with what Mrs. Brotherton has to say. As Teddy's mother, she has been in regular correspondence with him since his arrival in Scotland. She is very hopeful that everything will end well and the only harm done will be that we all had a good fright."

Lizzy was puzzled. What intelligence could Mrs. Brotherton possibly have? She was not aware of any messenger having come from Mr. Darcy, so what could account for it? Lizzy looked eagerly at Mrs. Brotherton and asked her to explain the reasons for her optimism.

"First, Miss Elizabeth, I want you to know that when Teddy arrived in Scotland, he went through weeks of training so that he would know how to act in almost any situation. Second, those two young men are not alone by any means. There are those who work for the estate manager as well as members of the community nearby who are ready to act in case anything goes wrong on the estate."

"Then why did Mr. Darcy go to Scotland?"

"Because he has a responsibility to the members of his pack, as well as to any others who may be affected by Rupert's actions, to find out exactly what happened. It is what a leader must do. But if you read the letter, you will understand that things may not be as dire as Mr. Darcy thinks. Upon closer inspection, I think you will agree with me that the master misread the first sentence. But before you read the letter, please allow me to explain that the term 'daybreak' is the process of transforming from wolf to human, just as the term 'nightfall' refers to the transformation from human to wolf."

At daybreak, there be reports of a large black animal sneaking about the rabbit hutches and that T and R be running about the countryside without his clothes. So MacGregor's gillie went looking. A shot rang out and R be hit in the arm. It's nary a scratch but MacGregor's man be swearing up and down that it be a wolf he took aim at. The laddies are with the laird to get it sorted. Robbie McDonald

After reading the letter a second time, Lizzy saw the reason Mrs. Brotherton believed Mr. Darcy had misread the letter. "*T and R be running about the countryside without* his *clothes.*" It was Rupert, not Teddy, who had been found without so much as a stitch on.

"When Mr. Jackson told me what was in the letter," Mrs. Brotherton continued, "it didn't make sense to me. Why would Teddy be running around without any clothes on? You see, Teddy only transforms for two days, while the gentleman transforms for four. So there was no reason for my son to be without clothes. Here is what I think happened. As he always does, Teddy was at the rendezvous point an hour before daybreak, but the gentleman wasn't there. Teddy then went back to the house, alerted the staff, and set out for the place where he thought Rupert might be, that is, the MacGregor estate. In the event a wolf is sighted by his neighbors, Mr. Underhill keeps black Labradors, Newfoundlands, and large black German shepherds on the estate."

"And they are all called Wolfie," Lizzy said.

"Yes, how did you know?"

"Just a guess. Please continue."

"I am sure Mr. Underhill went to the laird's house with the dogs in tow to show Mr. MacGregor what his gamekeeper had actually seen, and some money changed hands for the inconvenience to MacGregor's staff. The story of a wolf sighting will make the rounds of the alehouses for a while, but then it will be forgotten when something new takes its place. I am sure that is what happened. Teddy and I are very close, and if he were in danger, I would feel it here." The young man's mother pointed to her heart. "But I have no such feeling."

Lizzy went quiet while she sorted out all of this information, and it did make sense. It was her understanding that the Underhill estate had been a sanctuary for werewolves for more than two decades. Surely, this was not the first time something like this had happened because it seemed that as soon as Teddy had sounded the alert, everyone had sprung into action. It almost had the feel of a military maneuver.

"Thank you, Mrs. Brotherton. I do feel better. Your scenario sounds logical to me, and I now have reason to believe that it will end well for everyone." Lizzy smiled at Anne, and when Georgiana saw that Anne and Elizabeth were smiling, she stopped playing the pianoforte and rejoined the ladies.

A pleasant dinner was followed by a rubber of whist. After Georgiana had performed the piece she was to play at the dinner in Berkeley Square, they retired early. Lizzy could only hope that she would finally have a restful night, and she could barely keep her eyes open while Ellie brushed her hair.

CHAPTER 16

Lizzy did sleep well. She had decided that Mrs. Brotherton's interpretation of the events at the Underhill estate was correct and that she would not worry about the situation in Scotland until given a reason to do so. With that concern set aside, Lizzy now had to decide if she should remain at Pemberley and wait for William's return. Although Anne and Georgiana were excellent company, with three ladies, as well as Mrs. Brotherton, staring out the window waiting for Mr. Darcy's return, the days would drag on endlessly. On the other hand, if she returned to Longbourn, she would be able to take up her daily routine, which involved a lot more than sitting around reading books, doing needlework, and chatting. If she were to become the mistress of Pemberley, there would have to be changes made because she needed to move about, but with a purpose. Unlike Caroline Bingley, she did not consider taking a turn about the room, locked arm-in-arm with another fine lady, to be exercise. In truth, the lives of the women of the upper class could be excruciatingly boring.

At breakfast, Lizzy found that Anne's and Georgiana's spirits remained high, and they pleaded with Lizzy to stay in Derbyshire, at least for a few more days. Georgiana invited Lizzy to ride with her every morning after breakfast so that she might improve her skills.

"Will is an expert horseman, and he loves to ride into the

Peak to look at the different rock formations and to hunt for fossils and minerals," Georgiana explained.

Lizzy knew of her brother's interest in the geology of the region. In fact, because of all those afternoons spent in the parlor at Longbourn, she knew quite a lot about Fitzwilliam Darcy. Of course, there was one thing—one enormously important thing—that she had not known.

"Although I am an imperfect equestrian," Lizzy responded, "I am an excellent skater. Perhaps when the pond freezes, we could all go ice skating." Georgiana and Anne looked at each other, pleased that Lizzy was speaking of a future visit to Pemberley.

"Shall we go riding, Elizabeth?" Georgiana asked as she looked out the window at a cold gray day.

Lizzy was about to agree to the plan when Georgiana said that they would have to put off riding until later in the day. "We have company," she said in her bright, cheery voice, as she loved visitors. "Someone from Granyard Hall has come to call on us."

Lizzy had no doubt it was Lady Helen and under her breath mumbled to Anne, "Good Lord, what else can happen? I now know how Pharaoh felt when the ten plagues of Egypt descended."

A few minutes later, the beautiful Lady Helen swept into the room. Standing before the three ladies as if she were appearing on center stage at Drury Lane, she took off her gloves, hat, and coat, and after handing them to Jackson, announced, "My father has told me what happened in Scotland. How dreadful. I think we should all cling to each other, and so I shall stay at Pemberley until Mr. Darcy returns." After uttering that remarkable statement, she swept past her hosts and went into the drawing room.

The debate Lizzy had been having regarding her return to Longbourn came to an end as her visitor had decided the matter for her. "Lady Helen, that is very thoughtful of you," Lizzy said, sitting down opposite to her. "But for my part, I shall be leaving for Hertfordshire in two days."

Georgiana was about to say something in favor of Lizzy staying on, when Anne took her hand and squeezed it, and with the slightest shake of her head, indicated that her cousin should say nothing. As much as Anne would have liked to have Elizabeth remain, having Lady Helen in residence for three weeks was too high a price to pay, and she knew that once Elizabeth left Pemberley, the lady would return to Granyard Hall.

"Oh, I am sorry to hear that, but it is probably for the best," Lady Helen replied.

The best? For whom? It might be for you, Lizzy thought, *but not for me.*

"Would you like for me to send for some tea and cake?" Anne offered.

"No, thank you. I had a huge breakfast." She actually licked her lips at the memory.

And when Lizzy saw that, she smiled because she could picture a time when Nell would not sashay but waddle around Alpha.

"This whole thing could have been avoided if Alpha had only listened…"

"Lady Helen, there are servants about. Please refer to my cousin by his name," Anne cautioned her.

"Of course, my apologies. But it is true that I told Mr. Darcy that the gentleman in question was positively wild and beyond hope of reform."

"It is my understanding that William did decline," Anne

said, defending her cousin, "but the boy's father pleaded with *your* father, and it was only when Lord Granyard intervened that William agreed to host Rupert, albeit reluctantly."

"Yes, of course. No one is to blame except you know who. I am sure he will be exiled, and rightly so. My concern is what happens to me if Mr. Darcy does not get back in time for nightfall."

"But that is still three weeks away, and if my brother has not returned in time, then you could make arrangements with Mr. Cassel," Georgiana whispered. "You did that one other time. Remember?"

"Yes, I most certainly do remember it, and I found the whole arrangement to be dreadful. Mr. Cassel is the son of a nobody. It is bad enough that, on occasion, I have had to be out there with only Teddy, but at least he is a member of my family."

"But Teddy is an absolute treasure!" Georgiana cried. "There is nothing he would not do for the family."

"Yes, dear," Lady Helen said in a condescending voice. "He is a darling man, but his mother is your lady's maid. It is inappropriate."

If Nell considered being in Teddy's company to be inappropriate, then why did she allow Teddy to groom her, Lizzy wondered? And then she answered her own question. Teddy was a servant, and servants did such things for their masters and mistresses. And, of course, when the young lupine was not there and Mr. Darcy and Nell were alone, she would ask Alpha to brush her coat and, in doing so, create an aura of intimacy. What a clever girl.

"Does rank really matter when you are out in the wild?" Lizzy asked. "Don't you all have to act in concert?"

Lady Helen let out a puff of air to let Lizzy know how

absurd her question was. "Rank always matters, Miss Bennet, which is why I sleep next to Mr. Darcy." Lowering her voice, she continued, "And away from Teddy."

With each word spoken, Lizzy gained a clearer understanding of why Mr. Darcy had never considered Lady Helen as a possible mate, and it had nothing to do with her being like a sister to him or that she was boring. This exquisitely beautiful woman was an idiot. She had taken the precaution of whispering Teddy's name, but in a clear voice had said she slept next to Mr. Darcy. An unmarried Lady Helen sleeping next to Mr. Darcy! Oh, wouldn't the servants have fun with that one. Even Georgiana went wide-eyed, and if Anne clenched her teeth any tighter, they might be in danger of cracking.

"Perhaps we should continue this conversation in the study," Anne said in a voice lacking any warmth, "behind closed doors and out of hearing of any servants."

"Actually, I was wondering if I could have a word with you, Elizabeth? If you are agreeable, I would ask that you accompany me to the study." Without waiting for an answer, the earl's daughter stood up, leaving Lizzy to follow her.

Ah, yes, when it rained, it poured, and Lizzy decided that the past few days would have tested even the all-powerful Pharaoh, and her mind returned to the ten plagues. What were they?

She tried to recall the story from the Book of Exodus. She remembered some of them: turning the water into blood, locusts, lice, frogs, flies, hail, darkness, the killing of the first-born son. She was still missing two.

"Elizabeth, come sit beside me on the sofa, so that we might hold hands while we commiserate," Lady Helen said as Lizzy closed the doors to the study.

Boils! She now had nine of the ten plagues. Only one more. Darn! What was that last plague?

Once seated on the sofa, Lady Helen placed her hand over Lizzy's and looked into her eyes. Apparently, this was the look she used when she wanted to convey empathy.

"Killing of livestock! That is the last one," Lizzy said, snapping her fingers. "Sorry, I was trying to recall the ten plagues of Egypt, and when I looked at you, the last one just came to me."

"Did your parson recently preach on the subject?"

"No, I just happened to be thinking about plagues when we went into the drawing room."

Lady Helen, looking a good deal less comfortable, released Lizzy's hand.

"The reason I wished to speak to you in private concerns Mr. Darcy. I noticed at my sister's reception that when Mr. Darcy and you were together there seemed to be some interest," she said and paused for effect, "on your part."

Lizzy rubbed her forehead so that she might hide the smirk on her face. This might actually prove to be entertaining.

"Let us, for the sake of argument, pretend that Alpha..."

Oh, we are back to lupine talk. With one word, Lady Helen conveyed so much: *"I am in the pack, and you are not."*

"...pretend that Alpha is also interested in you. It would be ill advised for you to encourage him, and it is not just because you have no standing in society. For Alpha's safety and happiness, he should marry a she wolf."

"Safety? Please explain how I would endanger Mr. Darcy if a marriage should come about?"

"Have you not learned a lesson from this unfortunate incident? Does it not demonstrate how vulnerable we are? One misplaced step, one slip of the tongue, and we would all be exposed."

"For example, someone referring to Mr. Darcy as Alpha when there are servants about?"

"Exactly. That is a perfect example."

"But it was you who… Never mind."

"Did Alpha ever tell you about when we ran into the poachers?" Lady Helen asked.

"No, he did not."

"Well, these thieves came upon us when we were stalking a deer, and they ran into Lambton screaming that there were wolves in the woods. It was a very tense two nights because it happened at the beginning of nightfall. Oh, excuse me, you probably are not familiar with the terms used by werewolves, but it means…"

"I know what nightfall means," Lizzy said, interrupting.

"Forgive me. I have no way of knowing what Mr. Darcy has chosen to share and what he has withheld." Lady Helen did everything except stick out her tongue and say, *"So there."*

"As I was saying, as soon as Alpha returned to human form, he went into the village with Wolfie and smoothed everything over, but it was a near run thing. Another incident happened here in Derbyshire. A brother of a werewolf said something stupid in a tavern, and a rumor circulated that could not be tamped down. It was necessary for the werewolf to go to Ireland. Ireland!"

"What is wrong with Ireland?"

"Nothing, except the people. They are primitive and live in squalor."

"They live in squalor because all the best land is owned by absentee British landlords, and you do not have to go to Ireland to see such conditions."

Lady Helen took Lizzy's hand again, and in a headmistress

voice indicated that Lizzy should try to concentrate on the subject under discussion.

"And what of your family, Elizabeth? You could not share any of this with them. It would require that you keep a good portion of your life secret from your parents and sisters. I understand that you and your oldest sister are very close. Over time, you would be tempted to share something of your life with her, and if she told her husband... Well, you see the problem. Because of these concerns, it is the suggestion of the Council that male werewolves marry she wolves. You don't want to endanger Alpha, now do you?"

Lizzy turned her face away from the lady. Was it possible that she could do or say something that would expose Mr. Darcy's other life? And if such a thing occurred, it wasn't just Mr. Darcy who would suffer. Georgiana, Anne, the Fitzwilliams, possibly Charles Bingley and her sister would all come under suspicion. Lady Helen handed her a handkerchief, hoping that there were tears to be dried.

"Now, forgive me, Elizabeth, but I must speak my mind."

"I thought you already were," Lizzy said with an edge in her voice.

Ignoring Lizzy's comments, Lady Helen continued. "I would like your assurances that if Mr. Darcy should make you an offer you will decline it."

"Forgive me, but I also must speak my mind. I shall give you no such assurances because, to be quite frank, it is none of your business. Your rank does not entitle you to pry into my personal affairs." Standing up, Lizzy concluded, "I would never do anything that would endanger Mr. Darcy, and you have made your point. So let us now rejoin Anne and Georgiana."

Despite the exchange of words in the study, Lady Helen

remained for another perfectly awful two hours, but her threat to stay indefinitely was withdrawn. Lizzy felt bad for Georgiana, who had known her neighbor for her whole life and greatly admired her for her beauty and accomplishments, but by the time an afternoon of "everything about Lady Helen Granyard" had come to an end, the earl's daughter had sunk to a level nearing contempt in the estimation of Mr. Darcy's sister.

To ensure that Lady Helen would leave quickly, Anne, Georgiana, and Lizzy all walked with her to the door. After making her good-byes to Anne and Georgiana, the lady once again took Lizzy by the hand and led her away from the other two. *Could this woman be any ruder,* Lizzy wondered?

"I hope my openness and honesty has been of some help to you."

"It has," Lizzy admitted.

"And has it changed anything?"

"Oh, yes, it has changed everything."

CHAPTER 17

T HE THREE LADIES STOOD on the steps of the portico until Lady Helen's carriage went through Pemberley's wrought iron gate. A collective sigh of relief followed. Lizzy, who never stopped thinking about the plagues during her visit, felt as free as the Hebrews when Pharaoh finally told Moses that he would let his people go. Of course, they had all that Red Sea parting and wandering in the desert ahead of them, but one problem at a time.

"Lady Helen certainly makes the case for having a draw-bridge built," Lizzy said in an effort to lighten the mood. Although Anne and Georgiana laughed, it was a polite laugh, nothing more. When they went into the house, Mr. Jackson asked to speak to Anne, and so Lizzy and Georgiana returned to the drawing room.

"Georgiana, I can see that you are upset by Lady Helen's unfortunate comments, but in society, when a woman of her rank wants something, she usually finds a way of getting it. No quarter is given."

"But some of the things she said put my brother at risk," Georgiana said, still not believing the thoughtless words that had come out of the mouth of a fellow wolf.

"Her words put her at risk as well," Lizzy said, defending someone who did not deserve it. "She was so intent on making her case for William marrying her that she became careless."

"We have no worries on that account," Anne said as she came into the drawing room. "Apparently, Lady Helen's dramatic entrance put Mr. Jackson on his guard, and he sent all the junior servants belowstairs. Nothing she said was overheard by anyone other than Mr. Jackson."

"Will Mr. Jackson tell my brother?" Georgiana asked.

"Yes. I am afraid Nell is in for a reprimand of some kind."

"I am glad to hear it," Georgiana said with a fervor that surprised Anne and Lizzy. "I can understand her pursuit of my brother, and I can understand that in order to get rid of a rival, she would say anything to diminish Elizabeth. As Elizabeth said, no quarter is given. But it is what she said about Teddy that I find unforgiveable. My brother is always remarking on how attentive Teddy is to her in the wild, bringing her a mouse or rabbit because he knows she is always hungry. And has she forgotten the circumstances that resulted in Teddy becoming a wolf in the first place? He defended his master when a deranged werewolf lunged at him. I know that Teddy would do the same for Nell, and yet she talks about him in such a way," she said with tears in her eyes. "Would you mind if I went to see Mrs. Brotherton? I would take great comfort in her company."

"Please do, dear," Anne said. Although she was only seven years older than Georgiana, in her brother's absence, Anne had taken on the role of her young cousin's guardian.

After Georgiana left the room, Anne turned toward Lizzy. "This is not entirely Lady Helen's fault. If you are told from the time you are a child that you are better than everyone else, you should not be surprised that the child eventually believes it and becomes conceited. I think her mother would have kept her in check, but she died when Helen was five. Lord Granyard's next two wives, wishing to curry favor with the father, doted on her excessively. The product of so much unearned praise is now before us. I almost feel sorry for her because she will be reprimanded, and the rebuke will come from William."

"Do you really think he will admonish her?" Lizzy asked. She did not envy Mr. Darcy the task of disciplining a friend and neighbor.

"Without hesitation. He will not tolerate any behavior that jeopardizes another wolf. If he is willing to discipline the son of a prince, you can be assured he will not pause even for a moment to reprimand Lady Helen. But I have something else I wish to talk to you about." Anne took a letter out of her pocket. "Mr. Jackson just handed this to me. It is from my mother, and it is not unexpected. Because of concerns for my health, Mama is sending a man for me so that I might return to Rosings."

"I am concerned for your health as well," Lizzy said, looking at the circles under Anne's eyes and her pale complexion. "These past few days have been a trial for you, and you need to rest. Besides, you and I both know that the chances of William returning in three weeks are not good. It took him six days to get to Scotland in June when the weather was fine. What is the likelihood that he will have the same good fortune in November? But what will he do about the next nightfall?"

"I imagine he will go to the estate in Northumberland and stay with the family who provided food and shelter for the wolf and her pups. There is also another family in Yorkshire who will take them in. You need have no worries on that front. They are quite safe. But what are we to do about Georgiana? When it comes to her brother, she can be very stubborn, and she will think it disloyal for her to leave

Pemberley. I can just see her acting out, with great dramatic effect, William's return to an empty house." Anne closed her eyes, remembering her dropping to the floor in Elizabeth's bedchamber when she had heard her brother's mournful howl. "Before all this unpleasantness with Lady Helen, she would have stayed at Granyard Hall with Lady Elaine, but she will have no interest in doing so now."

"Are there no relations nearby?"

"The nearest relation is her father's sister, Aunt Marguerite, who lives near Leicester." Anne started smiling. "She is quite a character. I like her a lot, but she frightens Georgiana. She has been wearing widow's weeds for ten years, and she will tell you why. 'My husband died. I would like to think that he did that for me, so this is the least I can do for him.'"

Lizzy found that statement to be funny, and she started giggling and then laughing, and Anne joined in. They knew that it was not *that* funny, but it was proving to be cathartic. Of course, Georgiana would not find any humor in the situation, but while she was safely in the care of Mrs. Brotherton, the two ladies, now friends, could laugh as long as they liked.

After examining all the options, it was decided that Georgiana would have to choose between staying with Lady Elaine or Aunt Marguerite or going to Rosings with Anne. That afternoon, when presented with the choices, Georgiana was indignant, insisting that she was old enough to remain at Pemberley.

"I am not a child. In the spring, I will be out in society and will be encouraged to look for a husband, but you tell me that I cannot remain in my own home for a mere three weeks in a house teeming with servants."

"You do not have to argue your case with me," Anne said in a soothing voice. "I am just thinking what your brother will say to you when he finds you did not take our advice to stay with a friend or relation, and I am trying to think what I will say to him when he laces into me for leaving you alone in this great big house."

"This is so unfair," Georgiana said, pouting. And the sniffling began, and the tears flowed, but then Anne seized on the theme of her becoming an adult.

"Yes, it is unfair, but life is often unfair, and as an adult you will have your share of it. So what is your answer?"

But then a glimmer came into Georgiana's eyes. "There is another place I can go." Turning to Lizzy, she asked, "Now that Jane and Lydia are married, will there be room for me at Longbourn? I have not met your family, and it is always so much better when one can put a face to the names of people one has heard so much about."

Lizzy gave Georgiana such a look. "So Nell is not the only clever female in this part of Derbyshire," she said in admiration at little Miss Darcy's maneuvering. "Of course, there is room. You are very welcome to stay at Longbourn."

"Until my brother comes to Hertfordshire to get me."

"Yes, until your brother comes for you." And what would that mean for Lizzy?

CHAPTER 18

THE NEXT DAY AND the two days after that, Lady Helen sent a rider to Pemberley with a note asking if she should come for a visit. Lizzy was positive that the lady really did not want to pay a call. She just wanted to make sure that her rival really was returning to Hertfordshire. The thought of another morning or afternoon with Lady Helen hastened the packing, and everything was ready when the de Bourgh carriage pulled into the drive at Pemberley. Two days later, on a dreary autumn day, the three ladies and Mrs. Brotherton set out for Ashton Hall in Leicester, the first stop on their journey.

The house was a large unadorned three-story manor house built of stone but in no identifiable style. Attached to one side of the house was a turret with a flagpole flying a banner the color of sunrise that brought a smile to Lizzy's face. Lizzy would soon learn that the turret had been added to the manor house at the request of the newly married Lady Marguerite Ashton, its design influenced by illustrations from a book of French fairy tales.

Lady Marguerite's daughter Jeanne, a tall, pretty, and elegant lady, warmly welcomed the travelers to Ashton Hall and said that she hoped they would consider extending their visit, and it was soon apparent why she wanted her visitors to stay on. There was a war going on between her mother and her husband. George Wimbley was a man blessed with exceptionally good looks, but one with a wandering eye and a well-deserved reputation as a cad, and his mother-in-law was unhappy with her daughter for tolerating his dalliances.

"Kick him where it hurts and that will put an end to that," Lady Marguerite had told Lizzy as they sat by a fire following supper. "But Jeanne's afraid of losing him. Nonsense! You can't lose people like him; they always find their way home. But never mind about them, I want to talk about *you*. William has been writing to me for a year concerning this beauty from Hertfordshire that he fell in love with."

"Really? For a year?" Lizzy asked genuinely surprised, but pleased. "That would be when we first met at an assembly near my home."

"He also told me how he had mucked up the marriage proposal, but I told him that that did not matter as long as he got it right in the end. So tell me, dear, how well do you know my nephew?"

"I know that he is a good man and…"

"No, that is not what I am asking you. I want to know if you *know* him." She squeezed Lizzy's hand so tightly that it was getting mashed. What was she really asking? Surely, it was not about Mr. Darcy being a werewolf as Lizzy had been told that only Anne, Georgiana, and Colonel Fitzwilliam knew about his altered state. She finally just shrugged her shoulders and shook her head, indicating that she did not understand the question.

"Good!" she said, letting go of Lizzy's hand. "If you had just blurted it out, I would never have trusted you again. That shows you will protect him. The reason the others do not know that I am aware of his unique situation is I don't think of him in that way. To me, he is my wonderful nephew.

No need to go on and on about that other business. It would be like telling the Prince of Wales he is fat. He owns a mirror; he knows he's fat. And I am sure you are not the most pleasant person to be around when your courses begin. It is the same thing with him. He is different for those two days." She stopped talking and let out a hissing sound as her son-in-law went by, and he quickly walked to the far end of the room and sat next to his wife.

"I named my daughter after Jeanne d'Arc, a woman who led an army against the English and gave France a king, but who does she marry? A man who cannot pass a mirror without looking at his reflection. He has been unfaithful to her from the start. I am told his assignations are exclusively with women. You never know with these pretty men, so I thank God for small favors.

"Now back to my nephew. The reason I know about William is my brother told me what happened in the Black Forest. It gnawed at him, and he had to tell somebody. Since he knew that I was not on speaking terms with anyone in my family, his secret was safe with me. You see, David, William's father, felt responsible, and for the better part of a year, he dragged his son all over Europe looking for a cure because he did not want his mother to find out about the boy's transformation."

"But how did Mr. Darcy's father know where to go for help?"

"He was given a list by a German doctor, the one who treated him for the bite in Baden, but then they found Dr. Wilkolak in Edinburgh. His wife is a she wolf, and he studies the phenomenon. If there ever is a cure, he will know about it, and he will share it with the community."

"Did Lady Anne find out about William's condition?"

"Yes, God rest her soul. She was a frail thing for the last few years of her life, and when she learned what her son was, she passed out cold. But when she was revived, she told William that she would love him always no matter what, so when David said he had heard about yet another cure in Sweden, Lady Anne would not let the boy go. She told her husband that he was the only one who could not accept it, and he had to stop."

Since her arrival at Pemberley, Lizzy had been trying to come to terms with the idea that the man she loved was a werewolf. Because that subject had occupied all her thoughts, Lizzy had not given any thought to how his parents must have suffered because of their son's affliction. Her heart was deeply touched by his father's efforts to find a cure for his son and his mother's unconditional love, and when added to the depth of caring shown by Georgiana, Anne, and all who served him, a picture of a man worthy of her love and respect emerged.

Lady Marguerite handed Lizzy her handkerchief. "Now don't go all weepy. William needs a strong wife, someone who can deal with the unexpected and unpleasant, which reminds me, did you meet Lady Helen?"

"Lady Helen? Well, yes I did. She is quite… She is quite beautiful and a…"

"Pain in the wide end of a horse." Lizzy made no attempt to stifle her laugh. "God may have blessed her with great beauty, but as far as intelligence is concerned, he skipped over her entirely. She has been flirting up a storm with William ever since he came back from North America two years ago."

"Mr. Darcy was exiled to North America!" Lizzy asked. She could hardly imagine him breaking any rules, no less one that demanded disciplinary action.

"No, no, no. He was not exiled. He went there on holiday. With Georgiana in seminary, he thought it was a good time to go, and he went with Teddy and two others. They traveled from Scotland to Iceland to Greenland to North America, and in the far north of that frozen land, he developed a taste for caribou. But you can't get it in England. He tells me that reindeer is a good substitute."

Lizzy had never heard of caribou. If Mr. Darcy had a preference for the meat of the animal, she would have to learn more about them.

"It must have been a real challenge to live under such harsh conditions when he was not... You know, when he was not something else," Lizzy responded.

"It did test him, but he came back stronger than ever. He was already handsome, and so when he came home tall, dark, lean, and with all those muscles rippling under his coat, Helen wanted him. I still have not decided if he is pretending that he does not know that she is after him, or if he is so immune to her charms that he just does not see what a flirt she is. But once he set eyes on you, she did not have a prayer of securing his affections. You knocked the legs right out from under him. You should have heard some of the things he said about you."

"I can believe it. We had a rather rough start."

"A harsh word about you has never crossed his lips, and it was that rough start that convinced him that you were perfect for him. Anyone who would say no to the benefits of his rank and wealth and the prestige of marrying a Darcy and the grandson of an earl would be able to handle difficult times. I can tell a lot about a person just by looking in their eyes, and you have what is necessary to make him a good wife."

"I am not sure that is going to happen. There was an

emergency concerning someone in the community that required that he go to Scotland. He thought I should reconsider his offer while he was gone."

"Oh, Lord. He is being noble again. That is my fault.
In my tower, I have all these books about King Arthur and
all his knights, and we would go up there and read them
together. But in real life, no one is that good. If they were,
their presence would be intolerable. So if he says anything
like that again, you tell him you are not in the mood for any
noble speeches. As far as you are concerned, he asked you to
marry him, you accepted, and that is the end of it. You tell
him his aunt Marguerite said so."

CHAPTER 19

DARCY SAT ACROSS FROM Josiah MacGregor in a dark study in a dark house with candles casting shadows on wood-paneled walls lined with swords and muskets and the heads of a hundred red deer that reminded a hungry Darcy of how much he liked the taste of venison. It wasn't as good as caribou, but he definitely preferred it to squirrel or vole. But first to the business at hand.

When he had arrived at the Underhill estate, he was pleased to learn that both Teddy and Rupert had been released by the laird, but the estate manager had suggested that Darcy visit MacGregor in order to extinguish any lingering doubts about what the gamekeeper had seen in the woods. The next day, after hearing the whole of the story from Teddy and Mr. Underhill, including the alias he was to use, Mr. Darcy, who was to be addressed as Mr. Williams, set out to pay a call on the laird.

Darcy came prepared, and shortly after introductions were made, he suggested to MacGregor that there was no misunderstanding so great that it could not be resolved over a jar of whisky, and Mercer produced two glasses and a bottle of Scotch.

Because of heavy taxes imposed on the distilleries by the Board of Excise, most of the whisky produced in Scotland was illegally made, and Darcy, like most visitors and residents of Scotland, knew someone who could procure a few bottles of the spirits for the right price. A believer in free enterprise and minimal taxes on commodities, Darcy supported a private distillery near Jedburgh.

"I was in Scotland last summer in the company of a gentleman who had a private reserve of some spirits that are, shall we say, locally distilled, and he presented me with a few bottles to take home. This is the last of it," Darcy said as he poured the amber liquid into the glasses, and before the last drop splashed into the glass, MacGregor's hand was reaching for it.

"Mr. Williams, I am honored ta have such a fine gentleman in ma home," MacGregor began, "and it's unfortunate how ye came ta be here. There be no hard feelings on ma part, but as I telt Underhill tame and tame again, if he'd get rid a those big black dogs of his, ma servants wouldn't be havering aboot seein' wolves on tha property."

"That is good advice, sir. However, being partial to black dogs myself, I understand why Underhill wishes to keep them, but I will agree with you that they can look like wolves, which is probably part of their attraction."

"I dunna want ta give anybody tha wrong idea that I'm claimin' to be injured in ane way," MacGregor continued. When he had seen the expensive carriage with its matched pair of black stallions pull up to the front entrance, he had checked his shirt to see if there was any food left on it from the morning meal, and although he knew nothing about Mr. Williams, he recognized a gentleman when he saw one. The laird assumed that the crazed boy must be the son of someone important if his kin had sent a man of such quality to recover him, and he did not want to have some high and mighty from the South making his life miserable because their son had taken to crawling around on all fours on his property.

"But 'tis an odd business aw the same," MacGregor continued. "Aroon here, we're nat used ta someone loupin' naked in tha woods in freezing weather. We hae more sense than to do somethin' like that, and when tha laddie come into the house, I had ta put him in front a tha fire a'cause he was chilled to tha bone. Thomas, his man, took me aside and said that tha man was cracked," he said, tapping his temple. "I could tell by the way he blethered that he were a gentleman, but I didnae believe him for a minute when he said his da was a prince. But, I'll tell ye, he really thinks he *is* the bairn of a prince."

"Don't we all," Darcy said, and MacGregor thought that was so funny, he nearly choked on his drink.

"Another thing. Tha laddie knew he done wrong and was goin' to be skelped for it 'cause he started wailin' and sayin' tha he was goin' to be sent to Amerikay near the Hudson which, if I got my bearin's reet, is where the ships make port ta drop their wares in the city of New York. Now, I've n'er been ta Amerikay, sir, but the way he wa' carryin' ain, you'd think he was bein' sent ta tha North Pole. It cannae be that bad a place."

"As Thomas indicated, the gentleman suffers from a mental impairment," Darcy explained. "He has difficulty distinguishing between what is real and what is not. However, he has concerned parents who would be embarrassed if this episode became known. But I can see that you are a gentleman, someone I can rely on to be discreet and to keep this unfortunate situation quiet, and I would appreciate it if you would discourage any discussion by the locals."

"Ye hae ma word, sir. Yon gentleman's man, Thomas, gae us good reasons for tha poor laddie's behavior. Anyway, that storm has passed by. Tha excise man comin' in ta the glen frae the Sooth a looking fur mountain tay an' breakin' up stills is what everyane's blethering aboot. Takin' oor whisky is more important ta us than some lunatic runnin' aboot naked."

Darcy bristled at MacGregor's use of the word "lunatic." Yes, the moon did have its effects, but it did not make men run mad. After refilling the laird's glass, Darcy offered MacGregor some monetary compensation for the inconvenience caused by the young man.

Now in his cups, MacGregor declined any remuneration, but after Darcy continued to insist, the Scotsman took the notes spread before him, and Darcy left hoping that the government excise men would linger a while in the glen—anything to get people to stop talking about Rupert "loupin' aboot naked in the woods."

⚮

While Darcy had been inside the house soothing ruffled feathers, Metcalf, the coachman, had been removing every speck of dust from the carriage. A member of the Metcalf family had been driving carriages for Darcys for three generations, and it was Metcalf who had transported the she wolf and her pups from Northumberland, first to Pemberley and then to a port on the Irish Sea, a journey that could have proved disastrous if the wagon had broken down. Along with Mercer, a retired mail coach driver, Darcy relied on these men to get him to Pemberley or some other safe destination before the rising of the full moon. Neither man had ever disappointed him.

They had made the journey from Pemberley to the Underhill estate in five days—a day ahead of schedule. But that gain soon fell away because of Rupert, who was carrying on in such a manner that the only way to get him into a carriage to go to Durham, where members of the Council were waiting for him, was to tie him up, and that Darcy would not do. After sending an express rider to Durham with a letter explaining that they must come and get the bad apple, they waited, day after day, until the two Council representatives arrived. Because Darcy had no wish to witness his removal, Mercer and he had departed that same afternoon, but without Teddy.

In order to help calm the young miscreant, Teddy had offered to go with the Council men as far as Durham. That alone had served to calm the young man, but Teddy also told Rupert stories of his own sojourn in the far north of the North American continent. Because his appetite was second only to Nell's, when Rupert heard of the excellent hunting afforded by vast caribou herds and moose and the easy pickings of thousands of migratory birds and their eggs, his spirits picked up considerably, and he became more compliant. There were other inducements as well. Teddy spoke of the freedom of running over great snow-covered expanses and how he and his party had been invited into the homes of the natives, whose belief system included animals transfiguring into men, and because of that, the tension and danger of nightfall and daybreak were absent.

But while they waited, with the clock ticking away the hours, Darcy's attention turned to Elizabeth, and with a bottle of Jedburgh Scotch on the table next to him and David and Goliath at his heels, he reexamined his options. Yes, he loved her, more than he ever thought possible, but the reality was that he was a werewolf and she was a human. The situation with Rupert had served to demonstrate how vulnerable a population werewolves were. One wayward comment could end in disaster for the entire lupine community.

Even if there were no idiots like Rupert, there was still the physical transformation that took place every four weeks, and such thoughts caused Darcy to sink back into his chair. Of course, he would rather not be a werewolf, but he had accepted it from the beginning. And there were advantages to being a lupine. Although he relished the thrill of the hunt and roaming through the diverse landscapes of his property and the Peak, nothing compared to his time in North America. Because he had been tested mentally and physically by its harsh elements, when he had returned to England, he was confident in his abilities in both his incarnations. But with his adventure now behind him, he had decided it was time to choose a wife from among the she wolf population so that he might marry and raise a family. He had it all planned out until...

Darcy had arrived at Netherfield Park the very day of the assembly. It had been a mere two days since daybreak, and he had told Bingley that he was in no humor to go to a local dance. With his sense of smell still in a heightened state, the mixture of scents—most of them emanating from unwashed bodies with an added layer of perfume to disguise the odors— was unpleasant to say the least, but Charles would not be put off. Once they had arrived at the assembly, Bingley continued to press his friend, insisting that he dance. The result was that he had stated in a voice loud enough to be heard by others that "to dance at an assembly such as this would be insupportable." Worse yet, he had specifically singled Elizabeth out as being merely tolerable, but not handsome enough to tempt him to dance.

He was genuinely ashamed when he realized that Elizabeth had heard his remark, and when he turned around to gauge the effect of his rudeness, she had looked right at him and had actually smiled at his surliness. In that moment, he had felt a tug at his heart, but he needed to know more about the lady. So he had listened in on her conversations at Lucas Lodge and had found her to be an engaging conversationalist as well as someone who spoke with authority on a number of substantive topics. When she had called him out for his eavesdropping, he did not care because he had heard what he needed to hear. Added to all her charms and sparkling wit was a smile that had left him weak at the knees.

The result was that he followed her into Kent and badly botched the whole affair. As he walked to the parsonage, he practiced what he would say to her and thought that if an opportunity arose, he might even drop a hint that there was more to him than he was at liberty to disclose at that time. But when he went into the parlor and saw her sitting in front of a window, with its light creating an aura outlining her beautiful features, he forgot every line he had rehearsed. Instead, he concluded that it did not matter what he said. He was a werewolf, and this lovely creature would run away when she learned of his other incarnation. Instead of professing his love for her, he had presented her with a list of reasons why he should *not* marry her. In that way, he would not feel rejected when his secret was revealed.

A few months after his bungled proposal, Elizabeth came to Pemberley on the very morning of his return to human form. It was a glorious day, and after escorting Nell to the rendezvous point, he had decided to take a walk in the gardens. As he entered the lower gardens, there she was, sitting on a bench without her bonnet but with her eyes closed and her face pointed toward the sun. When she opened her eyes and found him staring at her, she jumped up from the bench and hurriedly returned her bonnet to its rightful place. He sensed her embarrassment, but he sensed something else as well. The message given out by her scent was unmistakable. She wanted him to take her in his arms and kiss her, and once again, he had reason to hope.

After her return to Hertfordshire, he had paid a call on her at Longbourn, which had gone very well, and with each subsequent visit, her scent and the way she moved her body let him know that she would be receptive to another offer of marriage, that is, if he were human. But between his monthly transformations and going to Northumberland and arranging for transportation for the she wolf and her pups, he had not seen her at all during the month of June. In July, he was in Scotland attending the gathering, and then Rupert had arrived at Pemberley. Although he had written a number of letters to her during their separation, when he had asked if she had received them, she said nothing more than, "Yes, they were properly addressed." Clearly, she had judged them to be unsatisfactory.

"Which reminds me that I must remember to write to Elizabeth and Georgiana before I leave Scotland," he said out loud, and after locating a writing desk where he could perform such a task, his thoughts returned to Lizzy.

It was Anne who had finally convinced him to reveal to Elizabeth his other incarnation, and it was a good thing that she had. When he arrived at Longbourn, Elizabeth was so annoyed at him for his peripatetic habits that if he had not had a plan in place, he believed that she would have shown him the door. As it turned out, Anne's scheme to reveal his lupine nature at Pemberley worked brilliantly, and the strength of his love eventually won her over.

If only he knew what was happening at Pemberley. Considering the circumstances under which he had been called away, he believed that he had done the right thing by providing her with an opportunity to change her mind. But would she take it? He dearly wished to know what was happening in Derbyshire. He would arrive at Pemberley shortly before the next full moon, but would Elizabeth be there to witness it?

CHAPTER 20

DURING THE LAST FEW days, Lizzy had been watching Anne de Bourgh for any sign that her health might be affected by all the emotional upheaval at Pemberley. During the carriage ride to Ashton Hall, Anne had contributed little to the conversation, stating that she preferred to listen to Georgiana speak of her debut or Lizzy's answers to her cousin's many questions about life at Longbourn. There was also a slowness in her movements that was a sign of fatigue, so when the weather went from dreary to dismal and the rains came, Lizzy suggested that they remain at Ashton Hall so that Anne could rest, and rest she did.

The first day after their arrival, Anne did not come downstairs until one o'clock in the afternoon, and Georgiana teased her cousin that she was picking up her bad habits. The second day was a repeat of the first, and it was then that Lizzy realized why Anne felt comfortable keeping to her bedchamber and foregoing playing cards after dinner. A weight had been lifted off her shoulders because Lady Marguerite was now in charge.

Although Lizzy thought Lady Marguerite was an absolute jewel, she greatly intimidated Georgiana with her outspoken opinions.

"Aunt Marguerite wants me to be strong like Aunt Catherine, but not bossy. Assertive like she is, but not scary.

A good hostess like Lady Helen, but not to be like her in any other way. Oh, and one more thing, she said that I should never marry anyone who is prettier than I am. Of course, she was referring to Jeanne and Mr. Wimbley."

The much maligned Mr. Wimbley had departed that morning to visit a relative who had suddenly taken ill. As Aunt Marguerite had explained it, "Once he realized that I would not stay in the dragon's den, which is how he refers to my suite of rooms, he hightailed it to his brother's house in High Wycombe, and Jeanne went with him to make sure he was visiting his brother and not someone else."

"I do not think Lady Marguerite had a very happy marriage," Lizzy suggested as a reason for her harsh treatment of her son-in-law.

"Oh, I know she did not," Georgiana said. "She made that quite plain when I asked how long Lord Ashton had been gone. She said that he had died ten years ago, but added, 'He had a heart attack brought on by… Oh, never mind, you are too young. Just let me put it this way, he did not die alone.'" Lizzy tried to suppress a smile, but Georgiana noticed. "I know I am young, but even so, I understood what she was talking about. I think it is awful when one's spouse is unfaithful. I do so hope that I shall marry someone who will be faithful to me. I want to be deeply in love with my husband and he with me."

So do I, Lizzy thought.

❧

After a five-day visit, Anne announced that she was prepared to resume her journey but hoped that she would be able to have a full day's rest at either Netherfield Park or Longbourn before going into Kent. Lizzy thought of the

palatial Rosings Park and decided that Netherfield Park was
the better choice—at least for Anne, and when Lizzy suggested to Georgiana that she stay with Jane as well until
Anne had departed, Georgiana agreed. In that way, Lizzy
would have time to speak with her mother, and she knew
what her first question would be. "Are you engaged to be
married to Mr. Darcy?" When she answered no, the inquisi-
tion would begin.

Although Lizzy had only been gone for two weeks,
she felt as if she had been away from Hertfordshire for a
month, and Jane hugged her as if she had been absent a year.
Despite the short interval, Jane, now in her fifth month, had
blossomed in her sister's absence, and there was no longer
any way to conceal her pregnancy. The proud father came
bounding into the room, greeting everyone with his irre-
pressible cheerfulness.

Lizzy was easily convinced to stay the night at Netherfield
Park. She would delay her mother's probing questions as
long as possible, but Jane was equally curious about recent
events and visited with her sister in her room after everyone
had retired.

"Lizzy, I do not know what to make of your short visit to
Pemberley. You seem to be in good spirits, but I suspect if
there was an announcement to be made that I would already
know of your engagement to Mr. Darcy because you would
be unable to contain your joy."

An announcement? Was there anything to announce,
Lizzy wondered. Mr. Darcy's chilling words before leaving for Scotland continued to echo in her mind: "Please
know that you owe me nothing. You are not bound to me."
Unsure of her future with the master of Pemberley, Lizzy
chose to remain silent.

"Mr. Darcy and I are not engaged," Lizzy said in a quiet voice. "He was called away on a family emergency, and since Miss de Bourgh's health became a concern, it was decided that we should leave Pemberley. But once Anne departs for Rosings, Miss Darcy will come and stay at Longbourn."

"Oh my! Won't that be interesting? The mistress of Pemberley will be staying at our humble abode," Jane said, laughing, but then she asked, "What happened with Mr. Darcy? I thought the purpose of his inviting you to Pemberley was so that he could propose at the Darcy ancestral estate."

"I am afraid things got off to a rather bad start. We both have strong temperaments, and we quarreled. However, it had the effect of clearing the air, and after that, my visit was quite pleasant. But then he had to leave. And I can see you are looking for more information, but I have nothing else to share."

"Good gracious! How long does it take for a man to utter the words, 'Will you marry me, Miss Elizabeth?' That is all that need be said. What is the difficulty? I simply do not understand the delay," Jane said in a raised voice, indicating her continued frustration with her sister's suitor.

"I think it will finally be decided when he comes to Longbourn for his sister, but until then, I am as much in the dark as you are."

❧

When Mr. Bingley's carriage pulled into the drive, everyone was expecting Jane and Charles to emerge, so no one came out to greet Elizabeth. But when Lizzy went into the drawing room, she was nearly overpowered by an exuberant Kitty and a squealing Mrs. Bennet. With Jane and Lydia married and Lizzy away in Derbyshire, Kitty had only Mary for companionship, and since the two sisters had nothing in common and no hope of that ever changing, evenings had been very dull for Kitty. The ruckus created by her welcome brought her father out of his sanctuary to welcome his daughter home.

"While you have been gone, not two words of sense have been spoken in this house," Mr. Bennet told his favorite daughter and gave her a peck on the cheek. "I look forward to a return of intelligent discourse."

Lizzy was delighted by the warmth of her homecoming, but then she turned around and saw her mother, who had been waiting for her daughter to burst out with the good news that she was to be married to the very wealthy Mr. Darcy. When Lizzy said nothing, she asked, "Well, are you engaged or not?" And the room went quiet in anticipation.

"Mrs. Bennet, she has only just walked in the door," Mr. Bennet said, scolding his wife.

"What has that to do with anything? She is either engaged or she isn't. So which is it?"

"I am not engaged, Mama," Lizzy said, looking at her father rather than addressing her mother.

"But I told you that you should not come home until you were betrothed. Why are you here? Why was your visit so short? That is the problem," she said, wagging her finger at her daughter. "You did not give him enough time."

"Mama, Mr. Darcy was called away on a family emergency."

"So what! You should have stayed at Pemberley until he came back. You may have lost him by leaving Derbyshire."

"Mrs. Bennet, if it is Mr. Darcy's intention to make our daughter an offer, then he will find Lizzy no matter where she is. If traveling the distance between Derbyshire and

Hertfordshire is an obstacle to their becoming engaged, then I must say that I would be reluctant to give my consent to the match."

"Mama, I could not possibly remain at Pemberley because Miss de Bourgh had to return to Rosings, and Miss Darcy came with her. They are both staying at Netherfield Park until Miss de Bourgh goes to Kent, and then Miss Darcy will come here."

"Oh my goodness!" Mrs. Bennet exclaimed. "Miss Darcy? Here at Longbourn? Why didn't you say that from the start? As long as we have her, Mr. Darcy must come here to recover his sister."

"Mrs. Bennet, you make it sound as if we are holding the young lady hostage." Mr. Bennet gestured for Lizzy to follow him into the study. After the door was closed, he poured a sherry for his daughter and a port for himself. She looked as if she needed it.

"What happened in Derbyshire?"

"A great deal," Lizzy said after taking more than a sip of sherry. "It is a lot more complicated than I ever thought it would be. After taking into consideration the prestige of the family, their aristocratic neighbors, the size of the estate, the number of servants, etc., I was quite overwhelmed by all the responsibilities expected of the wife of Mr. Darcy."

"Come, come, my dear. Those things are important, but if you love Mr. Darcy, it certainly should not deter you from marrying him."

"Papa, please do not say 'if I love him.' I do love him—so very dearly. But he is a complex man, and there were times when I did not understand what my role would be. I thought that I might not be exactly what he needs because… Oh, I don't know how to explain myself."

"If you are trying to say that he is a difficult man to be around, maybe he does not deserve you."

"Oh, no, Papa. He is such a good man, and he deserves a wife who will stand by his side through trials and tribulations."

"Trials and tribulations? What does Mr. Darcy know of such things? He lives in a grand manor house on an estate of thousands of acres with servants at his beck and call. He has wealth, prestige, and rank. He wants for nothing."

Lizzy looked away from her father, and tears filled her eyes. Mr. Darcy wanted for nothing—nothing except that he be wholly human, that he not live in fear of discovery, and that his every move not be dictated by the phases of the moon.

"My dear, something is bothering you. Please tell me what it is."

"Papa, it is not that Mr. Darcy does not deserve me. It is that I may not be what Mr. Darcy needs to live his life to the fullest."

"I do not understand you, child."

"I know."

❦

The days passed quickly. With Anne's return to Rosings Park, Georgiana had come to stay at Longbourn. After much discussion, the final accommodations were that Georgiana would sleep in Kitty's room because both were close in age, Mary would share Lizzy's room, and Mrs. Brotherton would have Mary's bedroom.

"Lizzy, it is so funny," Georgiana said, giggling. "I have such a big house with so few people in it, and you have a small house with so many people. Isn't that odd?"

Lizzy chuckled to herself. She had never thought of Longbourn as being a "small house," but to someone who lived in a grand country manor, the Bennet homestead probably did look small. Despite so many people living in tight quarters, Georgiana loved it. Having lost both of her parents by the time she was thirteen, and having only the one brother, who was ten years her senior, she was enjoying the energy and closeness of the Bennet family.

Georgiana was a perfect fit. Because Miss Darcy had access to an impressive library at Pemberley and had been educated at one of London's finest seminaries, she had a broad base of knowledge that Mary eagerly tapped into. Better yet, a friendship had developed between Kitty and Georgiana, and Miss Darcy was a more suitable companion for her than Lydia ever was.

When the young ladies walked into Meryton to pick up the mail at the inn, seventeen days had passed since Mr. Darcy had left Pemberley. In addition to letters from Mrs. Gardiner and Mr. Bennet's sister, there were letters for both Lizzy and Georgiana from Mr. Darcy that had been forwarded to Meryton by Mr. Jackson. Lizzy quickly tucked the letter into her reticule, but Georgiana broke the seal on hers, and when a smile appeared on her face, Lizzy knew that all was well, and she handed the letter to Lizzy.

My Dearest Georgiana,

We made excellent time and arrived a day earlier than expected. Rupert and Teddy are both well and send you their regards. However, there were some difficulties in arranging schedules, and so I must remain until those problems have been worked out. But I am confident that they will shortly be resolved, and I anticipate being back at Pemberley well in advance of my scheduled appointment. So there are no concerns on that account. Please give my best to Anne and Miss Elizabeth.

Yours, Will (writing from Carlisle)

"My brother thinks we are still at Pemberley," Georgiana said. "He will be disappointed when he finds that we are not there, but what could one do when Aunt Catherine sent a carriage for Anne?"

"Well, he will learn from Mr. Jackson the reason for our departure, and all will be well. Shall we go to the circulating library and see if anything interesting has come in on the London coach?" Lizzy asked, hoping that Georgiana would not mention that she too had received a letter.

As soon as Lizzy reached Longbourn, she went to the sitting room so that she might read Mr. Darcy's letter in private.

Dear Elizabeth,
All is well here. Things went much better than expected.
I look forward to seeing you when I return to Pemberley.
Yours, F. Darcy

Lizzy could hardly believe it. Three sentences! That was what she had been waiting for all this time? Such brevity was a message in itself. He had asked her to reconsider her decision to marry him when it was obvious it was he who was doing the reconsidering. She went to her father's study, and with fire in her eyes, she announced, "Papa, you were right. Mr. Darcy does not deserve me." She turned on her heel and left.

CHAPTER 21

THE SAME WEATHER THAT had delayed Georgiana, Anne, and Lizzy's departure from Ashton Hall had caused problems for Darcy as well. It had been necessary to take a detour around a washed-out bridge, and time was lost when they came upon an overturned wagon and a flock of sheep that had to be convinced to leave the road. By the time the village of Lambton came into view, all of Darcy's energy was spent, and he was looking forward to visiting with his sister and cousin, but most especially with Elizabeth. Had she changed her mind while he had been in Scotland? He would soon find out.

Part of a wolf's survival depended upon his ability to quickly assess his environment, and when the carriage pulled up in front of Pemberley, Darcy guessed that the house was empty. From the look on Jackson's face, he knew that he was right.

"Good day, Jackson. I shall be with you in a moment," Darcy said. "Metcalf, I will have no need of a carriage tomorrow, so please feel free to see to your personal affairs." He stepped back, indicating that he could proceed to the coach house.

"Mercer, please see to the trunks, and I shall want a bath. But after that, I do not want to see you for the rest of the day, and you may hear the same thing from me tomorrow.

Apparently, the ladies are not in residence, so I can go one day without shaving," he said, rubbing his scruffy chin. And although he had said that with a smile on his face, Mercer knew that his master was sorely disappointed to come home from such a difficult journey to find everyone gone. "Oh, one more thing. Please see that some of that whisky we bought in Jedburgh makes its way into my study.

"And now to you, Mr. Jackson. Shall we go in? I sense that you have something to tell me that I would not want others to hear?"

After directing Mercer to place the Scotch and two glasses on the table in front of him, he dismissed his valet, poured whisky into each glass, and handed one to his butler. "Sit down, Jackson. I am too tired to be staring up at you, and from the look on your face, I do believe you could use a drink yourself. But before we talk about what transpired at Pemberley while I was gone, I want you to know that I have a bottle of these fine spirits for you as well. Now, let us get down to business. Where are the ladies?"

After Darcy's butler explained that Lady Catherine had sent a carriage for Miss de Bourgh and that his sister and Miss Elizabeth thought that she should not travel alone, Mr. Darcy let out a sigh of relief.

"No need for a grim face, Jackson. That is actually good news because I had feared that Miss Elizabeth would reconsider my offer."

"Yes, sir, but there is more." Jackson spoke of Lady Helen Granyard's dramatic arrival at Pemberley, her reference to Mr. Darcy as Alpha, and her mentioning that she had slept beside him.

Darcy sat there stunned. "She said what? Was there anyone about? Did any of the servants hear her?"

"Only Mrs. Reynolds and I were on the ground floor during her visit. I had been put on my guard when Lady Helen practically ran up the steps and brushed past me in the foyer, and I thought that she might say something that the junior servants should not hear. So they were dismissed."

"What was she thinking?" Darcy asked, shocked by Jackson's revelation.

"Sir, it was my impression that she was not—thinking, that is. She had a purpose in coming here, and because of that, she gave no thought to her conversation being overheard."

"And her purpose was?"

"To convince Miss Bennet that she should not marry you. But then Lady Helen asked Miss Bennet to go into the study, and of course, I could not hear what was said behind closed doors."

"Was anything said by either lady when they came out of my study?"

"Sir, at that point, Miss de Bourgh and Miss Darcy had rejoined the two ladies, and the foyer was crowded."

Darcy knew that his butler was avoiding his question. "Jackson, you and I have known each other a long time, and we have a relationship based on your telling me the absolute truth. Even if you think I shall not like what you have to say, you must tell me."

"Very well, sir," Jackson said, shifting uncomfortably in his chair. "Lady Helen asked Miss Bennet if what she had said in the study had changed her mind. I assume she was talking about Miss Bennet marrying you, and Miss Bennet replied, 'It has changed everything.'"

"I see," Darcy said and looked down into his drink. "Well, I can't say I am completely surprised that Miss Bennet would reconsider. On the other hand, I am greatly surprised by Lady Helen's behavior. Do you know if Lord Granyard is in residence?"

"He is, sir. Lady Helen mentioned that the family will stay in the country until after the full moon, and then they will go to Lord Wilston's manor house, where they will remain until Twelfth Night."

"In that case, I shall have a letter ready for Cubbins to deliver to His Lordship in about an hour, and I shall go to Granyard Hall tomorrow. The full moon is in three days, and this must be dealt with before that time. Is there anything else I need to know, Jackson?"

"One other thing, sir. Miss Darcy did not go to Rosings with Miss de Bourgh. She is staying with Miss Bennet at Longbourn."

Darcy let out a quiet laugh. "My sister continues to plot and plan. Unfortunately, this time, it will not work out as she had hoped."

∽∾

As soon as Lord Granyard read Darcy's letter, he called his daughter into the library. "Mr. Darcy is coming to Granyard Hall tomorrow. He writes that he has an important matter of business to discuss with me. Do you know what this is about?"

Lady Helen bit her lip and smiled before saying that she could not possibly know the purpose of the visit.

"Don't be coy with me, Nell. Why is Mr. Darcy coming here?"

"I imagine he might wish to ask you for permission to court me." She broke out into a broad smile and clapped her hands.

"Court *you*? I doubt it very much. Other than you being a member of his pack, the man has never shown any interest in you at all. Additionally, I was given to understand that he is much taken with the woman he brought to Elaine's reception."

"No, she is merely a friend of Miss de Bourgh's," Lady Helen said, lying with a straight face.

"This is very odd, especially in light of his having told me that he thought of you as his sister. You and he have been out there in the wild together for three years, and all of a sudden he wants to court you? What kept him from asking for a courtship before today?"

"I think it is just a matter of it being the right time for him to take a mate. I am sure he is ready to breed."

"Well, if you say so," her father said, but he remained skeptical. "I do understand the logic of his wanting to marry a she wolf. But, Nell, if this has anything to do with the pack, my hands are tied. When you came under the Council's protection, we agreed to follow all of their rules, including the one about family members not interfering with Council business."

"Papa, I have done nothing wrong. I am sure there is a much more pleasant reason for Mr. Darcy's coming here."

After her father dismissed her, Lady Helen went upstairs and told Elaine about Mr. Darcy's visit on the morrow. "I am sure he is coming here to propose."

"Nell, I have no wish to throw cold water on your celebration, but it is my understanding from Georgiana that Mr. Darcy intends to make an offer to Miss Bennet."

"I can assure you that that will not happen. Miss Bennet told me that she would follow my advice and leave Mr. Darcy to marry one of his own. It was very foolish of him to think he could wed someone who is fully human. It is so rarely done. Besides, she has no understanding of what is involved in being a wolf and the precautions we must take."

"For instance, not referring to Mr. Darcy as Alpha as you did in the receiving line. You are lucky I was the only one who heard you."

"I agree that that was a mistake, but who would know what I was talking about if they did hear me?"

"Nell, you are not thinking like a lupine. Such terms are never used in public under any circumstance. Please understand that if Mr. Darcy's purpose in coming here is to propose, I most certainly will wish you joy, but he would be very displeased if he thought you had grown careless."

"But no one, other than Miss Bennet, heard me call Mr. Darcy Alpha," Lady Helen insisted.

"For your sake, I hope you are right."

CHAPTER 22

Lᴏʀᴅ Gʀᴀɴʏᴀʀᴅ ᴡᴇɴᴛ ᴛᴏ the window and stared out at the terrace and the gardens beyond. His title, his estate, his rank meant nothing in the matter at hand. The fate of his daughter, his beloved Nell, now rested in the hands of Fitzwilliam Darcy, and he had not felt such an emptiness since the death of Nell's mother.

"Darcy, will there be an official reprimand registered with the Council?"

"These are serious transgressions, milord. It was only because of Mr. Jackson's quick thinking that none of the junior servants were abovestairs to hear Nell's remarks. She actually said, 'sleeping with Mr. Darcy.' Although it has nothing to do with her being a lupine, if someone had heard such a statement, what conclusion would be drawn? That Nell is a loose woman, and that I am equally bereft of morals as I had seduced an unmarried lady of rank, a friend, and a neighbor."

"I understand, Darcy. It is just that she got it in her head that you wanted to marry her."

"I honestly do not know where she got such an idea as I have said time and time again that I think of her as a sister and as a member of my pack. I have not given her any encouragement because I am in love with another."

"Miss de Bourgh's friend?" Lord Granyard asked.

"Is that what Nell told you? That she was at Pemberley because she was a friend of Anne?" When Granyard nodded, Darcy shook his head. "This is truly distressing because she knows that is not true. Even so, Nell was able to convince Miss Bennet that it was not in her interest nor mine for us to become husband and wife. As distressing as that is, it is not the matter at hand. Without any thought that someone might overhear her, Nell referred to me as Alpha, and with her careless talk, she put me at risk, as well as my sister and your family."

"This is all my fault," Granyard said in a voice barely above a whisper. "I overindulged her, and as a result, she thinks that she should get everything she wants. I should have brought her up with a firmer hand, but when her mother died... Darcy, please do not reprimand her. If you do, for the rest of her life, she will be living under the sword of Damocles. One mistake and she will be exiled."

"Lord Granyard, over the past three decades, the Council has worked hard to protect the werewolf population in Britain, not an easy task. But one of the reasons for its success is everyone knows what will happen if they betray their fellow lupines with their words or actions. Nell is no different from anyone else in that regard. Her rank does not matter in the wild. Now, if you will, please ask Nell to come in."

While Darcy waited for Nell, he finished the port he had been nursing. If he were at Pemberley, he might have considered drinking the whole damn bottle. It was just a week earlier that he had had to deal with Rupert, and what a scene that had been. Rupert had got down on all fours and crawled toward Darcy before lying on his back to expose his belly, something he would have done in the wild. But the gesture had revolted him.

"Get up! For God's sake, you are the son of a prince and a member of my pack. Stop this disgusting display," Darcy had told him. "If you think that this will change anything, you are mistaken. You knew what the punishment would be for a second transgression, but you decided that since your father is the Prince of Wales you could get away with your slothful ways. You were on MacGregor's property because you wanted his rabbits. Why bother hunting if you can steal someone else's food? And in doing so, you came very close to being seen in your lupine form.

"If anyone had actually witnessed your transformation, do you know what would have happened? You would have been beaten to death, and after they had finished with you, they would have turned on Teddy. And then MacGregor's neighbors and the villagers would have been alerted to the werewolf in their midst, and because they knew that you were a guest of Mr. Underhill, they would have marched over to his house, and only God knows what would have happened. This very thing occurred in France, and the mob burnt the house to the ground."

But Darcy needed to get that horrible scene out of his head. Nell was not Rupert, and her transgression was serious, but nothing to compare to what Rupert had done. In all his years as a werewolf, other than Rupert, he had never personally known any lupine who had been subjected to Council discipline, and now it had been necessary for him to discipline a second member of his four-member pack. So what should he do? Nell's father was right. If he registered an official reprimand with the Council, she would have to watch every step, weigh every word, and would forever be looking over her shoulder. Considering the gossip-obsessed society she moved in, that might be a good thing. It might actually protect her from herself.

When Nell came into the room, Darcy recognized that Lizzy had been right. Nell was the most beautiful woman he had ever seen, and because she thought he had come to ask for her hand in marriage, she was dressed in one of her loveliest dresses. But before he even said a word, she knew that was not going to happen. Her father had warned her of Darcy's decision, and she had entered the room with head bowed.

"Mr. Darcy, I am so sorry," she said, sniffling. "I know there is nothing I can say to make up for my careless remarks, but you know I would never do anything that could harm the members of the pack."

"But you have already done such a thing."

"But Papa said that Mr. Jackson made sure that none of the junior servants were about."

"How fortunate for you—and me."

"What will happen to me?" she asked, twisting her handkerchief.

"In one way, you are the beneficiary of Rupert's stupidity because it allows me to compare the two situations. I have decided to reprimand you…"

Nell gasped. Short of committing a transgression so grievous that the wolf was immediately taken into custody and exiled, this was the worst thing that could happen for a first offense. Her sniveling gave way to copious weeping, but Darcy made no attempt to comfort her.

"Nell, allow me to finish," he said loudly in order to be heard above the sound of her sobs. "I have decided to reprimand you, but I shall keep the written report of your error at Pemberley. It will only be revealed to the Council if you should commit a second transgression. I have known this to be done in at least one other instance."

Nell came over and knelt in front of him and took his hand

and put it against her forehead as a sign of her acceptance of his decision. "Thank you. I will not disappoint you. I promise."

Darcy pulled his hand away. Such demonstrations were necessary in the wild, but he had never been comfortable with their use when he was in human form, and he helped her to rise.

"Please sit down because there is something else I want to talk to you about. It is the matter of your marriage. You are twenty-one years old, and the time has come to address this issue. Lord Angelsey is the only werewolf who is both British and your equal in rank, but you seem not to like him. I know of only four British werewolves who are members of the landed gentry, but, frankly, I cannot see you marrying any of them either."

"Are you sure that there is not another who is suitable?"

Darcy knew that she was referring to him, but if there had even been so much as a spark of interest on his part, that ember had been extinguished with her selfish pursuit of what was beneficial to her and to her alone.

"None that I know of. However, there are gentlemen of French, German, and Swedish origin in the various packs near the Welsh border. In the spring, I want you to go to Herefordshire and visit with Mrs. Evesham, and she will see that you are properly introduced to those gentlemen of suitable rank and age."

"Must I marry?"

"If you are asking me if I am ordering you to take a husband, the answer is no. However, the decision whether to marry a human or a werewolf has been taken away from you. I cannot risk your being careless with your husband's relations, so you must marry a fellow lupine, that is, if you choose to marry. But you are of a most agreeable temperament, and you are usually kind. I know that you have taken great care with your brothers and sisters, and so I imagine that you would want to marry."

"Yes, of course. I would want to marry and have a family."

"Then, as I have said, you will go to Herefordshire. In the meantime, I shall write up the reprimand, and you must sign it after daybreak."

"Yes, I shall do that. Is there anything else you want to talk to me about?" Nell knew that Mr. Darcy had every right to tear into her for trying to sabotage his relationship with Elizabeth Bennet, and now that she understood he had never wanted her, she was overwhelmed by a sense of remorse.

"No, that is all I have to say. My power over you extends only to matters pertaining to the lupine community. A discussion of personal matters would be inappropriate."

"Mr. Darcy, I am so sorry," Nell said with tears pouring down her face. "I only wanted to…"

"I believe you, so we will say no more about it. I shall see you at nightfall. Since this is the first bad weather we have experienced this autumn, and with only the two of us to hunt, we probably will have to be satisfied with small animals."

"I can ask my father to tie up a goat or a sheep, if you would like."

"You may, but do not do it on my account. It is no hardship for me to go without food for only two days. When I was at Hudson Bay, there were occasions when the only things available were berries and bugs, so I shall survive."

Nell grimaced, and Darcy knew that during their time in the wild they would be eating goat meat or mutton. But it did not matter. He had no appetite. Between Nell and Rupert, he had lost Elizabeth. So immediately after daybreak, he would leave for Hertfordshire to bring Georgiana home and to have one last look at the woman he loved.

CHAPTER 23

DARCY WAS SO WEARY that his muscles ached, and every bump in the road to Hertfordshire caused him to wince. But he wasn't the only one. Mercer, who was sitting across from him sleeping, was feeling unwell but had refused to remain behind at Pemberley. Metcalf was exhibiting the same stubbornness. Darcy had tried to convince the man that his son was capable of driving a carriage on a well-traveled road between Derbyshire and Hertfordshire. But Metcalf disagreed, and so he had two Metcalfs sitting in the driver's seat. Darcy wondered what he would do when these faithful servants, as well as Jackson, Mrs. Reynolds, and Mrs. Bradshaw, retired from his service. A worry for another day.

When he arrived at Netherfield Park, he was warmly greeted by Bingley, but then his friend always acted as if he had just got a new puppy. Being of a mercurial temperament himself, Darcy did not understand how Charles could be so even tempered all the time. Mrs. Bingley, however, was another matter. There was a coolness in her reception, and what, pray tell, did that mean? But he was too tired to probe. That evening he excused himself, citing fatigue, but he also wanted Mercer to retire, and as long as Darcy was up and about the man would not do that. An exasperated Darcy told his valet that his nursery maid had not hovered as much as he did, but it made no difference.

The next morning, an unshaven Darcy went to the stables and asked the groom to saddle Montcalm, Bingley's favorite horse. Because Charles had tamed the unruly animal himself, he wanted Darcy to ride him so that he might see what a wonderful mount he was, and this was the perfect morning to do that—clean, crisp, with a layer of hoarfrost on everything. Before speaking to Elizabeth, he needed to clear his head of the detritus that had accumulated there. Maybe he was misinterpreting what Elizabeth meant when she said that her conversation with Nell had "changed everything." Was it possible that it was a change for the better?

Forgetting about his scruffy appearance, he headed for Longbourn. He would know by her welcome if there were clear skies ahead or a storm on the horizon because Elizabeth was incapable of concealing her emotions. Her eyes, the way she moved her body, her scent revealed everything, and he pictured himself sitting in the Bennet's parlor drinking a hot cup of tea on this cold morning. While conversing with Elizabeth about all that had happened in Scotland, he would learn if she had reconsidered his offer of marriage. Hopefully, the visit would end with his asking Mr. Bennet for his daughter's hand in marriage.

※

A well-rested Lizzy came to the breakfast room full of vim and vigor and ready to take on a new day. Mr. Darcy's note had been liberating. He wrote that all was well, and so she wished him well. No more worries on that account. If the gentleman decided to marry Lady Helen, he would have a pretty wife and handsome children. Hopefully, they would inherit his intelligence, but that would be none of her concern. Besides, it was better this way. It made sense for Mr.

Darcy to marry a she wolf, because if he did not, he would eventually face nightfall alone as Nell would marry and leave Granyard Hall, and Teddy, who had indicated that he would not be content remaining a groom, would want to take on something more challenging. No, this was definitely better for everyone.

The previous day, Mr. Hill and his sons had cut off the lower branches of some pine trees so that the Bennets could decorate their parlor with evergreens. For the wreaths and garlands, he had also cut some sprigs of greenery with its red berries from the holly bushes. This was something the Bennet sisters usually did a little later in Yuletide, but Lizzy was eager to get started and enlisted Kitty and Georgiana's assistance.

Mary had resisted all pleas from her sisters for her participation. It wasn't until Georgiana asked her to join them that she finally agreed. Because Mary held Georgiana in such high regard, Miss Darcy had succeeded in convincing the third Bennet daughter to stop practicing her vocals so that she might concentrate on improving her fingering on the pianoforte. "So few people can do justice to both," Georgiana had told Mary. "I am of a mind that I would prefer to do one thing superbly than two things adequately." The Bennet family would forever be in Miss Darcy's debt.

The four ladies put on heavy leather gloves and coats with patches and were handed knives by Mr. Hill. Having been surrounded by servants since her infancy, Georgiana had never done anything like this, but the enthusiastic young miss stated that she hoped to start such a tradition at Pemberley.

Everyone had been working for about an hour when Kitty noticed that a rider had just turned into the drive. "Maybe it is an express rider."

"Oh, I hope not. An express rider never brings good news,"

Mary said, thinking of the rider who had brought them news of Lydia's supposed elopement with George Wickham.

Although Georgiana did not recognize the horse, she did recognize the rider. "It is William. It is my brother." She handed her knife to Kitty and ran down the drive to meet him. Darcy immediately dismounted and gave his sister a hug.

"You look wonderful, Georgie. Your cheeks are rosy, but so is your nose." He tweaked it, making her laugh.

"Is everything all right? How is Teddy?" They started to walk toward the house.

"Teddy is fine. He will stay with Rupert for a while, but then he will be back at Pemberley."

"Oh, Will, I am so happy to hear that everything went well. Would you mind if I went inside and gave Mrs. Brotherton the good news? She has been so worried about Teddy."

"Of course. Besides, I want to talk to Miss Elizabeth, so take your time."

As soon as Lizzy saw Mr. Darcy, she froze. Why had he not written to say when he was coming to Longbourn? Because she knew she would be working outside, she had not seen to her morning toilette. With her hair in a braid and with curls popping out every which way and wearing a patched coat, she looked like something the cat had dragged in. But when he got closer, she realized that he was not in his best clothes either. Obviously, he had not come a-courting.

After exchanging pleasantries, Mary and Kitty went into the house, leaving Darcy and Elizabeth to stare at each other. Finally, Lizzy spoke.

"I did not know you were in Hertfordshire, Mr. Darcy. You should have written and given your sister advance notice so that she would be packed and ready to leave."

"I will be at Netherfield Park for a few days, so there is

no hurry. Knowing of her fondness for you, I imagine she is perfectly agreeable to remaining at Longbourn for another two or three days."

"She is most welcome to stay here. She has been a delightful visitor, and we shall miss her when she leaves. But then all good things must come to an end. Isn't that right, Mr. Darcy?" Lizzy asked in a voice lacking in any warmth.

And with that Darcy's hopes faded. His first assessment of her exchange with Lady Helen had been correct. His leaving for Scotland had changed everything. She wanted no part of a life that involved being married to a werewolf. But then he hesitated. If that were the case, then why was she angry, and it was clear that she was. He would have anticipated regret, sadness, disappointed hopes. But anger? And for one of the few times in his life, he was genuinely puzzled. Apparently, he was already in hot water, so why not ask?

"You are angry," he said, stating the obvious.

Lizzy glared at him. "Oh, yes. I forgot. You can tell how I feel without me having to say a word."

The mystery deepened. "Didn't you get my letter?"

"A letter? No I did not get a letter. I did receive a three-line note, consisting of twenty-six words in its entirety. Is that what you are referring to?"

Darcy dodged the question. "I was wondering if you would come to Netherfield Park this afternoon so that I might…"

"So that you might what? Take your leave of me? It is not necessary, Mr. Darcy. I fully understand what has happened."

What did she mean by "take your leave of me?" Did she think *he* wanted to end their engagement? "I am not sure how to respond to that."

"Of course not. You are a man of few words and fewer letters."

Although her words stung, he was not unhappy with her being angry with him. Anger meant she cared. Right?

"I thought you might want to know what happened in Scotland."

"Of course," Lizzy said, looking down at the ground. Because she was so cross with him, she had neglected to ask about Teddy. She was pretty sure she knew what had happened to Rupert. Her embarrassment gave her pause, and she took the time to look at Mr. Darcy. There was no doubt he was exhausted, with dark circles under his eyes and a weariness about him that she had never seen before.

"You look awful," she told him.

He laughed. "You don't," he said with that smile she loved.

And a picture flashed before her of him sitting on the floor of his study after he had returned from his two days in the woods with her foot on his chest to keep him from making any further advances. He had wanted her so badly, and if she were a different sort of woman, she would have given in to him. And then she realized that her thoughts had brought about a physical change in her, and it was the same thing as saying out loud, "I want you—every inch of you." Her face turned crimson.

"When do you want me to come to Netherfield?" she asked, avoiding his gaze.

"May I send my carriage for you this afternoon? Let's say three o'clock?" From the lilt in his voice, Lizzy knew that he had noticed the change.

"Are you sure you want me to come today? Because the days have grown so short, if I leave that late in the afternoon, I will need to stay at Netherfield."

"If you do not have a problem with that, *I* certainly have no objection," he said as he moved the reins over Montcalm's head in preparation for his departure. "I look forward to see-ing you—preferably without the knife?"

Lizzy looked down at the weapon in her hand and chuck-led. "And maybe you will have shaved by that time."

"You do not like my stubble?" he asked, scratching his face.

"You look scruffy. My preference is that you have a full beard or be clean shaven."

Darcy was reassured. By her statement, she was telling him that whether man or beast, she loved him.

After mounting his horse, he tipped his hat. "Then I shall see you at Netherfield this afternoon. Oh, by the way, your Scottie has been looking out the window ever since I got here. You might want to reassure her that I am not coming into the house."

Lizzy looked at the window in the front parlor, and she could see Magic's face smushed up against the window. Even from such a distance, she could tell that the Scottie was very tense.

"I will go inside immediately or she will have an ac-cident. But one more thing before you go. When I come to Netherfield, I want you to know that I am in no mood for noble speeches. Your aunt Marguerite told me to tell you that."

Darcy bit his lip, and the furrowed brow returned. "Since it is never wise to disagree with Aunt Marguerite, I will con-sider myself warned."

CHAPTER 24

Magic was not the only one with her nose pressed up against the glass. As soon as Lizzy walked into the house, she was set upon by her mother.

"Well, what did Mr. Darcy have to say? Why did he leave? Are you engaged?"

Lizzy did not need this kind of attention. She wanted to digest what Mr. Darcy had said, but her mother was like a hound on the scent when she thought there was a possible suitor in the neighborhood.

"Mr. Darcy came to say hello to his sister and to inform me of the happy conclusion of events in Scotland. He left because he is tired from such a long journey, and we are not engaged. Did I answer all your questions?"

"I have no doubt that you let that fish get away. Just like Mr. Collins. You will have to start all over again, and Jane has not been particularly helpful in finding you a husband. Mr. Bingley has four brothers. Why have you not been introduced to them?"

"We *were* introduced to two of them. You have forgotten that the next three oldest Bingleys after Charles are his sisters and that James, whom we *did* meet at the wedding, is only nineteen years old."

"Nineteen years old? He is too young for you, but he will do nicely for Kitty." Lizzy could see the wheels turning. "As for you, young lady, since there are no young men in the neighborhood with a fortune sufficient to support you, we must look to Aunt Susan."

"If by 'looking to Aunt Susan,' you mean Mr. Nesbitt, I would rather have married Mr. Collins because whoever does marry Mr. Nesbitt will have to have a very large bed as the elder Mrs. Nesbitt will be sleeping between husband and wife."

The Nesbitts were neighbors of Aunt Susan, Mr. Bennet's sister, and because mother and son came to all their aunt's teas, Lizzy had been in the gentleman's company on several occasions. Excluding his resemblance to a stork, it was his habit of always sitting on his hands that made it impossible for Lizzy to take him seriously. Whenever Jane and she returned from a visit with Aunt Susan, they would have the best time trying to guess what Mr. Nesbitt was trying to stop Mr. Nesbitt from doing.

"You may jest all you want, Lizzy, but Mr. Collins is married to your best friend because you would not have him, and Mr. Nesbitt's attentiveness to his mother shows that he has a kind heart. He also has a good income and a good-sized house and will shortly be called to the bar."

"Mr. Nesbitt could live in Grosvenor Square and have ten thousand a year," Lizzy said to her Mama, "and I would not marry him. I would rather be a spinster living on the parish than marry Mr. Dalton Nesbitt." Turning away from her mother, she called upstairs to Kitty, Mary, and Georgiana to come outside so that they might finish cutting the holly. "I shall be going to Netherfield Park this afternoon to visit Jane. Mr. Darcy has been so kind as to offer his carriage."

"Oh, that is very good. You must stay overnight, and I insist that you remain at Netherfield Park until you are engaged."

"Shall I remain at Netherfield even if Mr. Darcy leaves?" There was something comical about her mother's doggedness. But wishing to end the conversation, she finally said, "I promise I shall not leave Netherfield Park until I am engaged, but if I have not returned by the spring, please do come visit me."

⤸⤹

Darcy's impression that Mrs. Bingley had given him a less than warm greeting the previous day had been correct. When he mentioned that he had ridden over to Longbourn, Jane had asked how her parents were.

"I was not so fortunate as to see either of your parents, Mrs. Bingley."

"Oh, that *is* unfortunate, as I am sure that was your purpose in going to Longbourn."

So sarcasm was a Bennet trait, Darcy thought. Although Elizabeth was better at it than her older sister, Jane had landed a good punch.

"I briefly spoke to Miss Elizabeth, and I am to send a carriage for her this afternoon."

"Now *that* is good news. I can never see enough of Lizzy, so it is a good thing for me that she did not remain in Derbyshire as long as I had anticipated."

Another jab. But since the tone of Mrs. Bingley's voice had softened, Darcy did not feel the sting as much as the first.

"Please excuse me, Mr. Darcy," Jane said, rising, "One of Lizzy's favorite dishes is mutton chops, and so I shall need to speak with Cook."

"More mutton," Darcy mumbled. During his last nightfall, without Teddy and Rupert to help in the hunt, Nell, who was not one to miss a meal, had asked her steward to make sure that a freshly killed sheep was left at a prearranged spot on the Granyard property, and he had eaten mutton on both days. But what was on the Netherfield dinner menu was the least of his problems. Trying to figure out what Elizabeth had meant by "not making any noble speeches" was his top priority; shaving was his second.

❧

Although Darcy had hoped to speak to Elizabeth upon her arrival at Netherfield, Mrs. Bingley had other plans for her sister, and most of Elizabeth's time was taken up with discussing what was required to prepare for the arrival of baby Bingley. Darcy knew that he was being punished by Jane Bingley for his dillydallying in asking Elizabeth to marry him, so he would just have to wait until after supper. But when the meal was finished and it was suggested that they play cards, Darcy had had enough.

"As much as I would enjoy playing cards, Mrs. Bingley, I am eager to acquaint Miss Elizabeth with some events that took place in Scotland. I was called away on a family emergency, and since she knows some of the parties, she expressed an interest in learning how things turned out."

It was only after getting a nod from Elizabeth that Jane finally agreed to retire for the evening and leave Lizzy and Darcy alone. Knowing that it was important that no one hear their conversation, Lizzy closed all the doors of the drawing room. She went and sat on the sofa next to Mr. Darcy, so that they would not have to whisper, an intimacy she was not prepared to engage in at the moment.

Darcy related every detail of what had transpired in Scotland, and there were times when Lizzy's heart dropped into her stomach, especially when she learned how close Rupert had come to being discovered in his lupine form.

After Mr. Darcy left Pemberley, she had asked Mr. Jackson to bring her every book on wolves and werewolves in the house. These tomes were concealed in the hidden room behind the study, and Lizzy had pored over them. The picture that emerged was that wherever wolves roamed, there was a concerted effort to exterminate them and that they had been successfully eradicated in all but the most remote areas of Britain.

Lizzy remained silent as Mr. Darcy spoke of his visit with the laird, waiting for Rupert's Council custodians to arrive, their arduous return visit, and Nell's reprimand.

"Disciplining Nell must have been difficult for you, and then nightfall came hard on the heels of your reprimand."

"It was awkward for the first few minutes, but Nell knew that there was a fresh kill on the property, and she could not wait to get at that sheep."

Lizzy started to laugh, and Darcy joined in. Nell's appetite had become a source of amusement for them.

"In the spring, Nell will visit the émigré population living near the Welsh border, and she should be able to find a mate as there are some aristocrats amongst them."

"Then Nell and you will not…"

"Will not what?"

"Will not be getting married?"

Darcy shook his head in confusion. "Me marry Nell? Why would you think that? I have never given one moment of thought to withdrawing my offer of marriage to you. It is you who have reconsidered. Jackson told me what you said after you and Nell came out of the study. You said that 'you had changed your mind.'"

"I said no such thing. My response to her efforts to separate us was that 'it had changed everything,'" Lizzy said visibly upset that her words had been misinterpreted. "After she told me of all the dangers werewolves face, I swore that, except for nightfall, I would never leave you again. It is as Ruth said to Naomi in the Bible: 'Entreat me not to leave thee or return from following after thee; for wither thou goest, I shall go, and where thou lodgest, I shall lodge. Thy people shall be my people.' That is exactly how I feel about you."

"Then you still want to marry me?" Darcy asked in a stutter, choking up after such a speech, and every frustration Lizzy felt since she learned that Mr. Darcy was a werewolf came to the surface.

"How dare you ask me such a question," she said, standing up and stepping away from him. "Without so much as a backwards glance, you left me at Pemberley with no words of comfort or an embrace to reassure me, and your noble effort to release me from my promise to marry you left me heart-sick." When he started to apologize, she told him that she was not finished. "I waited and waited for some word from you, and when it came, it was three lines of prose that you could have written to your solicitor." She made her hands into fists. "And then you come to Longbourn and play these cat-and-mouse games with me. I am so angry I could hit you."

"You may do so, but I warn you that I took lessons at Mr. Jackson's Boxing Academy."

"Do not think you can make me laugh and that all will be well, Fitzwilliam Darcy. These weeks have been pure torture for me. I did not know if we were truly engaged." Hot tears poured out of her, and when he offered his handkerchief, she refused it and went in search of one of her own.

"Elizabeth, you can be unhappy with me, but is it necessary for you to take your frustration out on my handkerchief?"

When Lizzy went to take it out of his hand, he pulled

her to him, and he held her tightly until she stopped fighting him. After he felt the tension leaving her body, he placed his hand on her head and brought it to his chest, and she put her arms around his waist and clung to him.

"You are not angry anymore," he said, and when she looked up at him, he traced the outline of her face with his fingers and kissed her forehead. "You must understand that I did not know what was happening in Scotland, so I had to leave immediately. The only reason that this situation did not end in disaster was Teddy did everything exactly right. If it had not been for him, I do not know what would have happened to Rupert. But there was no way for me to know that until I reached the Underhill estate.

"As for my letter, what could I write? After all that you had gone through in those two days after nightfall, I had to leave you to rush to Scotland to tend to another werewolf situation, so I thought it only right that you should have an opportunity to end our engagement. If I had written a love letter to you, it would have been the same as pleading with you to stay with me."

"Your letter to your sister was longer than the one you wrote to me," Lizzy said, after seeing the logic behind his staid missive.

"What was the point of writing the same thing twice?"

"Mr. Darcy, you have a lot to learn about women," she said, shaking her head in dismay. After drying everything that was wet, Lizzy took him by the hand and returned to the sofa. "I have had weeks to think about our marriage, and I have made a decision. I want to go to Gretna Green right away."

Darcy burst out laughing. This was a good sign. Lizzy had not lost her sense of humor, but after seeing the look in her eyes, he realized that she was serious.

"No," Darcy firmly said, "it was a terrible idea when I suggested it. It sounds even worse coming from you. Do you really want people to be looking at your belly for the next few months wondering if you are in a family way and *had* to get married?"

Lizzy thought of all the tongue-waggers in Meryton who would delight in speculating on a possible pregnancy. "No, I do not want that, so we shall do as you suggested and get a special license."

"Special licenses are expensive."

"I believe you said that you had a few pounds in the bank. Did you gamble away your fortune while you were in Scotland?"

"No, I am not a gamester, but I think your suggestion of having our banns announced in the village church is the right one. If we set a date for after the first of the year, that will give us ample time to make arrangements. You may wish to go up to London for your wedding clothes, and there is much to do to prepare for the wedding breakfast."

"After the first of the year? This is quite a change from the man who carried me to his sofa. Where has all that passion gone?"

"I can assure you I do not want for passion. If you knew what my thoughts were, you would run from the room."

"I know what your thoughts are, and I am still here." She gave him such a flirtatious smile that he felt his manhood rising, and so he crossed his legs, causing Lizzy to start laughing.

"Have you no compassion, you heartless wench?" he said amused, but uncomfortable.

"I do have compassion, and so I suggest that we marry in three weeks after the banns are announced."

"That will not work because it will bring us to within a few days of the next full moon. Surely you do not want your husband to leave you so soon after we are married."

"But you will *always* leave me for two days every month, and I will *always* be there to welcome you back."

"Very well," Darcy said, nodding his head in acknowledgment of her commitment to him, and after some quick calculations, he added, "shall we say December 24th?"

"Yes, I like that. You first told me of your other incarnation on the eve of All Saints' Day. It is fitting that we should marry on Christmas Eve. There is a symmetry in that."

"Now that we have set a date, please tell me what you would like as a token of my love. My mother's ruby ring, my grandmother's emerald necklace? Perhaps while you are in town, you will want to go to a jeweler and pick out a diamond ring. I shall get whatever you wish."

"I would be honored to wear your mother or grandmother's jewelry, but I have no need of diamonds. However, I would like something. A dog. Actually dogs."

"Do you mean a Scottie like Magic, except better behaved?"

"No, a Scottie is too small," she said, ignoring his cutting remark about her little terrier. "I was thinking about male and female Newfoundlands, not from the same litter, so that they may breed, and I must insist that David and Goliath have no say in the matter."

"Newfoundlands? They are enormous. But if you come and sit on my lap and give me a kiss, I will agree to your request. However, please do not think that you are fooling me as to the reason for you choosing Newfoundlands. You are trying to protect me, so that if anyone should report a wolf sighting, you would be able to produce one."

Lizzy leaned over and kissed him on the cheek. "Lady

Helen told me about how you were discovered by the poachers, and if you did not have Wolfie, who knows what would have happened. So, yes, the ring is negotiable; the dogs are not. As for sitting on your lap, I cannot, sir. You are not the only one who can sense things. In your present state, if I were to sit on your lap, I might risk my maidenhood."

"You need have no fear of being deflowered by me—not tonight anyway—but if you think you are leaving this room without kissing me, you are mistaken." Darcy moved so quickly that Lizzy had no time to flee. As he lay on top of her, she quickly settled into his rhythm. From the pleasure it gave her, she understood the freedom from society's constraints that he so enjoyed when he was in the wild, and she decided that for a little while, she, too, could be free.

❧

Lizzy stood still as Mr. Darcy returned her curls to their rightful place, and before tucking her lace back into her dress, she attempted to tie his neckcloth in the same way that Mercer would have, but her hands were not yet steady. If Mr. Darcy had not rolled off of her, she doubted that she would have stopped him. If the warmth she was feeling throughout her body was the result of his hands and lips, she could only imagine what it would feel like if he were to use everything in his arsenal, and the thought caused her to giggle.

"Why are you laughing?" he asked as he motioned for her to turn around so that he could make sure that her dress was not a wrinkled mess.

"I should be thoroughly ashamed of myself," she answered. "Although you did not act as a gentleman should, you showed more restraint than I did."

"I did so for selfish reasons. When you and I come

together as man and wife, we will not be listening for servants or a sister, and our time together will not be measured in minutes, but hours." Lizzy remained silent. "You have nothing to say to that?"

"What can I say? You can sense how I feel, and so you know that I find it to be an excellent plan," Lizzy said, blushing. "However, what I can tell you is that I love you more than anything in both your incarnations because you are a good man. I could not ask for better."

Darcy pulled Lizzy into one last embrace and held her there so that she would not see his tears.

CHAPTER 25

F OR TEN MINUTES, JANE and Charles had been watching Mr. Darcy pace back and forth in front of a window in the breakfast room. Jane had twice offered to prepare a plate for him, but he had declined and resumed his pacing. After seeing the look on Darcy's face when Lizzy entered the breakfast room, Charles jumped up, went over to his friend, and started to pump his hand.

"You are engaged. I am sure of it. When you said you would not ride this morning, I knew it was because you were waiting for Elizabeth. Welcome to the family, Darcy," Charles said and then slapped his friend on the back.

"Lizzy, is this true?" Jane asked. She had been anticipating this event for months, and she was not going to count this chick before it hatched.

"Yes, it is true." Lizzy hugged her sister. "Mr. Darcy and I are engaged or will be as soon as he can talk to Papa."

"Is it too early for champagne?" Bingley asked.

"It is never too early for champagne," Darcy answered, grinning from ear to ear, and a bottle was sent for.

"Mama will be very pleased," Jane said. "I daresay she will be ecstatic." She raised her glass to toast the happy couple.

Lizzy looked at her betrothed to see his reaction to Jane's reminder that Mrs. Bennet would soon be his mother-in-law. She still blushed with embarrassment at the memory of her mother's performance at the Netherfield ball, and she would never forget the look on Mr. Darcy's face when her Mama had blurted out that Jane's anticipated engagement to Mr. Bingley would throw her four daughters into the path of other rich men.

"Perhaps it would be best if I went to Longbourn alone and spoke with my parents. In that way, it will not be such a surprise."

"It can hardly be a surprise, Elizabeth. I have been sitting in your parlor for the past six months. My attentions were too marked to be interpreted in any other way, and since I was not asked by either parent to leave Longbourn at any time during that interval, I imagine I will have their blessing. Besides, I want to share our good news with everyone. So shall we go to Longbourn this morning?"

"Yes, but you do know that my mother will be…"

"Exuberant," Darcy said, finishing her sentence. "Yes, I expect as much, and I have come prepared. If your mother grows too shrill, I have little pieces of cotton in my pocket to protect my ears," he finished in a whisper.

"Shame on you for saying such a thing about my mother." But Lizzy started laughing. "All right then. We shall go to Longbourn, but you cannot say I did not warn you."

≈≈

When Lizzy got into the carriage, she sat in the middle of the seat, forcing Darcy to sit opposite to her, and he asked her to make room for him.

"I shall let you sit next to me, but first you must promise that you will not try to kiss me as you will knock my bonnet off, and my hair will look a mess. We cannot have a repeat of last night, and a lot can happen in three miles."

"I would never knock your bonnet off," he said, as he moved over to her side, forcing her to move over. "That would be inconsiderate. Instead, I shall do this." He pulled at the bow under her chin, and after Lizzy stopped laughing, she took her hat off.

After giving her a chaste kiss, Darcy took her hand, kissed it, and promised to be good. "There will be no repeat of last night. The next time I start something, I intend to finish it as last night's performance was a damn frustrating exercise. I have been waiting for so long; I can wait a little longer."

Lizzy wondered what Mr. Darcy meant by that remark? Because he was nearly twenty-eight years of age and a man of the world, she assumed that at some point he had had a physical relationship with a woman. It would be wonderful to think that he had not, but Lizzy had read too much to be naïve about what went on in the top tiers of London society.

"Are you saying that you have never…? I mean I have read about you in the newspapers. On a number of occasions, your name has been mentioned along with several young ladies and some not so young."

"If you are referring to Mrs. Clement, I did befriend her because the Prince of Wales treated her abominably. She had just come out of mourning for her husband, and the prince took advantage of her in order to make Lady Jersey jealous. I took particular offense at such a heartless act because he used his position as a royal prince to seduce her. It would be the same as me going to Granyard Hall, in human form, and subtly letting Lady Helen know that I would be pleased if she would tend to my needs. What the prince did disgusted me, and because Mrs. Clement was being snubbed by everyone in Lady Jersey's circle, I introduced her to another group of people.

"Honestly, if I so much as bump elbows with an unmarried lady, I am in the next day's paper as being in love with her," an exasperated Darcy complained. "And since you have admitted to reading such drivel, I am sure you have read about the boiling-hot romance I am having with the venomous Alexandra Banbury. At balls and breakfasts, I engage her in the most insipid conversations, and she acts as if I am reciting poetry. But I *never* call on her.

"As to your question of whether I have been with another woman, I shall tell you that I have, on occasion, been tempted to engage in sexual congress with a woman. But when it came to act on it, I could not do it. I attribute this to the fact that I am part wolf, and remember, wolves mate for life.

"As far as marriage is concerned, whenever I considered the subject, I thought that I should look for a wife from among the lupine population, and because we would have our other incarnation in common, I imagined that I would be content. But then I met you. You were the surprise that scattered my plans to the four winds. After the assembly, I could not stop thinking about you. When I finally decided to take the risk of courting someone fully human, I did not know how to win you, and I performed badly. I had just about given up on our ever being together when you came to Pemberley, and I could sense that you cared for me and that gave me hope. So I began again. And when you told me that you loved me..." Darcy paused because he had started to tear up, and he drew Lizzy to him. "I cannot tell you what that meant to me, and since you have seen my tears, I shall tell you that werewolves cry. In the wild, there is no shame in it. It is only when I am in human form that I am embarrassed by shedding tears."

Lizzy gave Darcy a long and deep kiss. "If you feel things deeply, why should you not cry? I do. You need never be embarrassed in front of me."

"Thank you for that, but I must change the subject." Because the next topic was one that cast him in an unfavorable light, he hesitated, but there was something that needed to be said. "In consideration of what you now know about me, you must find my reaction to your mother's... to your mother's..."

"Exuberance."

"Yes, your mother's exuberance to be a shocking example of intolerance, but I had never seen such a public display of..."

"Exuberance."

"Exactly. But in my defense, I did not know about the entail, which you must admit does explain a lot. Regardless, I was rude, and I apologize to you and hope that your mother did not notice my harsh looks."

"Oh, she didn't. That is the wonderful thing about Mama. Although Jane and I are often mortified by her behavior and have been embarrassed by her outrageous attempts to secure a match for us, she is oblivious to everything around her that does not concern the getting of husbands. And here we are at Longbourn, so you should go and sit in the parlor, and I will find Papa."

❧

Mr. Bennet was not at home, but Mrs. Bennet was in the kitchen going over the week's menu with Mrs. Smythe, the Bennets' cook. When her mother saw her, she gave Lizzy a sour look.

"You will never get a husband, Lizzy," she said, shaking her head in disappointment. "You only went to Netherfield yesterday, and here you are back again."

"But, Mama, you said that I could come home if I were engaged." Lizzy waited for that bit of news to seep in.

"What? Lizzy, what are you saying? Did Mr. Darcy propose?" When Lizzy nodded, she asked where he was.

"He is in the parlor, waiting to speak to Papa."

"Oh, no! Your father is meeting with the surveyor today. Isn't it just like him to be out on the farm when I need him the most," she said with her hands on her hips. "Lizzy, you must go into the parlor, and no matter what, you must keep Mr. Darcy here. You must not let him go away until he speaks to Mr. Bennet. Oh, here is Mr. Hill. Hill, you must find Mr. Bennet and tell him to come home at once. There is no time to lose, as we have a serious situation here that must be seen to immediately. It cannot wait one hour."

Lizzy stood behind her mother, shaking her head, so that Hill would know that the family was not in peril, and after the servant had gone in search of the head of the household, Mrs. Bennet went into the parlor with her daughter. Considering the way their courtship had gone, she was not taking any chances.

"Mr. Darcy, how good it is to see you again. You honor us with your visit," Mrs. Bennet crooned. "We always enjoyed it when you came to Longbourn. As soon as you went away, I always said to Lizzy, I wonder when Mr. Darcy will come back as he is such good company, and here you are."

It was at that moment that Kitty came into the parlor, but before she could sit down, her mother told her to leave. No one would be allowed to say a word to Mr. Darcy until Elizabeth was officially engaged.

"You have that piece of embroidery you have been working on for ever so long. Today would be a good day to finish it, and I *insist* you finish it in the sitting room." Kitty, who was used to seeing Mr. Darcy visiting Lizzy, was exceedingly puzzled. There was something going on here, so when she did leave, she sat on the stairs waiting for events to unfold.

"Now, where were we, Mr. Darcy?"

"I was about to tell you that I am happy to be here today, and if I may be so presumptuous…"

"Oh, go ahead. Presume all you want."

"I think you can guess the purpose of my visit, and since I am confident that Mr. Bennet will approve, I feel comfortable in speaking freely." After taking Elizabeth's hand, he continued, "I have asked Elizabeth to marry me, and she has accepted my offer."

Mrs. Bennet clapped her hands in joy and let out a squeal of delight. "Oh, I will confess that I suspected that you had an interest in Lizzy, but then I thought, that is Mr. Darcy of Pemberley, who has a great estate in Derbyshire, a house in town, fine carriages, and ten thousand a year, if not more…"

While her mother continued to list all of Mr. Darcy's many assets, Lizzy stared straight ahead, humiliated—again. But wishing to reassure Lizzy that all was well, Darcy squeezed her hand and made no attempt to interrupt the itemization of his property, even when Mrs. Bennet was wide and short of the mark. But then the gossip about Bingley had been wrong as well. He was supposed to have inherited a hundred thousand pounds, and because that was such an outrageous sum, when Bingley discussed the marriage contract with Mr. Bennet, he had to explain that although he had a generous yearly allowance, the lump sum settlement of his father's estate had been shared with his eight siblings.

"Mama," Lizzy interrupted, "I think it would be a good idea if we talked about the wedding breakfast. Because winter is upon us, Mr. Darcy and I have decided that we should have a simple…"

"Oh, the wedding breakfast," Mrs. Bennet said. "I had not thought about that yet. Because Mr. Darcy is so rich and is such a prominent figure, there will probably be hundreds of people coming from London and Derbyshire and who knows where else."

"Mama, please listen to me. Mr. Darcy and I are to marry on December 24th, and because of the season, we have decided to have a simple wedding breakfast with the family, but we shall return in the spring and have a great feast."

"December 24th! But nothing can be planned in such a short time. I thought… Lizzy, don't you want everyone to know how well you did in securing Mr. Darcy's affections?"

Sensing Elizabeth's suffering as a result of her mother's lack of decorum, Darcy decided to intervene. "Mrs. Bennet, there is a good reason for the delay in having an elaborate reception at this time. I want my dear cousin Miss Anne de Bourgh to be at the celebration of our marriage, but she will not be able to attend as her mother Lady Catherine will not permit her to travel in the winter. Furthermore, it is more likely that my aunt will attend if the date is pushed back until April or May." Darcy was hoping that delaying the wedding breakfast until the spring would give Anne and Georgiana ample time to work on his aunt.

Lizzy was spared any further embarrassment because her father had finished with the surveyor.

"Mr. Bennet, you have come," his wife said, and from her joyful expression, he understood that Mr. Darcy had finally asked Lizzy to marry him.

"Yes, Mrs. Bennet, I have come because I was led to believe that some disaster had befallen Longbourn. I am guessing that the cause for raising the alarm is a fire in the kitchen or perhaps one of our milk cows has died or Magic has gotten out again and is chasing the chickens. Which of these terrible events occurred in the short time I have been gone?"

"Mr. Bennet, how you do jest. Mr. Darcy has requested an audience with you." She arched her eyebrows to indicate that romance was involved.

"An audience. Well, then I shall receive the gentleman in my study. Allow me to lead the way."

In the past, Darcy had wondered how a man as sensible as Mr. Bennet could have such a silly wife, but if that was a typical exchange between them, then it was obvious that Mr. Bennet was amused by Mrs. Bennet's natural exuberance.

"Mr. Darcy, may I offer you a glass of wine?"

"No, thank you, sir."

"Then I shall not have one either," he said, sitting down. "I can tell that you are eager to get to the matter at hand, and knowing you to be of a taciturn nature, I suspect there will be no speeches. Mr. Bingley felt compelled to deliver an oration. Perhaps you prefer a simple declaration. Either way, you have my attention, sir."

"Thank you, Mr. Bennet. As you said, I am a man of few words, and so I shall get right to the point. I am very much in love with your daughter, and I am fortunate to have secured her love as well. Therefore, I have asked Elizabeth to marry me, and I have been accepted. However, I would be greatly honored if you gave your approval for the marriage."

"You have my approval, Mr. Darcy, because in these past few weeks, while you tended to your family's affairs, I have been a witness to Lizzy's unhappiness when deprived of your company."

"I experienced the same thing, sir."

"But I do have one reservation. You have been coming to Longbourn for the past six months, and each time you visited, my wife was convinced that you would ask our daughter to marry you. Instead, you departed, only to return a few weeks later, and the scene would be repeated. Something kept you from making Lizzy an offer. I would like to know what it was."

"I can easily understand how mystifying my coming and going must have been to you and Mrs. Bennet. So I shall explain as best I can. I had a recurring family situation that demanded my presence. That situation has been resolved— permanently. I cannot say anything else as it would be an embarrassment to the parties involved. If it were not for that, I would have proposed much sooner. I know that Lizzy has suffered as a result of my erratic attendance upon her, but I can assure you that she has suffered no more than I have."

Before saying anything further, Mr. Bennet mulled over Mr. Darcy's explanation, and after seeing the sincerity in the man's face, he said, "I find your answer to be satisfactory, and I will not pry into your private affairs." Even so, Mr. Bennet suspected the reason for his frequent absences might be that Mr. Darcy had a natural child hidden somewhere in the country. It would certainly not make him unique among the gentry. But how would such a situation be permanently resolved? It was all so puzzling, but knowing his daughter to be an excellent judge of character, he decided that since she had consented to the man's offer of marriage, surely she had deemed him to be a worthy partner.

"Thank you, sir. As for the marriage contract, I am to go to town shortly, and I will meet with my solicitor at that time. I can assure you that I will be generous and that you will be satisfied with the terms."

"I have no doubt of it, sir. So when is the happy day?"

"December 24th," Darcy answered, grateful that Mr. Bennet had not pressed him for the reason for his absences. "We are to see the vicar this afternoon."

"My goodness! That is just three weeks from now. Will you not have a courtship?"

"To my mind, the purpose of a courtship is for the couple to get to know each other better so that they will be sure that it is a good match for both. There is no question of our being well suited to each other, and I know that Elizabeth would agree with that statement. Thus, there is no reason to delay the marriage. We shall have a simple wedding and a breakfast with the family, but we will return in the spring and have a reception for all our family and friends."

"It seems that the matter was decided before I walked in the door, and since there is nothing left for me to say, I wish you joy. I do not know you well, Mr. Darcy, but I can take the measure of a man. Although you can be a snob," he said with a chuckle, "you are a decent man, and I believe you will take care of my little girl. I could not have parted with her to anyone less worthy." After shaking Mr. Darcy's hand, he concluded by saying, "That was the easy part. Now, we must go and share the good news with Mrs. Bennet."

❧

The house erupted in a joyous celebration. Kitty came out of hiding, and Mary put down her book. Every time Mr. Darcy looked at Elizabeth, he was smiling, even when he was talking to his future mother-in-law. However, it was necessary to leave this merry scene as there were things to do.

During the short walk to the church for their visit with the vicar, Darcy mentioned that he would be leaving to go to town and then on into Kent. Lizzy was dumbfounded. Was he actually leaving her again? From the look on his betrothed's face, he knew that he had better explain—and fast.

"I have to leave, Elizabeth. The next three weeks are going to be awful for me. Because everyone will know that we are engaged, they will all be watching our every move. I will be fortunate if I can hold your hand."

"I am to be deprived of your company for three weeks because you cannot kiss me whenever it pleases you?"

"There are other reasons as well," Darcy quickly added as he watched the muscles in her jaw clench. "I want to visit Anne. She writes that she is well, but I would like to see her nonetheless. I shall be taking Georgie with me because Aunt Catherine behaves better when my sister is in the room, and I shall need an ally when I tell my aunt that we are to marry."

Lizzy had to agree with that statement. While she was in Kent visiting Charlotte, nothing she said or did pleased the august personage of Lady Catherine de Bourgh. For someone as conscious of rank as she was, her nephew marrying a "nobody" could possibly end with her refusing to see him again. As much as she disliked the lady, she *was* the sister of Mr. Darcy's mother.

"After I visit with my aunt and cousin, I will send Georgie back to you as I must go to Herefordshire. When I reprimanded Nell, I told her that because of her poor judgment if and when she chooses to marry her husband must be a werewolf. Since she is a member of my pack, I feel it is my responsibility to go to Herefordshire so that I might be in a position to recommend a prospective suitor. I can assure you that I do not want to do this, but as the alpha male, it is my responsibility."

"That is fine. I have no objections." Lizzy's mood lightened immediately. In fact, she was smiling.

"You have no objections. Really?" Darcy found it difficult to believe that she could change her mind so quickly, but if she were angry, he would have sensed it. What accounted for the sudden change? "I am beginning to suspect that you will not miss me at all. You seem happy to have me gone."

"Oh, I *shall* miss you. Be assured of that. But far be it from me to interfere with the affairs of the pack, and if you say it is necessary to find Nell a husband, I certainly shall not stop you." And now Darcy understood.

CHAPTER 26

Because Mrs. Bennet lived life large, all Lizzy and Darcy's plans for a modest-sized wedding went out the window the day after their engagement was announced. The bride's mother did everything except hire the town crier to proclaim the couple's betrothal. As a result, the wedding breakfast that was to be held for "family and a few friends" ended up including everyone from the village and those who lived on nearby farms and estates. With the size of the wedding growing exponentially, Darcy sent for Mr. Jackson and Mrs. Bradshaw. With plans for the reception left in their capable hands, Lizzy departed with Mr. Darcy and Georgiana to visit Aunt and Uncle Gardiner, and she would buy her wedding clothes and accessories in town.

Before leaving, Lizzy reminded her mother that although Lydia was welcome to come to her wedding, Wickham was not. When Mrs. Bennet started to protest, Lizzy cut off any further discussion by saying, "Mr. Darcy would be displeased." Mama would never want to say or do anything that would "displease" a man who had ten thousand a year.

During the ride to London, Lizzy had another opportunity to see brother and sister interact, and it was quickly apparent that Georgiana considered her dear William to be her ideal for a man, and Darcy did not disagree with that assessment. He held himself to a high standard, and he expected no less from anyone who hoped to approach his sister when the season began in May. No mention was made of the difficulties involved in bringing someone into the family who would not be privy to Darcy's unique situation.

It was already dark when the carriage arrived at the Gardiner townhouse. Darcy was disappointed that he would be unable to visit with the couple, not only because he enjoyed their company but also because he was grateful to them for bringing Elizabeth into Derbyshire. If not for that holiday to the Peak, it was unlikely that he would now be holding Elizabeth's hand.

"Georgie, close your eyes," Darcy told his sister.

"Why should I close my eyes?" When Darcy gave her a knowing look, she shut them tight. Even so, he put his hat in front of his face as he kissed Elizabeth good-bye. After he had assisted her out of the carriage, he whispered that he loved her and that he would see her in three weeks, and after that separation, nothing would keep them apart.

Aunt Gardiner was disappointed that Mr. Darcy and Miss Darcy could not visit. Little did she know that the next day she would have a member of the extended Darcy family sitting in her front parlor.

❧

Mrs. Gardiner was enjoying her afternoon tea with her niece when her butler informed her that, "Antony, Lord Fitzwilliam, has presented his card and wishes to pay a call on you." After taking the card from Rothwell's hand, Aunt Gardiner took a quick glance at it before handing it to Elizabeth.

"His Lordship must have learned of your engagement to Mr. Darcy."

"Good gracious! Lord Fitzwilliam has come to pay a call on me? But how did he know where to find me?" Lizzy asked as she continued to stare at his card. "I can't imagine what I will say to him. Although I have never met him, I have certainly *heard* about him."

Any reader of *The Insider* or any of the pamphlets and gossip sheets sold on the streets of London knew of Antony, Lord Fitzwilliam. He had been married to Lady Eleanor, the daughter of the second Earl of Henley, for about a dozen years, and had been estranged from his wife for nine of them. But according to the newspapers, he did not lack for companionship. He was known to have had numerous affairs with married ladies of the ton, and rumor had it that he was currently having a robust romance with Lady Hillary Donwell, whose husband, Colonel Adam Donwell, was in Nova Scotia. While the colonel was in service to the Crown, his wife was servicing Lord Fitzwilliam. What could Lizzy possibly say to a known seducer and reprobate?

"Rothwell, please show Lord Fitzwilliam in," Mrs. Gardiner said, and after checking their dresses for wrinkles and their hair for stray tresses, both ladies stood up. And then came the grand entrance of the noble one. His Lordship handed his gold-tipped cane to Rothwell and held out his arms so that the butler might take off his coat. Not until he had removed his top hat and placed his gloves in it was he ready for introductions.

Although there was only a four-year age difference between Lord Fitzwilliam and his brother, Colonel Fitzwilliam, His Lordship looked older than his thirty-two years. The impeccably attired earl in his dark coat, tan breeches, and silk neckcloth showed the effects of the many late nights he spent gambling and carousing. However, with his blond hair, cornflower blue eyes, and mischievous smile, Lizzy understood why so many women fell for this devilish rake.

After apologizing for not giving Mrs. Gardiner any notice that he would be calling, Lord Fitzwilliam justified his unexpected arrival by saying that he absolutely had to meet the lady who had won the heart of his cousin.

"Darcy is a most particular fellow, so I had no doubt that you would be a beauty, Miss Bennet, and I was not wrong. I had hoped that we would be introduced by the prospective bridegroom. I did leave my card with Rogers, his butler, but Darcy chose not to respond," he said with a sigh before plopping down in a chair nearest to the fire as if he were in his own home, and who would have told him differently?

"Thank you, milord, for your compliment," Lizzy responded, "but as far as your cousin is concerned, Mr. Darcy has gone to Kent to visit with Lady Catherine and Miss de Bourgh," a statement that caused the earl to burst out laughing.

"I wish I had known that he was going to Rosings as I am in need of entertainment. One of my most intimate friends has chosen not to be so intimate, and it has saddened me." Mrs. Gardiner let out a gasp at His Lordship's comment, causing the earl to ask, "Mrs. Gardiner, what are you implying that I was implying?" his face a picture of innocence. But then he gave her such a smile that the lady blushed from head to toe. "Mrs. Gardiner, when I see beauty, I feel compelled to acknowledge it, and you are a very attractive lady, with such a rosy complexion. Is it always this rosy? By the way, is there a Mr. Gardiner?"

"Yes, milord. He is presently at his office," she answered, her voice faltering, "which is nearby."

"And what takes the nearby Mr. Gardiner away from his lovely wife?"

"He is a coffee broker, milord."

"A coffee broker? Excellent. Then I should like to get to know him. Unlike many members of the aristocracy, I do not snub men who engage in commerce as they are the future of England and will eventually have all the money. Monsieur Napoleon has called England a nation of shopkeepers. I have no quarrel with that statement. Unfortunately, I currently do not have any friends who are merchants. I mean, I do *know* merchants. One is waiting for me outside my door almost every day, but since I do not owe Mr. Gardiner any money and I love coffee, Mr. Gardiner would be a good friend to have. Is he usually absent for most of the day?"

After seeing her aunt turn beet red again because of the earl's suggestive question, Lizzy redirected the conversation. "Milord, as I said, Mr. Darcy and Miss Darcy have gone into Kent for a visit. He wished to personally inform your aunt of our engagement."

"It almost makes me want to rush to Rosings Park. I would pay good money to see how this scene plays out. You see, my aunt Catherine and I have a special relationship."

"Are you very close?" Lizzy asked, thinking it unlikely.

"We could not be any closer. Because if we were, it would end in verbal fisticuffs. If you have met the esteemed lady, you will certainly understand."

"I *have* met Lady Catherine," Lizzy answered, suppressing a laugh. "I dined with her on at least three occasions while I was visiting with a dear friend, Mrs. Collins, who is married to the vicar at Hunsford Lodge."

"I would be pleased to meet any acquaintance of yours, Miss Bennet. Unfortunately, since Mrs. Collins is married to a parson, it is most unlikely that we shall ever meet unless, of course, Aunt Catherine should go to her glory in the beyond.

I would most certainly attend her funeral, but since I know her to be in excellent health, it is unlikely that I shall have the pleasure of meeting your friend. But that is neither here nor there. You say that you have dined with my dear aunt. How did you get on? Did she like you?"

It was obvious that His Lordship used his engaging personality to ask any question that popped into his head, no matter how personal, and that he expected it to be answered. Lizzy, however, was of a different mind. "You would have to ask your aunt, milord."

"You are avoiding my question, Miss Bennet. Does my aunt like you?"

"She expressed her opinions, and I shared mine."

"Aha!" the earl said, gleefully. "If you had the audacity to express *your* opinions, then I *know* she does not like you, but that should not bother you. In fact, I would take it as a compliment."

Lizzy did not know how to respond, and thinking it best to ignore his statement, she asked if he frequently visited Rosings Park.

"Despite my deep attachment for my dear cousin, the lovely Miss Anne de Bourgh, I go but rarely because my aunt lives there as well. However, I do see Anne every time she comes to London, and she is an excellent correspondent who keeps me informed of family news, which is how I learned of your romance with my cousin."

"But that does not explain how you knew where to find me in town. I only came to London yesterday."

"My house is across the square from the Darcy townhouse, and my manservant saw the Darcy carriage. Gregg, whose charms are second only to my own, has been flirting with a housemaid in Darcy's employ, who spoke with a groom, who overheard a conversation between Darcy and his butler about seeing to the wishes of a certain Miss Elizabeth Bennet, who was staying with the Gardiners in Gracechurch Street. This should be a lesson to us all that we should never say anything in front of the servants that we do not want repeated. On the other hand, if one wishes to spread a rumor that is the most efficient way of going about it."

Lizzy now understood why Fitzwilliam Darcy became exasperated whenever he spoke about the head of the Fitzwilliam family. Darcy, through a clenched jaw, would express his frustration with a man whom he knew to have a fine mind and a caring spirit but who was completely undisciplined and denied himself nothing.

"Allow me to give you an example," Darcy had said during one of their conversations about the earl. "Antony was one of the few members of the House of Lords to voice his opposition to confronting the Americans on the high seas. I was in the visitors' gallery when he gave a speech warning that boarding American vessels and taking sailors off their ships would lead to war with the United States, and it might yet happen. It was an act of parliamentary courage, but did he remain in the House to discuss the matter with other members of the Lords? No! He went straight to his club, where he gambled the night away. Damn frustrating man!"

His frustration with his cousin was the reason Darcy had not mentioned Lord Fitzwilliam when discussing their wedding plans, but how could she not invite His Lordship to their wedding? The two were first cousins, and so Lizzy informed the earl of the date and place for the nuptials.

"You obviously have not consulted Darcy. He would not want me there," he said, pouting.

"If you wish to attend, you are welcome." Even though Lizzy knew that His Lordship was reeling her in, she was finding it hard to resist.

"Thank you so much, but it would probably be best…" But after pausing for a moment, he asked, "Do you know if the Granyards will be there?"

"No, milord. It is Mr. Darcy's wish that the reception be limited to immediate friends and family." Lizzy was content to remain ignorant of how large the wedding list had grown since she had departed Longbourn. "We shall have a reception for our friends and family in the spring at my parents' home in Hertfordshire."

"It is just as well then that I cannot go because if Lady Granyard is not going to the reception, there really isn't any point. Unless, of course, you are going," he said, turning to Mrs. Gardiner.

"Yes, my *husband* and I will definitely be going— together," she answered with a flutter. She had been relieved when Lizzy had taken over the conversation, but now he was speaking to her once again in a highly suggestive manner. "I do not think I mentioned earlier that I am the mother of four—two boys and two girls."

"Oh, I just adore children," Fitzwilliam said, cooing. "I have two little jewels of my own. Sophie is nine, and Emmy is eight. I do not see them as often as I would like because…" He sat up straight in his chair. "…because they live in a dark castle with a drawbridge guarded by dragons, and in the center of the castle is a throne where their mother, the Queen of Darkness, reigns. The castle is surrounded by a moat filled with crocodiles, which Lady Eleanor hand-feeds the pieces and parts of anyone who has ever crossed her. But, occasionally, I don my suit of armor and charge the castle.

After rescuing my children, I take them to Briarwood, my country estate. For a few peaceful days, we have the best time until their mother, riding in her black chariot with her hair on fire, comes for them. But children must have their mothers." After letting out a long sigh, he added, "Eleanor and I just don't get on."

Lizzy and her aunt looked at each other. *They don't get on? Who would have guessed?*

"But, Miss Elizabeth, I am sure you have much to do to prepare for your wedding," he said, rising, "and so I shall leave you. Hopefully, after you have married, you will invite me to your townhouse. I am sure Darcy pays his coal bills, so it will be a lot warmer in your home than it is in mine."

After being assisted by Rothwell with his overcoat and after putting on his top hat and placing his cane under his arm, he again addressed Elizabeth. "I shall conclude by saying that your soon-to-be husband is a royal pain, a stick in the mud, an enemy of fun, and the most decent man I know. However, on more than one occasion, he has pulled my derrière out of the fire, for which I am most grateful, and I ask that you be good to him because he deserves it and because he will always be good to you. He takes care of those he loves."

"I am in complete agreement with the part of your statement that mentioned Mr. Darcy's goodness, decency, and his attention to those he cares about, but as for being an enemy of fun, Mr. Darcy and you probably have very different definitions of the word."

"No doubt about that, Miss Bennet," he said chuckling, and after a quick kiss of Elizabeth's hand and a prolonged kiss of Mrs. Gardiner's, Antony, Lord Fitzwilliam, departed.

After collapsing into a chair, and with a sigh of relief, Mrs.

Gardiner commented on their extraordinary visitor. "I have never met anyone like him."

"I don't think there *is* another like him," Lizzy said, amazed at His Lordship's performance.

"Elizabeth, I do believe he was flirting with us."

"Oh, he wasn't flirting with me, Aunt Gardiner. He was flirting with *you*. Apparently, he only seduces married women. I am sure he has justified their seduction because they are not maidens."

"I can hardly believe that an earl was in my home, flirting with me, the mother of four children," Mrs. Gardiner said, giggling. "It really is too bad that Mr. Gardiner was not here to see it. However, I shall make up for his absence by providing him with every last detail of our afternoon." A dreamy smile appeared on her face, and while her aunt was thinking about their unique visitor, Lizzy was wondering how Mr. Darcy was faring in Kent.

⚶

"I forbid it!" an outraged Lady Catherine said. "You will never have my consent to marry that unfeeling, selfish girl. She will be the ruin of you in the opinion of all your friends, and she will make you the contempt of the world."

Darcy and Georgiana had been at Rosings Park for three days before any mention was made of Miss Elizabeth Bennet, and when her earlier visit to Kent was discussed during the evening meal, Lady Catherine had nothing good to say about such a headstrong young lady who dared to answer her questions truthfully. But on the fourth day, all was revealed, and the storm rolled in.

"Aunt, that is *your* opinion, and one I do not share," Darcy said in a calm voice. His aunt could go on as long as it pleased her. Since nothing she said would change his mind, he was determined not to become angry. She was his mother's sister, and as such, deserved his respect.

"Fitzwilliam, I am almost your nearest relation, and I can assure you that your mother would be opposed to this match."

"I disagree," Georgiana said in a soft voice as she came to her brother's defense. "I do not remember very much about my mother, and most of my knowledge of her comes to me by way of my father and brother, but this I do know. My mother and father were in love, and Mama would want for her son to be in love with his wife."

"Nonsense! Your mother's marriage to your father was arranged between the Fitzwilliam and Darcy families, one noble and the other with ancient ties to the monarchy. It had nothing to do with love. In your conversations with Anne, I have made note of your ridiculous romantic notions of men and women falling in love, but the reality is that only peasants marry for love, as they have nothing else to offer."

"You say that my parents' marriage was arranged, and I believe you, but the fact is that they did fall in love and that is what they would want for Will," Georgiana quickly rebutted, her voice growing stronger.

Darcy admired his sister's attempt to change the mind of their aunt Catherine, but she was up against a woman who had no experience with disappointment, except in her own marriage.

"Aunt Catherine, the thought of being estranged from you is painful to me," Darcy began, "however, if you will not receive Elizabeth at Rosings, then I shall not come here until you do. It is your choice."

"Fitzwilliam, I see that you have been taken in by Miss Bennet's arts and allurements, and in a moment of infatuation, you have forgotten what you owe to your family. She has drawn you in."

"'Drawn me in.'" Darcy said, smiling. She most certainly had drawn him in. "If that is how you wish to phrase it, I shall not quarrel with you. But I know this. I love Miss Elizabeth Bennet, and it is the kind of love that is strong and good and will weather all storms. I am less than a perfect man, but she has accepted me, with all my faults."

"Your faults? What nonsense. You have none. But Miss Bennet does. Not only is she presuming to quit the sphere into which she was born, she is dragging you into a family tainted by scandal. Do not think I do not know of her sister's patched-up marriage to the son of your father's steward. Of what are you thinking?"

Darcy was about to bring this conversation to a close when he saw Anne rise from her chair near the fire. "Stop! Mama, I insist that you stop!"

Anne had remained silent throughout the exchange. While watching the drama unfold, she had hoped that her dear cousins would be able to convince her mother to recognize the marriage without her becoming involved, but this had gone on long enough.

"Anne, please..." Darcy said, concerned for his cousin. After such an angry exchange of words, he would have to leave Rosings, but Anne would be left behind to deal with her enraged mother. He did not want that.

"No, William, I have something to say, and I mean to say it." Then she turned her attention to her mother. "Mama, I love you, and I loved Papa. But you did not love each other, and I can assure you that it was painful for me to have my father living most of the year in London while you and I remained here in the country. I do not want that for William.

"As for Miss Bennet, she is a warm, charming, gracious, and giving woman, and she loves William—deeply—and is committed to him with all of her heart and soul. She asks nothing of him, except his love. Now, you say that such an emotion exists only in the lower classes, but you are wrong because I have seen it with my own eyes."

For the whole of Anne's speech, Lady Catherine remained quiet. She loved her daughter more than anyone or anything, and she lived in fear of losing her at any moment to illness or disease. It was not her intention to upset her, but she was unalterably opposed to the mingling of classes and said as much.

"Mama, you do not go up to town as often as I do because if you did, you would see that trying to prevent the 'mingling of classes' would be like attempting to hold back the tide. Impoverished aristocrats are marrying their sons to the daughters of merchants *every* day. When I was in town on my return from Derbyshire, I learned of Lord Corman's engagement to a Miss Abernathy, whose father made his fortune in herring! Now, if the son of a duke can marry the daughter of a purveyor of fish, you certainly cannot object to the marriage of a gentleman's son to the daughter of a gentleman.

"And I have one more thing to add. William is not asking for your permission to marry. He is here as a courtesy to you. With or without your blessing, Elizabeth and he will marry on December 24th. I, for one, shall wish them joy, and if you wish to see Georgie and William again, you should do the same. Do you really want to be estranged from yet another family member? Is it not enough that Antony and you do not talk or that his sisters rarely visit because they are afraid of you? Think of the consequences before you say another word."

With that, Anne sat down, and the only sound was the clock ticking away the minutes. After an uncomfortably long silence, Darcy went over and took hold of his aunt's hand, but she would not look at him.

"I hope you will take Anne's advice because *nothing* will change my mind about marrying Elizabeth. However, I do not wish to impose upon your hospitality, so Georgiana and I will leave in the morning as there is much to do. Elizabeth and I will have a reception at Longbourn in the spring, and I hope you will attend." Darcy then signaled to his sister that they should retire.

The next morning, with her mother still in her bedchamber, Anne was the only one to see her cousins on their way.

"Oh, William, I wish I could be there for your wedding, but as you know, I do not travel well in the winter. By the way, when is the next full moon?"

"On the twenty-eighth. But you need not worry as Elizabeth borrowed a book on astronomy from the circulating library in Meryton and wrote down all the dates for the full moon for the next two years."

"Then you are obviously in good hands."

"Anne, you seem quite chipper this morning. Considering that things did not go well last night, I find your good cheer puzzling."

"Oh, I disagree. I think things went very well. You managed to have the last word with Mama. Can you ever remember that happening before? And because of that, I am hopeful that we shall see you in the spring."

Darcy nodded his head in agreement as well as in admiration of his fragile cousin who had taken the field and won the battle, if not the war.

CHAPTER 27

The day after Lord Fitzwilliam's visit, Lizzy and Mrs. Gardiner ventured out with Madame Delaine, Georgiana's modiste, who knew where all the best warehouses were located. Since Lizzy and Mrs. Gardiner's French was only marginally better than Madame's English, it proved to be an interesting experience for all parties, but by the end of the day, Lizzy had the material for her dress, and some of the "whatnots," as Mr. Darcy put it, to go with her bridal attire, all of which was put on his account.

"I told Mr. Darcy that Papa put away one thousand pounds for my dowry," Lizzy explained to Mrs. Gardiner, "but he said that because of Lydia's marriage to Wickham, he had no doubt that it would become necessary for her to ask our father for assistance, and the money for my dowry would be there to help her."

"That is very generous of Mr. Darcy, but of course he is a man with real assets, unlike Lord Fitzwilliam, who apparently does not have the money to pay the coalman."

An enjoyable morning was followed by an equally pleasant afternoon. When Lizzy arrived at the Gardiner residence, there was a letter waiting for her from Mr. Darcy. However, with the memory of his previous letter fresh in her mind, she put it in her pocket to be read in the privacy of her bedroom.

After supper, thirteen-year-old Margaret, the older of the two Gardiner daughters, treated her cousin to a number of delightful pieces, including a Scottish air, on the pianoforte. Following the completion of her performance, their governess escorted her four charges upstairs, and Lizzy and her aunt shared their shopping experiences with Mr. Gardiner, who was polite, but clearly uninterested in their excursion. To engage her husband's attention, Mrs. Gardiner told him of Lord Fitzwilliam's visit, and he laughed so hard that he nearly popped a button on his waistcoat. After wiping the tears of laughter from his eyes, he managed to sputter, "Do I have anything to worry about, Mrs. Gardiner? Should I work at home to keep the wolf at bay?"

That comment reminded Lizzy of Mr. Darcy's letter, and she excused herself. But before closing the door behind her, she could hear Uncle Gardiner saying to his wife, "All I can say, my dear, is that Lord Fitzwilliam has damn fine taste in women, and he has definitely put an idea in my head. Shall we retire early tonight?" Lizzy could hear her aunt giggling.

Once in bed, Lizzy stared at the letter. Surely, it must be better than the one he had written to her on his journey home from Scotland, and after another moment's hesitation, she broke the seal.

> *Dearest Elizabeth,*
>
> *Be not alarmed, on receiving this letter, by the apprehension of its containing any repetition of those words which were so repugnant to you when last I wrote. I write without any intention of paining you.*

And Lizzy hugged the letter to her chest and thought how clever he was to open his missive by mocking that first awful letter he had written to her when she was at Hunsford Lodge.

> *Being unsure if I would have the time to write to you once I was in Kent, I penned this letter while in town, and so it will contain no news, only my love.*
>
> *I have never written a love letter (and you can attest to that fact). So what do I say after I confess that my love for you is so strong that no wind could bend it nor rock could break it? I imagine that most gentlemen would make reference to that wonderful moment when he first saw his lady love. But I cannot do that because I was abominably rude to you at the assembly, and the first time I saw you smile was when you were laughing at me for being such a boorish man. I must also omit references to Lucas Lodge, the ball at Netherfield (where you were the prettiest girl in the room), and, most definitely, Hunsford Lodge.*
>
> *So I must move past our unfortunate beginning to the day I saw you at Pemberley. You were sitting on a bench without a bonnet. (Didn't your mother warn you about getting freckles from being out in the sun without a bonnet or parasol?) Your face was turned toward the sun, and because your eyes were closed, I was able to gaze upon your freckled countenance for several minutes. When you opened your eyes to find me staring at you, I thought that you might run away, but you did not, and in that moment you sealed your fate because I knew exactly what you were feeling, and it wasn't anger, animosity, or dislike; it was something quite different.*

Lizzy treasured the memory of her visit to Pemberley. She had been sitting in the garden, and with the sun warm upon her face, she had been thinking about the Hunsford letter. In it, Mr. Darcy had admitted that he had interfered in Jane and Charles's relationship, but not for the reasons she had suspected. And if he had failed to properly judge the depth of her sister's affection for Mr. Bingley, she had been completely blind to Wickham's true character. If Mr. Darcy's behavior had been less than exemplary, there was certainly enough criticism to go around, as she had these preconceived notions about him, every one of which had proved to be wrong.

But on such a beautiful day, thinking unhappy thoughts was unpardonable, and so she had set them aside. While waiting for her aunt and uncle to come down the garden path, she had been thinking of what it would be like to be embraced and kissed by the handsome owner of this beautiful estate, when she sensed that someone was nearby. Upon opening her eyes, she found Mr. Darcy standing not more than twenty feet from her, holding his jacket and with his shirt opened, and she had been both embarrassed and…

"Oh my God! That's what he meant by, 'I knew exactly what you were feeling, and it wasn't anger, animosity, or dislike; it was something quite different,'" She remembered the sensation that had spread throughout her body when she had seen his exposed chest and the heat she had felt that had nothing to do with the sun. And he knew it! She quickly scanned the letter to find her place. Were there other revelations to be found in its pages?

And because I knew what you were thinking, I felt comfortable in engaging you in conversation, and for the first time since I left Kent, I had hope. There was, of course, a major hurdle to be overcome, and after I saw your face when I revealed all, I again despaired. But on that first night of nightfall, when you came out onto the terrace, I saw a ray of light in a bleak landscape. And you know the rest.

Do I need to tell you how much I want you? How I suffer each night because I sleep alone? When I told you in the study that I wanted to taste and touch every inch of you, I was not speaking figuratively...

Lizzy felt her temperature rise, and she used the letter to fan herself and wondered what her wedding night would be like? On more than one occasion, Lizzy had overheard her mother's conversations with Aunt Philips and the other hens from Meryton speaking of their own wedding nights. Although they were laughing when they shared their "pointed" comments and their "probing" questions, they still spoke of the discomfort and embarrassment they had experienced that first time.

Would she be embarrassed? She did not think so. William had talked about how Nature provides for its creatures. If stripped of the overlay of shame and guilt placed on making love by society, it could be a pleasurable experience for both men and women. But would it hurt? That was a different matter altogether. When he had lain on top of her in the study at Pemberley, his manhood seemed to be a third of the length of a broomstick, but again, he had explained that Nature prepared a woman to receive a man *if the woman was receptive.* Lizzy decided to stop thinking about it. She would know soon enough and continued reading.

At night, as I lie awake, I think of the words from Shakespeare's forty-third sonnet:
All days are nights to see, till I see thee.
And night's bright days when dreams do show thee me.

My darling, you have become the reason for my existence. Without you, there is no Fitzwilliam Darcy.

                             Yours always, Will

Lizzy let out a sigh, quite pleased with the contents of the letter, and as she tucked it under her pillow, she thought how few nights there were left when he would sleep alone.

CHAPTER 28

WHILE MADAME DELAINE WAS measuring every inch of her person, Lizzy was imagining a shop where you could buy a ready-made dress. A tuck or two, a shortening of the hem, and a bit of added lace, and she would be done, but she dare not speak her thoughts aloud, as Madame had already mentioned her contempt for the inferior work of some of the other dressmakers, at least that was Lizzy's translation of her heavily accented English.

Buying the shoes, boots, gloves, shawls, and chemises was a lot more fun, and she particularly enjoyed visiting the milliner's shop, where she donned turbans with tassels and hats with ostrich plumes sprouting everywhere. But with Mr. Darcy's satirical eye, she could just imagine his comments about such exotic head coverings. He had already voiced his opinion on the overly wide brims of her poke bonnets, saying that she wore them not to keep the sun off of her face but to keep his lips off of her mouth. How wrong he was about that.

Two days later, Aunt Gardiner and Lizzy returned to Madame Delaine's boutique for Lizzy's first fitting, and when she saw the emerging form of her dress within the fabric, she was very pleased, and so she suffered in silence as Madame pinned away.

When aunt and niece got out of the hackney at Gracechurch Street, they saw a carriage parked outside the

Gardiner townhouse, and Lizzy immediately recognized it as belonging to Mr. Darcy.

"Ah, Miss Darcy has returned to town," Lizzy said, smiling. She had developed a deep attachment for Georgiana as she was all that a sister should be, but when she went into the parlor, there sat not Miss Darcy but her brother. After an exchange of pleasantries, Mr. Darcy told Mrs. Gardiner that his sister was upstairs with her eldest daughter, and when she learned that Margaret was teaching Miss Darcy how to trim a bonnet, she said that she would check on their progress.

Knowing of Mr. Darcy's ardor, she sat on the sofa across from him.

"I thought you were to go directly to Herefordshire," Lizzy stated, somewhat concerned. She wanted nothing to interfere with his task of finding Nell a husband.

"Well, I had to come through London anyway, and so I decided to break my journey for a day or two. Are you complaining?"

"Of course not, but you will go to Herefordshire, will you not?"

"Elizabeth, I thought you would be happy to see me. Instead, it seems that you will be pleased to see me on my way. I have not pressed on in my journey because I missed you. Three weeks was too long. What was I thinking when I made those plans?" And then he became suspicious of her reasons for wanting him out of London, but in Herefordshire. "Is this about Nell?" Of course it was, and Darcy shook his head in disapproval. "Your silence speaks volumes. Once again, I will tell you that I have no interest in the lady. You have nothing to worry about."

"I believe you, and I do not want to talk about Nell. How did things go with your aunt Catherine?"

"Better than I would have thought."

"Really!" Lizzy said pleased. "I feared that it would not go well at all. So she approves of our marriage?"

"I would not put it that way."

"Are you saying that although she does not approve of our marriage, she will not stand in our way?" Lizzy asked in an unsure voice.

"She did not say that either."

"Well, what did she say? Is your good news that she did not throw a vase at you or hit you with her cane?"

"A vase was not immediately at hand, and her infirmities prevent her from wielding a cane in such a way as to cause injury."

"Oh, now I see that your purpose in going into Kent was to hone your skills as a wit."

"I have been so easily found out," he responded, but when Lizzy started to twiddle her thumbs while waiting for an explanation for his optimism, Darcy explained Anne's supposition that since her mother did not have the last word, it was a sign of her acquiescence.

"You bring me thin gruel, sir," Lizzy answered, unimpressed, "but it is a better conclusion than what your cousin anticipated when he called on me."

"Richard is in town?"

"No, not the colonel, but his brother, Lord Fitzwilliam. He paid a visit earlier in the week."

"Good God! You did not say anything, did you? Because telling him anything is the same as releasing it for publication."

"Of course not. That is an insulting statement, Will. Your welfare is my first concern."

"I am sorry," he quickly added. Knowing that she would never do anything that would endanger him, Elizabeth had a right to be insulted. "It is just that he has a way of wrapping people, especially women, around his little finger, and I can see from your expression that you were taken in by his charms."

"I must confess I was amused by his wit, but it is the same as when troupes of acrobats and jugglers come into the village. They are very entertaining, but you would not want them to linger too long."

Lizzy shared with Mr. Darcy the details of His Lordship's visit, including his flirting with Mrs. Gardiner. When he offered to apologize for his cousin's behavior, Lizzy assured him that her aunt had enjoyed every minute of it and had shared it with Mr. Gardiner. But Lizzy did want to know if Lady Eleanor really was the Queen of Darkness and if Lord Fitzwilliam was truly broke.

"I am sure Antony told you that Lady Eleanor drowns kittens in her moat or is guilty of performing other such monstrous acts, but it is just another example of a failed arranged marriage. Although she is not the Queen of Darkness, Eleanor is definitely one of the most unpleasant people I know. As to your second question, the earl is not broke. He is one of the very few of England's elite who wins more at the gaming tables than he loses. Unlike most other members of his club, he knows when to leave the tables."

"Then why does he not pay his bills? Apparently, his townhouse is freezing because he owes the coalman for past deliveries."

"Because he has a liquidity problem. Winning at cards and collecting the money are two different things, but when Antony finally does get the money, he will pay Mr. Blackmun, the coalman, first. Once he is paid, word spreads quickly that the earl has money and that they can expect Gregg, his manservant, to come 'round and pay his debts."

"What a terrible way to live."

"It is terrible, but it is the way business is done in town. I hope you did not invite him to the wedding."

"I did," Lizzy answered, and when she saw Mr. Darcy's look of displeasure, she quickly added, "How could I not invite him when we were sitting in the same room discussing our wedding? But he is not coming, which raises another question. One of the reasons he will not be attending is because Lady Granyard will not be there. Surely, he is not having an affair with her."

"Not now, he isn't. But he did have an affair with her when she was Lady Boyle. But do you see what has happened?" he said in an exasperated voice. "Instead of us talking about our wedding, we are talking about Antony. This happens every time. The only people who can upstage him are the royals, and not all of them either. But no more about Antony. Did you read my letter?"

"Yes, I did," Lizzy said, and her whole demeanor changed. "You know, I should burn it. You should not write such things. The part about our wedding night was really improper." But Lizzy could not keep the smile out of her voice.

"In two weeks' time, I promise not to write anything of the sort. Words will be replaced by deeds."

Lizzy's physical response was immediate, as was Darcy's, and he spanned the distance between them in two steps. After lifting her out of the chair, he kissed her as if they had been parted for months instead of one week. But Lizzy removed her arms from around his neck, and after sliding them down his chest, she gently pushed him away.

"You have such power over me. I cannot hide anything from you," she said, her voice unsteady.

"Do not speak to me of power. You have brought me to my knees."

"In that case…" Lizzy pulled his mouth toward her, and because she was a head shorter than he was, he lifted her off her feet and kissed her until his arms ached.

"I cannot stay away from you, Elizabeth Bennet, and so I will make short work of my business in Herefordshire, and as soon as I have done so, I shall go to Netherfield and remain there until we are man and wife. Actually, I have no choice. Georgiana speaks of nothing but Kitty and Mary and you, of course. Whenever you are ready to return to Hertfordshire, she will leave London with you, but she will stay at Netherfield with me."

"That is probably best. With all the preparations for the wedding breakfast, there will be too much going on at Longbourn." Or so she thought.

CHAPTER 29

WITH EXACTLY ONE WEEK to go before the wedding, Lizzy and Georgiana arrived at Netherfield Park, but when they came to the gated entrance, their driver had to yield as a slow-moving wagon moved in front of him. When Georgiana recognized the driver as Abel Metcalf, Lizzy knew that her wedding reception was not going to be held at Longbourn, but here at Netherfield.

"You should have written to me, Jane," Lizzy said as soon as she was in the house. "I had no idea that the guest list had grown so long. Here you are an expectant mother doing everything, and I am doing nothing and I am the bride."

"You need not concern yourself on my account," Jane reassured her sister. "I have done very little. Mr. Jackson arrived two days ago, and he has met with our butler, Mr. Cleveland, and between the two, they have taken care of everything as well as seeing to the needs of all of the servants who have come from Pemberley to help. Mr. Jackson said that this is nothing to him, as he has been with the Darcys since he was a boy, and when Lady Anne was alive, the family was frequently on the move—visiting other families at their country houses, going to town for Christmas and the season, to Weymouth to sea bathe, and back to Pemberley. These pleasant memories brought a smile to his face."

"You must be mistaken, Jane. Mr. Jackson never smiles. It is not in the butler's handbook."

From the day Lizzy had met him at Pemberley, Mr. Jackson had shown her nothing but kindness, and she had developed a deep affection for him because of how protective he was over his master. But she had never seen even a tiny crack in his somber facade. When Lizzy had mentioned this to Mr. Darcy, he answered by saying that he knew for a fact that Mr. Jackson was capable of smiling. "One time, Mercer caught him in the act, but he only performs this exercise when he is belowstairs, and only in the company of the senior servants, and then only once or twice a year as he does not want to overdo it, or so I am told, having never actually witnessed the phenomenon myself."

"But why does he not smile abovestairs?" Lizzy had asked. "He must occasionally be amused by something he has seen or heard."

"It is quite normal for senior servants not to smile as they bear heavy responsibilities. You cannot judge the servants here at Pemberley based on your relationship with Mr. and Mrs. Hill. Such familiarity would not work on such a large estate. When you think about it, Pemberley is as large as some villages, so Mr. Jackson must be very strict in order to keep his young staff in line."

"Well, if Mr. Jackson actually did smile," Lizzy told Jane, "I am sorry to have missed it, as it happens as frequently as the appearance of Mr. Halley's comet."

Lizzy shared with her sister all that she had done in London. "Madame Delaine is an accomplished dressmaker, and while her nimble fingers performed miracles on my wedding dress, Aunt Gardiner and I went from shop to shop, having the best time, all at Mr. Darcy's expense."

"By the way, where is Mr. Darcy?" Jane asked, looking around. "Is he with Charles?"

"He is not here. He had some business that required his attention, but he will be here in a day or two."

Jane was not pleased to hear that Mr. Darcy was once again absent. She had grown used to Charles's boundless energy and his need for movement, but it was nothing compared to Mr. Darcy's meanderings. At least her husband remained in the county, but that was not the case with Mr. Darcy. He was always coming and going, but only God knew where he went.

"Lizzy, I do so hope he will not be running about the country once you are married. Your courtship was unorthodox by anyone's standards, except, perhaps, for those men who travel the roads to sell their wares."

"Please do not worry, Jane. You must understand that Mr. Darcy's wealth is not derived exclusively from his properties and that he has investments in other companies and manufactories. Up to this point, he has been personally involved in their management, but he will not do so once we are married." All of this was true. It just did not have anything to do with what was happening in Herefordshire.

"I am very glad to hear it, and I shall hold him to it as a husband should be by his wife's side. Now, as to the preparations for your wedding, Mr. Darcy's cook arrived with Mr. Jackson. Prior to her coming, she sent such detailed instructions to poor Mrs. Blanchard that she was quite overwhelmed, but Mrs. Bradshaw assumed command and went into Meryton to talk to the butcher and the greengrocer and everyone else who will be providing whatever is needed. I have been warned that she is very demanding and brooks no interference in her kitchen."

"Then we shall not interfere," Lizzy said. "Besides, Georgiana is now here, and she knows how to get around Mrs. Bradshaw," or so Lizzy hoped. "She is speaking with her right now, so I shall join her, as I feel that I should do *something* since it is my wedding."

But it was not to be. As predicted, Mrs. Bradshaw politely told Lizzy that she was the bride and needed to tend to her own role and to leave her to do her work. This was said in a tone of voice that left no doubt that Lizzy had been dismissed, but it was a good thing that she had been shunted aside, as Mr. Darcy came to Longbourn the next day.

❧

Because it was such a gray, rainy day, Lizzy and Mr. Darcy could not go for a walk and were thus confined to the parlor with Kitty, Mary, and Mrs. Bennet. The gentleman tried to appear to be interested in their discourse, but he really did not want to hear Mary summarize the vicar's Sunday sermon, nor was he interested in Kitty's visit with Maria Lucas, and he most especially wished to be spared the reasons for the onset of Mrs. Bennet's flutters. All the news he had to share with his betrothed remained unspoken, that is, until Mr. Bennet took mercy on the couple and offered them the use of his study.

"Finally, we are alone," Darcy said as he pulled Lizzy into an embrace, and the two remained in each other's arms saying nothing. When Darcy did kiss her, it was a quick brush of his lips across her cheek. "I am at a point where if I were to kiss you on the lips it would have such an effect on me that I would risk embarrassing myself."

"I am in a similar state, but you probably already knew that. So let us sit on the sofa, and you may tell me of your trip to Herefordshire. How did it go?"

"Very well," he said, nodding his head for effect.

"As well as it went with your aunt Catherine?"

"Much better," he answered, laughing. "I may have found Nell the perfect husband. He is the son of a French aristocrat, twenty-six years old, reasonably handsome, of good height and build. The whole family, their servants, *and* their chef had to flee their estate in Provence because of revolutionary mobs roaming the countryside. It seems that the Reynards are gastronomes. I spent the better part of one evening talking to Vicomte Reynard about nothing more than meats, sauces, truffles, wine, brandy, et cetera."

"Oh, that does sound promising. I really do want Lady Helen to be happy, but I also want her gone, and not for the reason you might think. I was truly distressed at how indiscreet she was at Pemberley, and I would be constantly on edge, fearing that she would say something that would reveal your situation. With Rupert gone, it will be just you and Teddy, and he is completely reliable."

"Unfortunately, that is no longer true as Teddy will soon be leaving Pemberley for good."

"But why? If Nell marries Monsieur Reynard and Teddy leaves, then you will be all alone."

"Which is exactly the way I want it. Rupert was a menace, and Nell is annoying. Teddy and I could get by on a rabbit or partridge or, God forbid, not eat at all, but if there are three of us, Nell always wants to go after a deer and that causes problems. You cannot leave a carcass out in the woods that has been torn apart by animals as it will cause alarm bells to ring, but it is nothing to her as she gets in her carriage at daybreak and returns to Granyard Hall. But Teddy, Mercer, or I must go out and bury the deer or sheep or whatever she has devoured."

"I certainly understand why you want Nell and Rupert to leave the pack, but why Teddy?"

"I had an opportunity to speak with Teddy while I was in Herefordshire. He is there because that is where Rupert is being held prior to being transported, and it was he who came to me. At Pemberley, the explanation for Teddy's monthly disappearances was that Rupert was the son of a nobleman, and once a month he was permitted to go see his father, and Teddy would accompany him as his manservant. That situation no longer exists, and you cannot have a groom go missing once a month. It would make Teddy's life very difficult with the other grooms, and it might possibly invite comment. I cannot have that. Now that I am to be a married man with a family, I will not take any unnecessary risks and that is what I told the Council."

"The Council was in Herefordshire?"

"Yes, Rupert remains a problem because you cannot have someone who was so public a figure just drop out of sight. The Council is made up of two werewolves and one man. It was decided that Mr. Clark, the human, will take Rupert to London where he will be seen, and when spring comes, word will have got around town that he wants to go to North America, and Teddy will go with him."

"Oh, poor Mrs. Brotherton! Can the Council force him to go?"

"It is not a matter of *forcing* him to do it; he wants to do it. In fact, he turned down an opportunity to become alpha male. The pack in Herefordshire has grown too large, and it must be divided. The position was offered to Teddy, but he declined. He told me that he wants to make his fortune in the New World where rank does not matter. His plans are well thought out, and I told him that I would provide him with seed money if he wants to start a business. I will be sorry to see him go, but go he must."

"I will miss Teddy, as will your sister, and his mother will be truly heartsick. I do understand why he must leave Pemberley, but I do not like to think of you out there by yourself."

"That is because you do not yet understand my other life. When I am a wolf, I enjoy doing those things that wolves do. I like to hunt and run and chase and play in the snow. It is not a hardship for me, and when the weather is bad, there is a cave where I take shelter."

Darcy could see that Lizzy was unhappy, and so he put his arm around her shoulder. "It is only two days a month," he said, trying to reassure her. "So let us speak of other things, as there is another topic I wish to talk to you about." Darcy's face changed from comforting to uncomfortable because he did not know how Lizzy would react to what he had to say.

"I have mentioned before that wolves have a heightened sense of smell, and because of that, I know when… I always know when you are about to start your courses."

"Good grief, Mr. Darcy! That is no subject for a man, not even a husband!"

"It is for this man because I also know the days when you are fertile. Please allow me to explain why this is important. My mother died shortly after she was delivered of a stillborn child. Bearing children is very taxing on a woman's body, and so I want to limit the number of children we have because the thought of losing you… What I am trying to say is that I shall know when not to come to your bedchamber."

"Are you telling me this now because I shall be fertile on our wedding night, and we shall not lie together?" Lizzy asked in near panic.

Darcy started to laugh. "No, I made sure of that before

agreeing to the date. Actually, it works out perfectly. You will begin your courses tonight or tomorrow at the latest, and so you will be finished by our wedding day, but you will not yet be fertile."

Lizzy covered her face in embarrassment. "This really is too much—for you to know when it is my time."

"But it is all a part of the natural order. There is no need for you to be embarrassed, and there are advantages. I will be more understanding of your moods." As soon as Darcy said it, he knew that he had erred.

"My moods?"

"Occasionally, your mood does alter. For example, when I went to Longbourn to invite you to Pemberley, you were, you know…"

"Oh, I see. So the reason for my unhappiness was not your coming and going without explanation for six months. It was because of my courses."

"No. That is not what I am saying."

"Well, what *are* you saying?"

"Merely, that it was a contributing factor."

"No, Mr. Darcy, it was not a contributing factor. By the time you had come back to Longbourn from your last disappearance, I had been angry with you for three weeks."

"I stand corrected," he quickly responded and sealed his lips together.

"That is all you have to say?"

"Elizabeth, there is no way I can win this argument, so I apologize for any past, present, or future transgressions."

"You are a quick learner, Will Darcy," Lizzy said smiling, and she kissed him on his cheek.

CHAPTER 30

I N THE MIDST OF all the hubbub caused by the wedding preparations, Lizzy could almost forget that the man who would shortly be her husband was also a werewolf, but when the snow started to fall on the morning of December 22nd, Lizzy was jolted back into the reality of a life lived by the lunar calendar and the necessity of reaching Pemberley by the afternoon of the twenty-eighth.

"Elizabeth, I know what you are going to say," Darcy said as soon as they were behind the closed doors of the sitting room. "You are concerned about the weather, and because I know that you worry about such things, I am going to tell you exactly what will happen in the next few days." They walked hand-in-hand to the sofa.

"Because of the snow, we will leave early on the morning of the twenty-fifth. This is now a hard and fast date, and all entreaties for us to remain must be firmly rejected. We will leave Netherfield at dawn, but we will not have far to go—only about twelve miles—where we will change from my carriage to a coach. Mercer has already left to see to these arrangements.

"The ride will be less comfortable than in my carriage, but the coach can go faster and will have horses better suited to our purpose. Our first night will be spent with Mr. and Mrs. Gowland. Although they are paid by the Council, you are not to engage them in conversation. You will call me sir, and you will be addressed as madam. Georgiana is miss, Mercer is my manservant, and Metcalf is the coachman. No names are to be used. I have stayed with the Gowlands before. The rooms are small, but clean, and their home is amply provisioned.

"I am afraid that you and Georgie will be very tired from traveling, but we will leave first thing in the morning and press on to my aunt Marguerite's house. Weather permitting, we will stay there just the one night before leaving for Pemberley. If all goes well, we will arrive home with plenty of time to spare. If necessary, I can transform at Ashton Hall. I have done so on three occasions, so a plan is already in place. Since Jeanne and George Wimbley are in town, there is only Aunt Marguerite in residence, and she knows what to do."

All the while Darcy was talking, Lizzy was holding his hand, and she felt as if she had not taken a breath since he began speaking. He was making it sound as if every contingency had been considered, but what if the snow prevented them from reaching the Gowlands' refuge?

"There is another Council house along the route, but I would more likely take you, Georgie, Metcalf, and Mercer to an inn, and I would stay outside."

Lizzy shook her head, and tears began to pool.

"Darling, please remember that I spent two years near Hudson Bay. By the end of my first winter, I lost a quarter of my weight, but I survived. If I can survive in one of the most hostile environments in the world, I can spend two nights in the woods in the English countryside, but I do not think any of those things will happen. We had a light dusting of snow this morning and nothing since. I am taking all of these precautions because of you."

But when her expression remained unaltered, he

continued. "Elizabeth, I would never have asked you to marry me if I did not think you were strong enough to deal with my altered state and all that goes with it. You are afraid for me because everything is new to you, but after a few nightfalls, you will not give it a second thought. My sister is an example of this. While you are sitting here worried, Georgiana is at Netherfield playing cards with Jane and Bingley.

"However, there are things you can do to help. When we are this close to nightfall, I will ask that you do everything I ask as soon as I ask it. If I say we must leave now, please stand up and leave with me. If I say that you must remain and I must go, you must not argue. Do you understand?"

Lizzy nodded because she could not speak.

"Elizabeth, the day after tomorrow, we will marry unless…"

And Lizzy put her fingers to his lips, "Entreat me not to leave thee or return from following after thee; for wither thou goest…" But that was all she could manage to get out before he pulled her into his embrace.

❦

The following morning, while Jane and Lizzy were discussing the next day's nuptials in their once-shared bedroom at Longbourn, Bingley and Darcy were visiting with Mr. Bennet, who was trying to stay clear of his wife. Mrs. Bennet was running hither and yon but in her husband's opinion, to little effect, and so he had lured the two young men into his study for a discussion of Napoleon's expansion of his empire on the Continent.

While the men plotted strategy for military campaigns, the sisters discussed a much more important subject and one that was foremost on the minds of all brides. What would her wedding night be like? Jane confessed that first night she had found the whole ritual to be embarrassing and that she had insisted Mr. Bingley extinguish the one candle that had been left burning so that she would not bang into something if she needed to use the chamber pot during the night.

"I would rather have had a bruise the size of a goose egg than for Mr. Bingley to see me without any clothes on." With that statement, the giggling began. Jane assured Lizzy that although there was some discomfort, the deed was done in just a few minutes. "But I should warn you that the scene was repeated during the night and again in the morning. You could say that the sun and Mr. Bingley rose at the same time." The sisters collapsed onto the bed laughing. "By the time I got out of bed to see to my toilette, I was an old hand at it."

But Jane's laughter ceased when Lizzy informed her that Mr. Darcy and she would leave Netherfield Park immediately after breakfast on the twenty-fifth, and her response was exactly as anticipated.

"But why must you depart on Christmas morning? Is it absolutely necessary for you to leave for Pemberley the day after you are married? I do not understand the need for such haste."

"Mr. Darcy promised his aunt Marguerite, who lives near Leicester, that we would visit. Lady Ashton is the elder Mr. Darcy's sister and the only one left from that generation of Darcys."

"That is all well and good, but why must you see her at this time?"

"Because Mr. Darcy wishes it, and I am agreeable to it, and that is all there is to be said." Lizzy said this in a harsh tone, but it was necessary for her sister to know that this was not a subject open to discussion. "Jane, if Mr. Bingley had asked you to do this on the day after your wedding, you would not have said no. I do not wish to begin our marriage by denying my husband the first thing he has asked of me."

"Well, I hope that Mr. Darcy will allow you to return to Longbourn when I am near my confinement," Jane said with a catch in her voice.

"Oh, Jane, please. I would not miss the birth of Baby Bingley for anything. I shall be here. I promise."

But Jane was now clearly unsettled. "Please forgive me, Lizzy, but there is something I must say, even at the risk of offending you. I have thought for some time that there is something unusual about Mr. Darcy. I cannot put my finger on it, but he has a tendency to stare. When he does, it is almost as if he knows what a person is thinking. The other night, just as I was about to ask Mr. Bingley to bring me a cup of tea, Mr. Darcy went and poured a cup for me, saying that he could tell that I was thirsty. Another time, he retrieved my fan because he knew that I was overly heated when I had said nothing about it. It was very kind of him, but I swear he sensed..."

"I understand why you have that impression," Lizzy said, interrupting, "but contrary to what you think, Mr. Darcy is not staring at you but through you. I have mentioned this to him, and he is trying not to do it. But old habits are hard to break. I think part of the problem is that you are comparing Mr. Darcy's quiet nature to that of Mr. Bingley's more animated disposition, but one should not be criticized for being overly attentive to another's needs."

"You do understand that I only want what is best for you." Jane began to cry, which was something she was doing quite frequently now that she was in her sixth month.

"Then your wish has been granted as I *do* have the best. Mr. Darcy and I are perfectly suited to each other. He loves me deeply, and when I am with him, there is no one happier than I am." Lizzy stood up and offered her sister assistance in rising. "Now, you must return to Netherfield Park. Tomorrow is my wedding day, and you are my matron of honor. I want you well rested so that you will enjoy the wedding breakfast. I do believe that half the county is attending."

"Only half?" Jane said, smiling, and she went in search of Charles just as Darcy came looking for Lizzy.

"If you are beginning to think about what you will need for our journey," he whispered, "make sure you have your gloves, muff, boots, extra stockings…"

"Sir, you have told me what to expect, and I shall pack accordingly. You should really take your own advice and stop worrying. Since my mother has turned our wedding breakfast into a spectacle to rival a harvest festival, I plan to enjoy myself."

By this time, Georgiana had come downstairs, accompanied by Kitty and Mary. The siblings had already received an invitation from Mr. Darcy's sister to come to Pemberley in the spring. *After nightfall*, Lizzy said to herself, and she realized that every plan she made would have that contingency attached to it.

After seeing the Bingley carriage turn out of the drive, Lizzy pulled her shawl tightly around her and looked up into an obsidian sky punctured with a thousand points of light and a waxing moon poised over a distant wood. Although Mr. Darcy had told her that in time the rising of a full moon would not merit a second thought from her, she knew differently. The welfare of her husband and her family depended on her being acutely aware of the moon's every phase.

CHAPTER 31

"THANK YOU, MAMA," LIZZY said as her mother tightened her stays, "but Jane and I have already had this conversation." She could hardly believe that her mother had chosen the morning of her wedding day to have "the talk" with her daughter.

"But you might encounter a very different situation than Jane's as Mr. Bingley is of a slight build when compared to Mr. Darcy, so…"

"Mama, at this point, there is nothing to be done, and I wish to enjoy my wedding day without thinking apprehensively about my wedding night." Lizzy gave a silent prayer of thanks when Kitty arrived and handed their mother a letter.

"Oh dear!" Mrs. Bennet said after briefly scanning its opening paragraph. "It is from Lydia. She will not be coming to the wedding after all, as there are no funds to pay for her coach fare. It is too bad that she did not write sooner as there is nothing to be done now." She continued perusing the letter. "Oh, goodness me! There is more news. Lydia is to be a mother, and she expects to be delivered of her child in midsummer. How wonderful! I shall be a grandmother twice over in the new year."

Lizzy made no comment. Her sister's announcement that she was with child should have been joyfully received, but how could it be when it was coupled with the news that she did not have enough money to pay the coach fare to come to her sister's wedding. As her father had so succinctly put it at the time of Lydia and Wickham's marriage, "Lydia has married one of the most worthless men in Great Britain." No good could come out of such a union, and the letter proved it.

But then Mrs. Bennet burst forth with the happy news that Lydia would shortly be coming home, as Mr. Wickham's regiment was to go to fight in the Peninsular campaign. With Wickham gone, there was no point in Lydia remaining in Newcastle. Although her mother was happy that her youngest daughter would be coming back to Longbourn, Lydia's sisters were not, not even Kitty, who had learned a lesson from her sister's mistakes. Everyone understood that with Lydia's arrival the house would be topsy-turvy once again. But this gray cloud did have a sliver of a silver lining for Lizzy: Mrs. Bennet had left the bedroom to share the good news with Mr. Bennet, and all discussion about Mr. Darcy's size had come to an end.

❧

Darcy had been up since dawn, and with Mercer gone to see to the arrangements for their journey, he had to dress himself, which was no hardship, except for the damn neckcloth, and he enlisted Bingley's assistance in tying the knot.

"We are all fools to have that peacock, Beau Brummel, dictate fashion," Darcy complained. "This thing around my neck is little different from the bows that Georgiana wore in her hair when she was a little girl. Why must it be so complicated?"

"Calm down, Darcy. You know that this has nothing to do with your neckwear. You are a nervous bridegroom, and there is no need to take your frustration out on poor Mr. Brummel."

"You mock me, Bingley, and having been in my position, what, seven or eight months ago, you should be more sympathetic."

"I do not recall being this nervous—certainly not about the ceremony. Perhaps you are looking past the festivities to your wedding night."

"Why do you say that?" he asked anxiously. "What do you think will happen? Will it be unpleasant?"

"Not for you, it won't."

"Damn it, Bingley. I am not here for your amusement."

Bingley found it difficult to suppress his laughter, but since his friend was in desperate need of calming, he told Darcy of his own wedding night, including the darkened room, Jane with the covers up to her nose, his wife lying in their bed as stiff as a board, and fumbling about in the dark.

"But, Darcy, you have to allow that it is a rather curious thing for a woman. Jane and I were not permitted to be alone at any time during our courtship, but on our wedding night, she is supposed to be comfortable disrobing in front of a man? Not likely. You will find that it takes patience and a great deal of talking about love."

"I am finding this whole business of the terrors of the wedding night to be ridiculous. Why should a woman hide beneath the covers in trepidation of a physical act that has gone on since the time of Adam and Eve? It is a part of the natural order. Men and women were created so that they might reproduce. 'Be fruitful and multiply.' It is a Biblical injunction."

"Is that what you are going to whisper in Elizabeth's ear? 'Darling, I come to you tonight by Biblical injunction, so that we might reproduce.'"

And even Darcy had to see the absurdity of his statement. "I cannot wait for this day to be over."

⌇

Darcy decided to follow Bingley's suggestion and have a glass of wine, and he had just poured himself a tall one when Colonel Fitzwilliam arrived at Netherfield. Because Richard had been unsure if he would receive permission to leave his regiment, Darcy was more than pleased when his cousin entered the room. However, his pleasure was short-lived because right behind him was Antony, Lord Fitzwilliam.

"Oh, God, just what I need," Darcy said to himself, and he added more wine to the glass.

Antony immediately sought an introduction to Mr. and Mrs. Bingley, and it was quickly apparent why women loved this irredeemable rascal.

"Mrs. Bingley, I had the good fortune to make your sister's acquaintance while in town, and I thought, what a beautiful young lady my cousin is to marry, but here I come to find that Miss Bennet has a golden-haired equivalent residing in the country." He continued on in that vein, and although Jane had been told about the black sheep of the Fitzwilliam family and his shameless flattery, she could not help but smile, especially since she was in need of compliments as she felt as wide as a barn door.

As much as he was enjoying the company of the lovely Mrs. Bingley, Antony tore himself away so that he might speak with his cousin to reassure him that he had not come to make mischief.

"Darcy, I promise to be on my best behavior. Besides, I do not think there is anyone here to misbehave with, so I shall limit myself to flirting with Mrs. Gardiner."

Darcy rolled his eyes but decided it was best not to say anything. It only encouraged him.

"Oh come, Darcy, don't give me that look. I daresay Mrs. Gardiner enjoyed my winking at her. I do not know of any woman who does not like to be reminded of a time when a man flirted with her. Such little pleasures keep one young. But I have come with only one purpose in mind and that is to wish you joy. Honestly, I did not think you would ever marry."

Darcy gave his cousin a sideways glance. "Why not?"

Antony looked about to see if their conversation could be overhead before continuing, "Because your wife would have to be a very special person, now wouldn't she?"

"What are you talking about?" Darcy asked, as he felt his heart quicken. Had Richard betrayed him by telling his blabbing brother of his situation?

"I know that you do not have a high opinion of me, Darcy, and with good reason. You think that I am incapable of keeping a secret, but I have kept yours for eight years." Following Darcy's eyes as he looked across the room at Colonel Fitzwilliam, he continued, "Richard did not tell me. It was Anne." At first, Darcy felt his heart sink, but knowing what an incurable gossip the earl was, Anne must have had a good reason for revealing so dark a secret.

"Do you remember the time when Anne was so ill that she thought she was going to die?" Darcy nodded, and a vision of Anne lying in her bedroom at Rosings fighting for every breath appeared before him. It was only by God's good grace that she survived. "It was then that she asked me, as the head of the Fitzwilliam family, to take care of you. So I have watched you all these years from a distance, and as far as I could tell, you required no assistance from me. But when I learned from Anne that you were engaged, I was concerned—for both of you—which is why I called on Miss Bennet while she was in town."

"You have no reason to be concerned on Elizabeth's account. She knows everything as she has seen me in my altered state."

"Then I have nothing else to say except to offer my congratulations to you on finding true love," Antony said. "In my short visit with Miss Bennet, I saw something: a strength of will and character. And I knew that you had found the perfect wife, and I envy you that. But I want you to know that if either of you ever needs assistance, I will be there to help you in any way I can. I also want you to know that I will take your secret to my grave. Not even Richard knows that I know. The less said, the better, even to my brother. Let me conclude by saying how much I admire you. Something like that would have brought a lesser man to his knees—me, for instance."

Antony took out his pocket watch and showed it to Darcy. "You have about one hour before you leave the ranks of one of England's most sought-after bachelors. Do you know how many hearts you are breaking by marrying Miss Bennet? Alexandra Banbury has taken to wearing dark colors."

"How is it that anyone in town knows I am to be married? I have made no announcement." Antony looked at the ceiling, studied his nails, straightened his collar, and in every way looked uncomfortable. "You cannot help yourself, can you?" Darcy asked.

Antony merely smiled, but as he started to walk away, Darcy pulled him back. "You and I have had our differences, but you should know that if I did not care, I would not bother."

"Of course, I know that, but as for our having differences, I know your lectures are for the purpose of making me a better man. However, I have no intention of reforming. Our time on earth is so short that it would be a sacrilege to go through life as a virtuous prig. Now, here comes my brother, so I shall have a glass of wine." The brothers bowed in passing.

"Good grief, Darcy. You are not even a married man yet, and you are already mellowing. That is the longest conversation you have had with Antony in years, and you only rolled your eyes once. That is a record, I am sure."

"There are times when he can actually be helpful. I assume you came in Antony's carriage, so if he was the only means of your getting here, I am glad to have him. But where the devil did you stay last night?"

"At the coaching inn, the Roost, about four miles from here."

"I cannot picture Lord Fitzwilliam sleeping on a well-worn mattress in a coaching inn."

"You do not have to picture such a scene because he did not sleep on any mattress. He came prepared with his own pillow and blanket, and after spreading out his overcoat, he lay down and went right to sleep. So I slept in the bed and escaped without so much as one bedbug bite.

"On another matter, on the way up to town," the colonel continued, "I stopped at Rosings Park and visited with Aunt Catherine and Anne, and our cousin looked very well; she was lacking that gray pallor she usually has in the winter. She sends you her love and is looking forward to visiting Pemberley in the spring."

"Did Aunt Catherine have a message for me?" Darcy asked.

"Actually, she said that she hopes the weather stays

fine—not necessarily for you, but for everyone, and there is reason to hope that she will come around. Apparently, after Georgie and you left, Anne and her dear Mama had a long talk, and Aunt Catherine stated that she hopes you will be happy. Although she doubts you will achieve domestic felicity, she wishes to be proved wrong."

Darcy nearly spit out his wine. "Aunt Catherine wishes to be proved wrong? Yes, and Antony wishes to stop sleeping with married women."

"However, bringing up a touchy subject was not my reason for making my way over here. I have come to execute my responsibilities as your best man and to make you aware of the time."

"Richard, I can hardly believe it. I am actually getting married." Darcy's whole demeanor changed at the thought of his marrying Elizabeth. "Just like any other man, I shall have a wife and family. I did not think…" Darcy could hear the catch in his voice and looked away from his cousin.

"Come on, old boy," Richard said, slapping Darcy on the back. "We are to church, as your bride awaits."

CHAPTER 32

WHILE MRS. BENNET PRATTLED on during the ride to the church, Lizzy and her father were lost in thought. Mr. Bennet still had a nagging feeling that there was more to Mr. Darcy's lengthy absences than either the bride or groom cared to reveal, but whatever the cause, Mr. Bennet was sure his daughter knew of the reason as the couple seemed to have formed a bond that was usually reserved for those who shared a secret.

Lizzy's mind was more pleasantly engaged. She was thinking about Mr. Darcy and how fortunate she was to have found such a man. While most men would be offended by her impertinence, Mr. Darcy found it amusing, and he had often told her how much he admired her strong character. She would be brave for him and not give into her fears, but he must do the same and not be overly protective of her or he would hear about it.

When Lizzy entered the church vestibule, she was met by Jane, who was wearing a panel attached to her pale yellow dress to hide her pregnancy, but even with her bulging middle, she looked particularly lovely as yellow was her best color. However, on this day, the most beautiful Bennet sister was Elizabeth. Her wedding dress was white satin with a gauze overdress and trimmed with Brussels lace matching her waist-length mantilla. Her only jewelry was a single strand of pearls that Mr. Darcy's mother had worn on her wedding day.

Standing near the altar was the bridegroom, whose impatience to be married was providing amusement for the guests, but even if he had made note of the whispers, he would have ignored them as his mind was fixed on one thing: his ardent desire to make Elizabeth Bennet his wife. He even ignored the tittering of Mrs. Gardiner and Aunt Susan, Mr. Bennet's sister, who were listening to Lord Fitzwilliam describe his own nuptials.

"I was in the vestry, but they found me," the earl explained, "and after being dragged from my hiding place, Eleanor and I were united in wedlock—the emphasis being on 'lock.' We promised to stay married for better or for worse, richer or poorer, in sickness and in health, until death do us part, and by God, we have lived up to those vows. She is richer; I am poorer. She is hale and hearty, while I am sick whenever I am in her company. It could be better, but it could not possibly be worse. And because we are both too stubborn to die, we remain married."

But Darcy heard none of this. He had just taken out his pocket watch when the church doors opened. As he caught sight of his bride, a sense of well-being surged through him. As Elizabeth drew closer, he knew that she was feeling exactly the same thing, and their hearts beat as one.

❦

Except for the absent militia, Netherfield was as crowded as it had been on the evening of the ball, and Elizabeth and Darcy had to squeeze through the throng to greet all of their well-wishers. While moving amongst their guests, Lizzy heard snatches of conversation, all complimentary, about how well the two eldest Bennet daughters had done in the business of getting husbands, but among those bits of overheard dialogue was her mother informing her friends that ten thousand pounds was not even close to the true amount of Mr. Darcy's yearly income. How did Mrs. Bennet know that? they asked. She replied, if his assets were not substantially larger than that sum, how could one account for the large estate, the house in town, the carriages, the clothes, etc., etc.?

The Fitzwilliam brothers were enormously popular and covered both ends of the spectrum. While Lord Fitzwilliam entertained the married women with his double entendres or stories about his unhappy marriage to Lady Macbeth, the colonel, handsomely accoutered in his regimentals, had all the local beauties surrounding him, much to the chagrin of the Lucas boys and the other youths of Meryton. But Georgiana put a smile on the lads' faces when she offered to play a jig on the pianoforte so that they might dance, and Kitty's response was immediate. She stood in front of the colonel so that he would have to ask her to dance first.

But before the day got away from him, Darcy was determined to have a conversation with Jane Bingley. He understood why she was unhappy with him. In addition to interfering in her relationship with Charles, he had insulted her sister with his ungracious proposal, and when he had returned to renew his efforts to win Lizzy, his behavior was so erratic that at a minimum it invited criticism, but more alarmingly, it had aroused her suspicions.

When Darcy approached, Jane, who was sitting in the parlor in order to avoid the press of people, was having a conversation with Mrs. Glenn, who had recently become a grandmother, but the older woman kindly left the two to have their talk.

"Mrs. Bingley, I know that you have reservations about your sister marrying me, but…"

Jane blushed at this revelation. "I am sorry Lizzy repeated what I said. I thought our conversation was confidential."

"Your sister did not betray your confidence. I am afraid on this subject your face is an open book, and I understand the cause for your concerns. I was not the best suitor, but I would ask that you put aside all prejudice and judge me from this day forward as I intend to be the best of husbands."

"Sir, please understand that I only want my sister's happiness, and since Lizzy has informed me that she cannot be happy without you, I wish you joy."

"Be assured, Mrs. Bingley, that you and Charles are always welcome at Pemberley, and I know that Elizabeth and I will be welcomed at Netherfield Park. I anticipate a lot of time being spent on the road between Hertfordshire and Derbyshire. We shall visit so often that our carriages will leave ruts in the road."

By the time Mr. Darcy returned to his wife, Jane was reassured. The dour gentleman from Derbyshire really could be quite charming, and she had absolutely no doubt that he loved Elizabeth. But she would hold her brother-in-law to his promise to allow Lizzy to visit frequently because if Lizzy did not come to her, she would go to Lizzy.

❧

By evening, when the last of the guests had departed, not so much as a cake crumb was left, only a few scraps of meat remained on the platter, and the punch bowl had been emptied and replenished several times. Lizzy was glad she had instructed Mr. Jackson to make sure that enough food was set aside for the servants so that they might join in the celebration.

"I really should go downstairs and compliment Mrs. Bradshaw for the wonderful job she did today," Lizzy said as she collapsed into a chair, "but I am too tired."

"No need," Darcy answered. "She already knows it as there is nothing modest about Mrs. Bradshaw, but we shall thank everyone when we get to Pemberley."

The mention of Pemberley was Jane's cue to suggest that the newlyweds remain at Netherfield until the day after Christmas. "It will be so much fun. We shall all sing Christmas carols and have punch and light the Yule log. Besides, after all of the busyness of today, you will be so very tired," Jane said, addressing her sister, and Charles nodded in agreement.

Darcy said nothing. Instead, he looked to Elizabeth.

"Jane, thank you for your offer, but we must adhere to our original plan."

When Jane started to protest, Georgiana interrupted. "Mrs. Bingley, I am the reason we must depart tomorrow morning. At my request, there is a certain person who has been invited to Ashton Hall by my aunt Marguerite, and he will be there on the day after Christmas." She looked at William in such a way that it gave the impression that Georgiana had tried to put something over on her brother. Jane, not wishing to cause trouble between the siblings, said no more, and an uncomfortable silence followed until Jane said that she wished to retire.

Lizzy walked with her sister to the staircase and kissed her on the cheek. "Jane, do not be upset with me, please. I promise I shall be here for the baby, if not sooner."

"I am not upset with you, Lizzy. It is just that you have not even left, and I am already missing you. But you are as tired as I am. Would you like for me to help you take your hair down?"

"Thank you, but that will not be necessary."

"Is Mrs. Brotherton to help you undress?"

"No, I can manage."

"Lizzy, don't be silly. You cannot unbutton your own dress. I shall send Mrs. Grover to you."

"No, thank you, Jane. I really can manage."

"Oh, I see," Jane said, blushing, now realizing that Mr. Darcy was to provide that service. "Well, you always were braver than I, so I shall say good night."

It was not a matter of her being brave. It was a matter of trust, and Lizzy trusted Fitzwilliam Darcy.

❧

While Darcy brushed her hair, Lizzy told her husband of the embarrassing conversation she had had with Jane.

"I am sure I shocked her by not having a lady's maid help me to undress."

"But why should you be some quaking creature hiding under the covers? It is so different in the wild. When I was in North America, I lived very close to a pack of wolves, and the mating pairs would have a splendid courtship of nuzzling and nibbling and sleeping side by side, and before they performed the act, they whipped their tails at each other and jumped all about. It was a joyous experience, not something to be got through."

"Are you going to whip your tail at me?" Lizzy asked. Darcy immediately put down the brush. After helping Lizzy out of her dress, he tried to untie her stays, but they were knotted.

"Who tied your stays?" Darcy asked.

"My mother laced me up."

"Oh, I see. Your mother hopes to delay the inevitable."

"Don't be silly. I am sure it was unconsciously done."

"Hmmm." Darcy tried to unknot the laces, but the stays stayed on. "I am going to have to cut the ties."

"Oh no, you are not. These are the only stays I have with me."

"Then borrow another from Jane tomorrow."

"How am I supposed to explain that? My husband could not wait and cut right through my ties?" Lizzy started to laugh, which only made the chore more difficult.

Finally, he walked with her to the bed and told her to bend over.

"Sir?"

"By bending over, you will round your back, and it will be easier that way." Finally the knot came undone, and Lizzy was left standing in her chemise.

"I have a very pretty nightgown," she said, looking down at her plain cotton gown.

"You are going to get out of this nightgown to put another one on?" Darcy asked confused.

"Well, it is silk and very pretty. I bought it in London."

"Do what you want, but it seems redundant to me."

"Will, you are not being romantic at all. This is not how I pictured my wedding night."

"So you have been thinking about our wedding night?" he asked, slipping his hands around her waist. "So have I."

"I am sure my thoughts were quite different from yours."

"Really?" Darcy asked as he ran his hand along her neck, exposing her shoulder.

"Yes, really."

"Lizzy, be honest." But his wife said nothing, refusing to confirm the obvious. "After you remove your stockings, why don't we get in bed?"

"Can I not leave them on? My feet are cold." Her feet were the only part of her body that was.

"I shall warm them up for you." He reached up under her nightgown and rolled down the first stocking and then the second. After doing so, Darcy quickly shed his boots, breeches, and blouse before climbing into bed with his wife. When they were both under the covers, Darcy ran his hand down her body before reaching under her nightgown.

"You said you were going to warm my feet first," she said, whispering in his ear.

"They will be warm in a minute. I promise," and he pulled the covers over their heads.

CHAPTER 33

DARCY TRACED THE OUTLINE of Lizzy's face with the back of his hand. He hated to disturb her at such an early hour, especially since they had so little sleep. He would have preferred to wake her up by making love to her again, but they had to get started on the first leg of their journey. It had been a mistake to agree to the December 24th date for their wedding. It would have been better if he had insisted that they wait until after his transformation, and he should have allowed more time to get to Pemberley. He had wanted their first nightfall together as husband and wife to go smoothly, without any hiccups, but here he was trying to rouse his wife from her sleep when they should have been lying in each other's arms.

Lizzy placed her hand on her husband's and kissed it and waited for him to return her kiss, but when she opened her eyes, she saw that he was dressed and ready to leave. She quickly sat up and looked up into his beautiful green eyes.

"I shall get ready quickly, Will." After hugging her, he said that he would be back in fifteen minutes to take her overnight bag downstairs. Lizzy went to the mirror and grimaced at what she saw. Because her hair was so curly, she braided it every night except, of course, last night. As a result, she looked as if she had been struck by a bolt of lightning. "He must really love me or he would have run away," Lizzy said, smiling.

A very sleepy Jane and Charles were waiting for them in the breakfast room. As requested, only tea, coffee, and porridge had been prepared for the travelers, and Georgiana, who was known to sleep half the morning away, looked as if she might fall face first into her bowl.

Despite it being Christmas morning, Jane had a long face on her, and because his wife was sad, Charles looked equally forlorn. In order to avoid tearful good-byes, Lizzy made quick work of breakfast, and after kissing Jane and hugging Charles, she walked straight out the door and into the carriage. Darcy lingered a little longer, but if they were to arrive at Mr. Gowland's house before dark, they needed to leave now.

Mrs. Brotherton and Georgiana barely managed to remain awake for the twelve miles to the inn where they changed carriages. There was nothing pretty or comfortable about their new conveyance, but it would get them where they needed to go and quickly. As expected, Mercer had everything ready, and after a brief respite, the four travelers got into their coach with Mercer driving and Metcalf remaining behind with the Darcy carriage and horses.

The motion of the carriage soon rocked Georgiana and her lady's maid to sleep, and with no one to see them, Lizzy slid over so that she might cuddle with Darcy. After she had unbuttoned one of his buttons, she slipped her hand inside her husband's coat. Yes, after last night he was definitely her husband, and the memory of their wedding night brought a smile to her face.

As soon as they had gotten into bed, they had immediately begun to make love. Not wishing to cause his wife any pain, Darcy had entered her slowly, but that was the only slow thing they did. Not having anything to compare it to, he was afraid things were going too fast. But when Lizzy wrapped her legs around his and pulled him deeper inside her, he realized that she needed this as much as he did, and he surrendered.

Lizzy had rested her head on his chest, and in the silence, she could hear his heartbeat. She could also hear the change in his breathing, letting her know that he had fallen asleep, and she had dozed off as well. But neither had slept for long, and she soon felt his weight upon her once again.

As the night wore on, with the fire nothing more than glowing embers, the room had grown cold, and Lizzy moved next to her husband for warmth; he pulled her closely to him so that their bodies took the same shape. That was all it took, and since they were only half awake, their lovemaking had a dreamlike quality to it, and it was slower and sweeter, and he was beginning to know how best to please her. Everything she did pleased him.

As the carriage continued to rumble toward the Gowlands' residence, Darcy and Elizabeth spoke of their wedding day. He told her how beautiful she had looked, and she returned the compliment. They spoke of the children they would have, but not before their first anniversary. Lizzy was in agreement with her husband on this because she had seen the effect Jane's pregnancy had on her marriage. Now, all talk was about their little bundle, and as she had grown bigger, Jane tired easily. Lizzy did not want that—not yet.

When Darcy shared with Elizabeth that Antony had known of his other incarnation for eight years, she wasn't all that surprised. "When he visited Aunt Gardiner, I had the impression that he was not there just because he was being nosy, which he most definitely is, but because he wanted to take my measure. Now I know why. He was trying to protect you."

"Not just me. He wanted to be sure that you knew I was a werewolf, and he came away believing that you did because you were so protective of me."

"Yes, I was," she said and kissed him. "Did you see him flirting with Lady Lucas? He had bitten into an apple, and he said as delicious as it was, his preference was for fully ripened fruit. She was so shocked that she dribbled punch down her dress, and then she started to laugh. After providing amusement for Lady Lucas, he took up with my aunt Gardiner exactly where he had left off in town, and he had her giggling once again."

"Yes, he certainly can be charming."

"And my goodness, Colonel Fitzwilliam could barely move for all the young ladies clustered about him."

"To which he made no objection, I might add. He is as big a flirt as his brother, but when it comes time to marry, he will marry money as he has expensive tastes. Because of that, I feel sorry for him; his chances are slim that he will love his wife." He kissed the top of Lizzy's head.

By the time the coach pulled into the Gowlands' yard, the sun had already set, and darkness was upon them. It had taken them longer than expected because, unlike the light dusting of snow at Longbourn, a few inches had fallen farther north.

The coach was met by Mr. Gowland, who immediately pulled Mr. Darcy aside, and from his expression, it was obvious that he was being told something he did not like. Instead of helping the ladies out of the carriage, he climbed back in.

"There is a stranger inside who sought refuge because of the weather, and it would have been wrong for Mr. Gowland to turn him away. I do not think there is anything to be alarmed about, but I would ask that you not speak, or if you must, please do so in French. Just as a precaution, I shall ask that our meals be served in our rooms."

Lizzy entered a large room with a long table that served as kitchen and dining area, and at the end of a bench sat the unexpected visitor. He immediately jumped up, bowed to the visitors, and introduced himself as Jacob Linley, who had been recently appointed to serve as curate in a parish near Watford. Upon hearing this, Lizzy relaxed, as he definitely had the look of a clergyman about him. When he spoke to her, she pretended not to understand him, and to discourage any further attempts at conversation, Mrs. Gowland quickly led the ladies upstairs.

The bedroom was simply furnished with a bed, wash-basin, and small table with two chairs. Because the wood had been dampened by the snow, the fire was producing little heat. Georgiana and Mrs. Brotherton's room was a little better, and so they decided to have their meal in there. The three ladies were seated in front of the fire when Lizzy heard Mr. Darcy's heavy footfall on the stairs, and he came in the room and closed the door behind him.

"I am going to join Mr. Linley for supper to make sure he is who he says he is, but your meals will be sent up short-ly. Even though I find nothing alarming about the gentle-man, I do not like the idea of someone who is not in the community staying in a Council house. Because of that, we shall leave earlier in the morning than expected," he said and went downstairs.

"Do not worry, Elizabeth. My brother is a very cautious man," Georgiana explained as soon as her brother had de-parted. "I can assure you that if he thought anything was amiss, we would not stay here tonight."

Lizzy agreed, but it was a rapid initiation into a world where anyone who did not belong to the "community" was considered suspect until proved otherwise.

After their meal, and with her coat still on, Lizzy went back to her room to see if she could do something to get the fire to give off more heat. She was making some progress when Darcy came into the room carrying some sticks and twigs, and he immediately took the poker from her. After deftly moving the logs about, he threw some of the kindling on the fire and flames shot up.

"I learned how to make a good fire when I was in Hudson Bay because you did not dare let it die out or *you would die.*" He brought one of the chairs close to the hearth. After his wife sat down and after tucking her coat between her legs and away from the fire, he apologized for the poor accommodations. "The only other time that I have been here, I was alone. It was fine for me, but I must admit it is quite primitive for a lady. With our early departure, I forgot to wish you a happy Christmas." After looking around the room, he added, "Not the cheeriest of places to spend our first Christmas."

"It is fine, and since this will be the first full day of my being Mrs. Fitzwilliam Darcy, I am having the happiest Christmas of my life. Besides, it is only for the one night."

"Not even that. I want to leave before Mr. Linley gets up. Metcalf has arrived, and he will remain behind until the curate leaves to make sure that he heads south toward Watford. Both Mercer and Metcalf are sleeping downstairs, so Mr. Linley cannot go anywhere without one or the other knowing of it."

"For someone who isn't concerned about the curate, you are certainly taking a lot of precautions."

"I am always on the lookout for someone who is not where he belongs. It is instinctive; I cannot act in any other way."

The thought of a life lived looking over one's shoulder sent a shiver down her spine, but she, too, would have to learn to recognize when someone did not belong.

"You are shivering. I am sorry it is not warmer in here."

Lizzy stood up and put her arms around her husband's neck and pulled his face to hers. "Why don't you warm me up the same way you did last night?"

CHAPTER 34

THE TRIP FROM THE Gowland house to Aunt Marguerite's was uneventful, and with Mercer perched outside on the driver's seat, no one complained about the chilly interior. As soon as the house came into view, Lizzy looked out the window to the top of the turret, and once she saw the pale orange flag flying, she felt a sense of relief. Even if something unexpected happened and Mr. Darcy had to transform here, he would be safe.

Darcy's aunt was waiting for them at the door and ushered all of them into the library, where a blazing fire awaited them, and after making arrangements for Mercer to be served a hot meal, Marguerite followed her guests inside.

"Make yourself at home. We are all alone here, Jeanne and her… Jeanne and her… I never can get it out," she said, shaking her head. "The pair of them is in town. I have ordered some hot soup to be served right away, and then we shall have a nice supper. But first, tell me all about the wedding."

After getting the nod from her sister-in-law, Georgiana described everything the bride had worn, right down to the tiny pearls on her satin slippers, and then provided descriptions for Jane's dress as well as her own and spared no details for her brother's attire, even noting his expertly tied neck-cloth, which caused Darcy to chuckle. He would have to tell Charles that if he ever found himself in financial difficulties, he could hire himself out as a manservant. While his sister recreated the wedding breakfast for her aunt, Darcy smiled at his wife, thinking how gracious she was to allow Georgiana to provide the details of the most important day of her own life.

After supper, they all returned to the library, the warmest room in the house, but shortly thereafter, Darcy asked that the entire party be excused as they had had very little sleep since the wedding. Aunt Marguerite indicated that was fine for her niece and nephew but gestured for Elizabeth to sit beside her on the sofa because there were a few things she wished to discuss with the new Mrs. Darcy. When Darcy tried to protest, his aunt cut him off.

"Did you and Elizabeth share the same room last night?" she asked.

Darcy looked confused. They had only been married two days; of course they had shared a room. "Yes, we stayed at a Council house."

"All right then. That should hold you for a while. Off you go. I want to talk to your bride."

Knowing his aunt to be a mule and that he would not win any argument with her, Darcy departed, but he was not happy about it. What could she possibly have to say to Elizabeth that he could not hear?

Once Marguerite was sure her nephew was gone, she asked Lizzy how everything went on their wedding night.

"Fine," Lizzy answered and said no more, but Marguerite continued to look at her as if waiting for some horrific confession. "Truly, everything was fine."

"I am glad to hear it," she said, putting her hands over Lizzy's, "because my husband nearly put me through the headboard, but we worked it out. When we first got married, he was actually very considerate, and I have often wondered what would have happened in our marriage if I had been a little kinder. Maybe he would have held off sleeping with other women longer than he did. But I wasn't, and he didn't, and he's dead.

"Now, you don't have to worry that I am going to keep you away from William. After we finish our talk, I shall go to Jeanne's room, where I shall stay until after you leave tomorrow morning. Hopefully, in the spring, you will come back for a visit, but there are a few things I want you to know about William as a man and as a wolf." She plunged right in.

"First, it is important that you differentiate between the two natures. If it is the middle of the lunar month and William is in a bad mood, it has nothing to do with his being a wolf, so don't start making excuses for him. You should treat him no differently than any other annoying man.

"The other thing I want you to think about is William's ability to know what everyone is feeling. It tends to make him overprotective, especially where Georgiana is concerned, and you can help her by not letting him hover constantly, especially since she will soon be coming out. For yourself, this ability to know everything about you might prove to be disconcerting. Women are not used to men being attentive to our needs, but there is a way to get around it."

"Really?" Now Lizzy was very interested. Most of the time, she did not mind Mr. Darcy knowing what she was thinking or feeling, but every minute of every day was a bit much.

"The strongest sense for a wolf is his smell, so you have to introduce other scents to confuse him. If you use lavender water everywhere you sweat, it makes it a lot harder for him to figure out what you are thinking or feeling from your own scent.

"Second, wolves have superior vision, which is important

in hunting, and you also need to keep in mind that he can see in the dark. So if you are thinking about getting out of bed during the night to hide his birthday gift, he will see where you put it.

"Now, this is the important part, so pay attention. It is the combination of smell and sight that allows him to know what you are feeling, so if you do not want him to know something, use the lavender water and do not look at him. I would suggest you keep your needlepoint basket handy. In that way, you will be looking at your hands, and he will not get suspicious. Putting a sachet of potpourri in the basket would not hurt either."

"How do you know all this?" Lizzy asked. Yes, it was true that Aunt Marguerite had known that her nephew was a werewolf from the beginning, but she doubted that they had spent enough time together for her to draw such detailed conclusions.

"Do you know about Wilkolak, the doctor who lives in Edinburgh?"

"I have heard his name mentioned. I believe he does research on the werewolf population."

"Yes, that is true, but he also meets with the Council to update them on his findings. About five years ago, Darcy asked if I would host a Council meeting here. The doctor is now in his fifties, and it would be helpful if he did not have to travel as far as London. After he had reported to the Council, we had a nice long talk while the others turned their attention to business matters."

"Business matters?"

"Yes, it takes a lot of money to keep up these Council houses and to feed and house those werewolves fleeing the Continent. For those who cannot afford it, they also pay for passage to North America, and the three Council members have all their travel expenses paid because they are constantly on the go. William is a big contributor, and I give them two hundred pounds a year myself. But to get back to Dr. Wilkolak. Before he returned to Edinburgh, I told him that the next time he had to meet with the Council, he should bring his wife. She is a she wolf, and she was already one when he married her. In fact, she saved his life. Everything I know about werewolves, I learned from the Wilkolaks."

"Mrs. Wilkolak saved the doctor's life? How did she do that?"

"Thirty years ago, he was traveling the Great North Road on his way to Edinburgh when he was attacked by highway-men. They beat him up and left him for dead on the side of the road. It was a full moon, and Jenny Giffords, who lived on a nearby farm, found him and lay down beside him to keep him warm. At daybreak, she went back to the farm and returned with her father and a wagon. While he was recover-ing, they fell in love. He went to Edinburgh and continued on with his medical studies, but then he turned his attention to finding a cure for his wife. In his search, he has studied hundreds of wolves, and he knows everything there is to know about them, including that one werewolf immediately recognizes another.

"One day, the Wilkolaks passed the Earl of Nordland, who was getting out of his carriage, and Jenny Wilkolak and His Lordship looked at each other, and that is all it took for them to recognize what the other one was. He arranged to meet with the pair of them, and Jenny said that once he ut-tered the words, 'I am a werewolf,' he began to cry. The poor man had been a wolf for five years and thought he was the only one in Scotland. After hearing what Dr. Wilkolak was doing, he agreed to fund all of his research, and it is on his estate where the wolves have their gathering in July. He is gone now, but his son continues to provide money for the program and to preserve the property for the wolves."

"And that is how the Council got started?" Lizzy asked.

"Yes and no. There was already a patchwork of smaller councils in place, but once they got Nordland's support, they were able to actually go out and find other werewolves and bring them into the community. But let us get back to your situation because I know William is pacing the floor waiting for you. Dr. Wilkolak said that as much as he loved his wife, he found it unsettling to have her know everything about him, so he started experimenting. For example, when he wants to concentrate on something that he does not want his wife to know about, he cooks the evening meal because it throws Jenny off the scent. He always wears scented powder to confuse her sense of smell, and when you meet him, you will see he still wears a powdered wig. He added that the way he gets around her visual acuity is to look out the window while they are talking, so that she cannot see his eyes, or to be writing something while she is talking to him.

"Getting all of this to work will take time and practice, but the longer William and you are together, the easier it will become because you will know him better. Now, I have a present for you." She went to a chest and took out a bottle. It was lavender water. "You will have to be clever about this because you do not want him to figure out what you are doing, but no man should know all there is to know about a woman."

"Yes, I agree. A woman's nature should be a mystery to a man." Lizzy pulled the top off the bottle and put some lavender water behind her ears, and with a smile on her face, she said, "We shall see if this works. I certainly hope so."

≈

"You smell pretty," Darcy said as Lizzy came into the room.

"Your aunt wanted to give me this." She held out the bottle of lavender water for him to see.

"That is all she wanted?" Darcy asked, doubting it very much. You do not chase a groom away from his bride of two days so that you can give her lavender water.

"No, she wanted to tell me that if you are a grouch, it has nothing to do with your being a wolf. It has everything to do with your being a grumpy Fitzwilliam Darcy."

"That's it?"

Lizzy went to the window and pulled back the curtain. "Will, come here. You can see the man in the moon."

"Yes, the two of us will soon be together," he answered while slipping his hands around her waist.

"It will be Nell, you, and the man in the moon," Lizzy said, correcting him. Oddly enough, Nell's presence was a comfort to her. She did not like to think of him as a lone wolf.

"Oh, yes, I forgot about Nell." The idea of being with Nell instead of his wife was a decidedly unattractive prospect, but he needed to talk to her about Monsieur Reynard.

Lizzy turned around and started to untie his neckcloth, and he responded by unbuttoning her dress. After slipping it off of her shoulders, he traced the outline of her neck with his tongue. She immediately responded to him, and he took her by the hands and walked backwards with her toward the bed.

After they had made love and Mr. Darcy had fallen asleep, Lizzy lay awake smiling. She was thinking how fortunate she was to have such a thoughtful and giving man as her husband, and his desire to please her was evident while they were making love. For her, the intimacies of the marriage bed had proved to be a pleasant surprise. All the old wives' tales she had heard, and even Jane's rendition of her wedding night, had proved to be untrue—at least for her. But there was a second reason she was smiling. Her very first effort at creating a distraction to overcome Mr. Darcy's superior senses had been successful. When she had walked to the window, he had been unable to look into her eyes, and so he had failed to notice that she had avoided answering his question about his aunt. So the werewolf in Fitzwilliam Darcy could be got 'round, and that was a good thing to know. On the other hand, when she did want him to know something, that was easily done as well. Lizzy was beginning to think that she might have the best of both worlds.

⤜∼⤛

When Lizzy awoke, she found her husband gone from their bed. This was becoming a habit, one she hoped to break once they got to Pemberley. Since Mr. Darcy said that he wanted to leave the first thing in the morning, she wondered why he had not awakened her, and when she looked at the mantel clock and saw that it was ten thirty, she nearly panicked. Because of the late hour, it was unlikely that they would be able to reach Pemberley by dark. But when she went to the window and opened the drapes, she understood why he had allowed her to sleep so late. Snow was falling, and no one was going anywhere. It looked as if Mr. Darcy would experience nightfall at Ashton Hall.

After performing her morning ablutions, Lizzy was about to ring for a maid when her husband walked in, and right behind him was a serving girl carrying a tray. After the girl left, he came to Lizzy and kissed her.

"I had hoped to serve you breakfast in bed," Darcy said to his bride. "I assume you have looked outside."

"Yes, I see that it is snowing."

"We will have to remain here until it stops, and then Mercer will decide if we may leave tomorrow, which depends on whether the temperatures remain above freezing."

Lizzy was unhappy with the idea of not getting to Pemberley in time for nightfall, but she did not want Mr. Darcy to know that. "Since we are delayed for at least one day, how shall we spend the day, dearest? A sleigh ride perhaps?"

"No, I do not think we should go outside at all. It is a soft slushy snow, and we will get soaked. Since Metcalf has not yet arrived with our luggage, we have nothing to change into."

"That is true. Well, let us see what is here in the room. There is a volume of Walter Scott's poems on the mantel. Would you like for me to read aloud to you?" Darcy shook his head. "Shall we invite your aunt, sister, and Mrs. Brotherton to play cards? All right, no cards. What if we go to the drawing room? Georgiana or I could play a tune on your aunt's spinet." Darcy continued to reject all her ideas.

"What about charades? Compose riddles? Sing carols?"

Darcy shook his head at every suggestion.

"If none of these appeal to you, what do you suggest we do?" Lizzy asked in an exasperated voice.

Darcy pointed to the bed.

"We cannot spend all day in bed!" Lizzy said, shocked. "What will your sister and aunt think if we remain closeted in our suite?"

Darcy picked his wife up, cradled her in his arms, and then carried her to the bed. After he lay down next to her, he whispered, "They will think we are newlyweds."

CHAPTER 35

WITH A NEARLY FULL moon to light his way, Mercer checked on the conditions of the road that ran outside the gates of Ashton Hall. Because the temperatures had remained above freezing, the snow had turned to slush. As a former coach driver, he determined that there was a good chance that they could reach Pemberley with a few hours to spare if they were on the road by four o'clock in the morning. So at three o'clock, he knocked on his master's door to let him know he thought that they should attempt it. Darcy agreed. If it was necessary for them to stop, there was a Council house between Ashton Hall and Pemberley where the others could spend the night, but it was Darcy's preference to be home in time for nightfall.

When Darcy went back inside their room, he found Lizzy was already getting dressed, and she told him that she would go wake Georgiana and Mrs. Brotherton. She, too, wanted to be at Pemberley in time for Mr. Darcy to prepare for nightfall. With everyone moving apace, an hour later, they climbed into the carriage.

Because of their hasty departure, Lizzy would be unable to say good-bye to Mr. Darcy's cantankerous aunt. In addition to being lively and unpredictable, it seemed as if Aunt Marguerite was the keeper of the family's secrets, and she looked forward to returning to Ashton Hall in the spring. As

Mercer drove down the tree-lined drive, Lizzy looked out the carriage window and saw a light in the turret window, and although she could not see Lady Ashton, she knew that she was wishing them Godspeed.

"How long do you think we will be on the road?" Lizzy asked her husband.

"The journey is usually between six and eight hours, but the conditions of the road will slow us down. There is also an incline that will require that we walk in order to lighten the load. So let us say ten hours and that will leave me plenty of time to prepare."

Lizzy was not reassured. Who knew what the conditions of the road were farther north, and Darcy seeing her anxiety sought to put her mind at rest.

"It is not necessary for me to be at the manor house in order to transform. The Granyard property runs to the south of my estate, and the Rutland property runs south of that. Because Lord Granyard keeps a pack of hounds and is a good friend of the Duke of Rutland, he has asked that Rutland not allow traps or spring guns on his property. So there are no worries there. Additionally, as lords of the manor, we three are responsible for a twenty-mile stretch of road from the manor houses, so I can assure you that once we reach the Rutland property, you will see that the roads are in excellent repair."

This information provided little comfort. Elizabeth had not given any thought to the awful devices that landowners and gamekeepers used to keep poachers and trespassers off their properties, and she said a silent prayer that they would reach Pemberley at Mr. Darcy's estimated time.

Once they reached the incline, the four passengers got out and were greeted by the songs of several chickadees in the branches above them, and this gift brightened the mood of the travelers.

"The incline marks the southernmost boundary of the Granyard property," Georgiana said, and she put her arm around Lizzy's shoulders. "So now we have no worries. We will arrive at Pemberley with time to spare. Let us walk quickly so that we might get there all the sooner."

After the passengers returned to the coach and as they made their way through the snow-covered Derbyshire countryside, Darcy said, "I hope you were not expecting a grand welcome. With Mr. Jackson and Mrs. Bradshaw still in Hertfordshire, Mrs. Reynolds is the only member of the senior house staff at Pemberley. I do not think I mentioned to you that it is a Darcy tradition to spend Yuletide in town, so most of the servants are put on half pay and they go home to their families. Even when we are in residence, we keep to the first floor, as the public rooms are very difficult to heat and are always cold."

Lizzy could testify to the chilly public rooms. During her November stay, she was rarely without her shawl and frequently found herself standing in front of the fireplace.

"Since we are so close to nightfall, I would like to keep our arrival as subdued as possible," Lizzy answered, and she squeezed Darcy's hand.

"But we shall have a grand welcome once the servants return," Georgiana piped in. "Everyone will want to meet the new mistress of Pemberley. Knowing how considerate you are, I am sure you will try to remember everyone's name, but it will take time as there are so many of them."

Since they were discussing the servants, Darcy decided it was a good time to tell Lizzy that Ellie could not serve as her lady's maid. "I know you are disappointed," he said, after seeing her expression, "but your attendant must be someone from the community."

"I am very fond of Ellie," Lizzy replied.

"It is important that you be able to speak openly when you are in your bedchamber. That would not be possible with Ellie. While I was in Herefordshire, I found two ladies, both in their late twenties, who I think would serve you well. They are French but speak passable English."

"But Ellie will think she did something to displease me."

"I know you like her very much, but Mrs. Reynolds made it clear to Ellie that her attendance on you was temporary and would last only as long as your visit. No promises of a permanent position were made, but knowing that you would be concerned on her behalf, I have asked Mrs. Bradshaw to begin training her as an undercook."

"Ellie is to work for Mrs. Bradshaw? But Mrs. Bradshaw is so…"

"Yes, she is. But if Ellie chooses not to marry and to move up in service, this will be her way of achieving that end because if she can work for Mrs. Bradshaw, she can work for anyone. However, until you choose a lady's maid, Mrs. Brotherton will assist you."

"But you employed Mrs. Younge for Georgiana," Lizzy said, continuing to press on Ellie's behalf.

For Darcy, there were so many things to think about. Discussing Mrs. Younge was a very low priority for him. But Elizabeth needed to understand that every decision he made factored in his unique situation.

Georgiana, who had openly discussed with Elizabeth Wickham's attempt to lure her into an elopement, chose to answer the question.

"Mrs. Younge served as my companion only when I was

in town. Before the fiasco in Ramsgate, Mrs. Younge had been an exemplary employee. I am sorry to say that her misjudgment of Wickham's character cost her her position. But please understand, Mrs. Younge was *never* at Pemberley."

"Does that answer your question, Elizabeth?" her husband asked her.

"I do understand the logic behind your decision, and my French is definitely in need of improvement." Darcy nodded his head up and down, lightening the mood considerably. "So the matter is settled, and I shall have a French maid."

The coach arrived at Pemberley at two o'clock, and Lizzy was never so glad to see any place in her life. With two hours until nightfall, the newlyweds would have some time together before he would have to leave her.

After receiving a warm welcome from Mrs. Reynolds, Darcy and Georgiana led Mrs. Fitzwilliam Darcy to her suite, and brother and sister looked at her to gauge her reaction to the room that had once served as Lady Anne's bedchamber. Looking about the room, Lizzy suspected that nothing had changed since their mother's death ten years earlier, and that fact was quickly confirmed by Georgiana.

"Before my parents married, my father hired Robert Adam to redecorate the public rooms and my mother's bedroom suite. It was Papa's wedding present to her, as she was a great admirer of his work."

"I, too, am an admirer of Mr. Adam's work. Jane and I toured Syon House and Kenwood House with my aunt and uncle Gardiner, where we saw other examples of his designs."

"Then you approve of your accommodations?" Georgiana asked eagerly.

"How could I not approve? It is the most beautiful room I have ever seen, and pale green is my favorite color." She turned and smiled at Mr. Darcy. "In fact, it comes very close to matching the color of a certain article of clothing I bought as part of my trousseau." When Darcy returned the smile, she knew that he understood that it was the color of the nightgown she had attempted to wear on their wedding night.

Mrs. Reynolds entered the room to ask Mr. Darcy if he wanted his dinner to be served in the mistress's sitting room. Like everyone who was privy to Mr. Darcy's secret, the housekeeper knew exactly what was required before each nightfall, and her master liked to eat a light meal before going out. But it also served as a reminder that he would shortly be leaving, and because of that, Georgiana excused herself so that her brother and sister-in-law could be alone.

"My wife and sister will eat in here, Mrs. Reynolds, but as for me, there is not enough time."

What does he mean there is not enough time? The sun will not set for another hour.

When they were alone, Darcy asked Elizabeth if she had any questions about the impending transformation.

"Only one. What time is daybreak?"

Darcy looked relieved that she wanted no specifics of the actual experience of changing from man to beast. "Daybreak is at 8:06. But there are things I must do before I enter the house and that usually takes about thirty minutes. Add to that the thirty to sixty minutes I remain in my study, I should be upstairs and ready for my bath between nine thirty and ten o'clock. As soon as I am dressed, I shall come to you. Is that agreeable?"

"Of course. I look forward to your return." She tried to hold steady because she feared that she would start crying at any moment.

"Lizzy, promise me that you will not leave the house while I am gone," Darcy asked. "I mean, at night, you should not leave the house at night. You will not be able to see me, as I will stay clear of the manor and the stables. It is risky to do otherwise." Lizzy agreed. His coming to see her on the terrace had been a dangerous thing to do. "Now I must go."

"But it is only three o'clock. The sun does not set until four," she said, and her face showed her confusion.

Darcy pulled her into his arms and whispered, "Please believe me when I say that I must leave." She nodded, but clung to him for another minute, and in that minute she knew that he *must go now* because she could feel a tightening in the muscles in his back that had not been there a moment earlier. "I love you," he whispered, and she detected a deepening of his voice as well.

Lizzy released her hold on him and stepped away to show him that she would not try to prevent him from leaving. If she had any doubts that the transformation had already begun, they were quickly put to rest. Instead of kissing her good-bye, he rubbed her nose with his, and then he turned away from her and left without saying another word.

After she heard the door close behind her husband, Lizzy stood still as if frozen to that very spot, and tears poured down her face. She made no attempt to stop crying or to be brave. Nature had imposed this forced separation upon them, and there was nothing she could do about it. And so she cried and cried, and because of her sobbing, she did not hear Georgiana come into the room, and seeing Elizabeth's distress, Georgie went to her and put her arms around her sister-in-law and held her until there were no tears left to cry.

❧

Embarrassed by her loss of control over her emotions, Lizzy excused herself and went to a sitting room adjacent to her bedchamber. As her nerves steadied, she decided that she would have to look at her husband's monthly departures in the same way as that of a woman who was married to a man in the military. When Mr. Darcy needed to leave, she must be strong or she would fail him as a wife.

When Lizzy returned to her room, she found Georgiana pouring out two cups of tea. She had obviously anticipated her sister-in-law's distress, and Lizzy was glad she had.

"Elizabeth, I know how difficult this is for you, but I can assure you that it will become second nature to you. It might even have its advantages. My brother can be very intense at times, and you may welcome a respite now and then."

"Yes, I am sure you are right," Lizzy said, trying to smile, "and it *is* only two days."

"Did you know that it has started snowing again? Which is a good thing?" Georgiana quickly added. "Whether man or wolf, Will loves the snow. I am sure that as soon as he returns, he will have you out for a sleigh ride or to go sledding, so I shall warn you that he goes up to the very top of the hill near the gazebo, and swoosh, down he comes at a frightening speed."

Lizzy also loved the snow as well as sleigh riding and ice skating. Like her husband, she needed to move about, and if they could go sledding shortly after his return that would be a perfect way to lift their spirits and help them to forget all about nightfall.

"By the way, I owe you my thanks for telling Jane that you were the reason we had to leave for Pemberley on Christmas day," Lizzy said. "That was very quick thinking on your part."

"Not really. You see I heard your sister telling Mr. Bingley that it was her intention to try to persuade you to remain at Netherfield, and so I had time to think of a story in case one was needed. I think of it as telling a white lie, which I will do without hesitation in order to protect Will."

"Georgiana, when did you realize your brother was a wolf?"

"I feel as if I have known about his other nature my whole life. My parents were very clever in the way they went about it. Mama would tell me stories about wolves who became men, not the other way around, and that it was better to be a wolf than a human. I loved those stories, and so one day she asked if I would like to meet such a creature. Well, you can imagine how excited I was to actually get to meet a wolf-man, which is the term that was used in the stories. One day, Mama, Papa, and I went into the woods, and this beautiful black animal came bounding up to me and nudged me with his nose."

Ah, so he has had that habit for a while, Lizzy thought.

"Of course, I started to giggle, and seeing that I was amused, he started to run around in circles and to jump over logs or in the air. This doglike creature was putting on a performance just for me, and when he stopped playing, I looked into his eyes, and I knew the animal was my brother. Obviously, there is a dramatic physical change during trans-formation, but the one thing that does not alter is the wolf's eyes. You would never mistake Will for any other male wolf because of his beautiful gray-green eyes. But once I was let in on the family secret, Mama and Papa impressed upon me the importance of never telling anyone, explaining that not everyone liked wolf-men and some bad people might want to harm Will."

"That *was* very clever. Your parents went about it in ex-actly the right way," Lizzy said, impressed by their handling of so difficult a subject.

For another hour or so, Georgiana amused Lizzy with

stories of staying with her aunts Catherine and Marguerite while her brother was in North America.

"It was a matter of choosing your poison," Georgie said, laughing. "Except for being deprived of Anne's company, I was actually glad when I had to go back to seminary."

After assuring Georgiana that she had completely recovered following her tearful exhibition, Elizabeth insisted that her sister-in-law retire.

"I know you are exhausted because I am, so if you will undo the buttons on my dress, I can see to the rest." She kissed Georgiana on the cheek. "Thank you for all you have done in making me a part of your family and in helping me to better understand your brother."

"It will get easier. I promise," Georgiana said, taking hold of Lizzy's hands.

"Please stop worrying. Go to bed and forget all about my emotional display. You will not see another." And Lizzy meant it.

❧

There was nothing Lizzy wanted more than to fall into a deep sleep so that the hours would pass quickly, but after tossing and turning and turning and tossing, she left her bed, put on her robe, and after lighting another candle, she stepped into the hallway to have a closer look at her new home and the portrait gallery. Unfortunately, her little candle failed to cast enough light so that she could actually view the portraits, but there were niches containing *objets d'art* all along the gallery as well as on both sides of the double wrought iron staircase that were visible by candlelight.

In one niche, there was a reproduction of *Laocoön and His Sons*, trying to break free of sea serpents, and in another, the lovely *Aphrodite of Knidos*. She imagined that the elder Mr. Darcy had bought *Aphrodite* for his wife, and Lady Anne had purchased *Laocoön* for her husband, which would account for the dramatic differences in their subjects.

She was studying two glazed Chinese vases when she heard someone approaching, and she turned to find Mercer walking toward her.

"Mrs. Darcy, is there anything wrong?" he asked anxiously.

"No, not at all, Mr. Mercer. It was just that I could not sleep, and so I was admiring some of the pieces in the Darcy collection. I did not mean to wake you."

"I'm a light sleeper, ma'am. Mr. Darcy accuses me of having a 'mother's hearing' and says I worry too much. But if you are having difficulty sleeping, may I suggest a glass of sherry?"

"Yes, thank you, I would like a glass."

"Shall we go into the study?"

After lighting some candles, Mercer immediately went to the fire, and in the ashes he found some glowing embers, and soon there was a small but sufficient blaze going.

"If you would like a drink, Mr. Mercer, please help yourself, and do sit down."

"If you don't mind, I'll have something less sweet, ma'am." He poured himself a glass of port and sat on the edge of his chair, as if being comfortable in the presence of his mistress might be viewed as being disrespectful. She hoped to put him at his ease by asking about his service to Mr. Darcy.

"Excuse me, ma'am, but you don't have to make small talk with me. I can see that you are troubled, and all I can say is that it will get easier with each nightfall."

"That is what Miss Darcy says as well," she answered, her voice trailing off.

"Meaning no disrespect, ma'am, but Miss Darcy's situation

is a little different from ours. She grew up knowing what her brother was, but it wasn't that way with me and you. First, we come to know him and then to like him and then to love him before learning of his burden, and it hurts us to see Mr. Darcy having to carry this weight on his shoulders, especially since he don't complain about it or ask why this had to happen to him. He just goes out there once a month and does whatever is necessary to protect Lady Helen and any other wolves who might be on the property."

"Mr. Darcy made me promise not to go out of the house at night," Lizzy said, "but would there be any harm in going up to the glade tomorrow?"

Mercer shook his head no. "Right now, with you being newly married, he probably wants you to see him only in his human form, not as some creature of the night."

"Yes," Lizzy said, nodding in agreement. "I see the wisdom in your advice." She went quiet for a moment, and another idea came to mind. "When I was last here, Mr. Darcy asked that I put a candle in the window if I was willing to accept him as he was, and I am ashamed to say that I did not do it. But I could do it tonight. I am not sure he will see it, but I would like to do it nonetheless."

Mercer's response was immediate. "I'll get a candle." After doing so, he led her to a sitting room in the front of the house which was directly over the portico. After pulling away the drapes, he said, "If you set the candle on that table, he'll see it right away, that is, if he's about."

"Thank you, Mr. Mercer. You may go back to sleep. I wish to stay here for a few minutes longer."

Lizzy went to the window carrying the candle and looked at the falling snowflakes. If the snow continued to fall at this rate, there would be several inches by morning, and she would have something to look forward to because she loved snow-covered landscapes. When the coach had turned into the Pemberley property, she had seen a great white expanse broken by denuded oaks and pine trees groaning under the weight of the newly fallen snow. She wondered if, in her role as the mistress of Pemberley and Mrs. Fitzwilliam Darcy, she would be permitted to throw snowballs and to make snow angels as she did with her sisters. She certainly hoped so.

After one last look at the moonlit scene, she left the candle on the table and stepped away from the window, but before she reached the door, she heard a howl pierce the night. Quickly returning to the window, she waved the candle back and forth. A second howl followed, and there was nothing mournful about it.

CHAPTER 36

CLEAR SKIES AND MILDER temperatures followed in the wake of the storm, and it was a perfect day to make a snowman. Elizabeth and Georgiana enlisted Mercer's help, and the result was a fine-looking snowman with a button nose, two eyes made out of coal, and crowned with one of Mr. Darcy's old top hats.

"It is one of William's *old* hats, isn't it?" Lizzy asked Georgiana.

"Well, it is now." The two ladies dissolved into laughter.

The snow had proved to be the perfect antidote for Lizzy's emotional exhaustion, and because somewhere in the woods behind her Mr. Darcy and Nell were also enjoying the snow, she was happy as well.

While building the snowman, Lizzy asked Mercer how he occupied his time when Mr. Darcy was away "doing other things."

"Even with the master gone, there is still a lot to do, but I do have the evenings to myself. So I decided to tackle something I didn't know anything about, and I learned how to make fishing flies. I'm proud to say that when Mr. Darcy steps into the streams hereabouts, he's using one of my flies."

"What a marvelous idea, Mr. Mercer. I could view Mr. Darcy's absences as an opportunity to make improvements in those areas where I am lacking, such as riding a horse. I could also work on my French. Since I am to have a French maid who speaks passable English, it would be nice if she had a mistress who spoke passable French."

After decorating the front lawn with numerous snow angels, the ladies, soaked through to the skin, were walking back to the house when two rabbits dashed out in front of them.

"For their sake, let us hope Nell does not see them," Lizzy said, and the giggles began anew.

While Georgiana played a beautiful piece on the pianoforte, Lizzy was looking out the front window and noticed a carriage coming down the drive. Instead of following the U to the front entrance, the carriage continued on to that part of the drive that led to a courtyard and the servants' entrance.

"It must be Mr. Jackson and Mrs. Bradshaw," Lizzy announced, which caused her to bite her lower lip. She was now the mistress of Pemberley, and when Mr. Darcy was away, she was supposedly in charge of the house, or so he had told her.

Seeing the anxious look on Lizzy's face, Georgiana joined her at the window. "I know you are thinking about Mrs. Bradshaw, but you should not worry. When she brings you the menus, agree to everything she says. That is what I did. And why should you not? She knows more than anyone else, and she will tell you so. Aunt Marguerite, Aunt Catherine, and Mrs. Bradshaw were all cut from the same cloth, and there is no changing them."

Within the hour, Mr. Jackson sought out his mistress, first, to present her with letters from her mother and sister and, second, to tell her that because of the poor roads, Mrs. Bradshaw had insisted that the silver, china, and crystal be left behind. "Abel Metcalf remains at Netherfield Park for the purpose of..."

"Guarding the plate?" Lizzy asked.

"Of course not, ma'am," Jackson quickly answered. "Please understand that it is our responsibility to ensure that everything is returned to its proper place here at Pemberley."

"I am teasing you, Mr. Jackson. I know how diligent you are in making sure that everything is exactly as it should be, but if Abel is at Netherfield Park, who was driving the carriage?"

"I was, ma'am. It has been a while, but I don't mind saying that I can still drive a carriage. It is said belowstairs, and behind my back, that I am the Jackson of all trades." Mr. Jackson smiled, and Lizzy wished that Mr. Darcy had been there to witness it.

"Ma'am, on behalf of the staff," Jackson continued, "may I say that it is an honor to serve you, and once everyone has returned after Twelfth Night, it will be my privilege to formally introduce you to those who are in your service. Of course, I should point out that David and Goliath do not consider themselves to be a part of the staff, and you will need to deal with them directly."

"Mr. Jackson, you are quite a wit," Lizzy said, chuckling.

"Yes, ma'am. If you say so."

⁂

Georgiana and Lizzy spent a pleasant evening playing cards, but immediately upon saying good night, Lizzy returned to the front sitting room as she had done the previous night. After lighting a candle, she waved it in front of the window for several minutes and looked for any hint of movement, but after seeing none and hearing no howl, she returned to her room. It was her intention to sleep for a few hours before going to the study to wait for Mr. Darcy's return. She was not sure if he would approve, especially since he had told her that he would come to her as soon as he had bathed, but he had not specifically told her *not* to go to the study. Either way, it did not matter. She was determined to be there when he came home.

When she awoke during the night, she jumped out of bed and crossed the room to view the mantel clock. It was only six o'clock, two hours to daybreak. Because she did not want to risk missing him, she decided to spend the rest of the night in the study.

After sliding out of her chemise and slipping on her green silk nightgown with its matching robe, she went to her dressing table, brushed her hair, and pulled her tresses back with the pearl combs Georgiana had given to her as a wedding gift. As she ventured down the hallway, she avoided those areas of the floor that squeaked, and although she was able to walk past Mercer's room without alerting him, she suspected that he knew of her plan. Her hunch was confirmed when she went into the study and found a fire burning and a blanket folded neatly on the sofa. After draping herself in the blanket, she put her head on the arm of the sofa and was soon asleep.

❧

As Darcy waited with Nell at the rendezvous point, he was trying to hide his annoyance. By her excessive whimpering, she let him know that she was not happy with his taking them so close to Pemberley or with his howling twice on the first day of nightfall. Obviously, she did not realize how important that candle in the window was to him. Or maybe she did, which would explain why she had chosen to hunt on the far side of the Darcy property. No matter. He did not have to see the candle to know that Elizabeth had lit another one for him.

Darcy signaled his displeasure with her sulking by leaving as soon as Lady Helen's maid stepped out of the Granyard carriage. Usually, he would brush against her side or lick her muzzle before leaving, but she would receive no such attention from him this daybreak.

Despite the snow, Darcy made excellent time in reaching the cave where he would begin his transformation from lupine to human form. Because so much of the geology of the Peak District was porous limestone, the whole area was pockmarked with caves and caverns, and it was because of these natural shelters that there were still Darcys on the property.

During the Civil War, the Darcys, who had remained loyal to Charles I, had fled the manor house when Cromwell's men descended upon the estate looking for royalists. After the Restoration of the monarchy, the family returned to Derbyshire to find the house a ruin, and a new Pemberley, built in the Palladian style, rose from the ashes. But with the war and their narrow escape a recent memory, a tunnel was dug leading to this cave, and after further alteration, it was connected to a stairway and a room accessible only from the study. Once Darcy reached the cave, he knew he was safe.

As he waited for his transformation to be completed, all thoughts were of Elizabeth. He pictured her in her bedchamber sleeping on his side of the bed while hugging a pillow and dreaming of those moments when they lay in each other's arms. When they were finally reunited, perhaps he could convince her to keep to their room for the remainder of the day.

As he lay on a sheepskin cloth, he could feel the start of the last and most uncomfortable part of his return to human form. It was where his buttocks flattened so that his legs could lengthen. Once he was bipedal, he would have to spend several minutes stretching the muscles in his legs and lower back as daybreak was much harder on the body than nightfall was. But the greater challenge was to readjust his mind so that he was thinking like a human and not a predator.

After putting on his shirt and breeches and running a comb through his hair, he ate mint and rinsed his mouth, and then made his way to the study. As he looked at his pocket watch, he thought, just one more hour, a mere sixty minutes, and he would be with his bride.

❧

As soon as Darcy slid open the panel, he knew Elizabeth was in the room. As eager as he was to see her, he did not want this. Because his mind was still in a state of transition, he would remain in the secret room until the mental phase of the transformation had been completed. But he made the mistake of stepping into the room to look at his wife, and in doing so, awakened her. She immediately stood up and started to come to him, but he held out his hand to keep her from getting any closer.

"Elizabeth, I want you to go back to your room and wait for me there." He could hear the gruffness in his voice, but there was nothing he could do about that; the vocal chords were one of the last things to change. But his statement only caused her to step closer to him.

"I must insist that you leave. I am not yet fit company." But her scent reached him and he could make out her form beneath her nightgown, and he felt his manhood growing. "Go now. Quickly. I could hurt you," he warned. But she stood rooted to the spot, and so he stepped forward and grabbed her by the arm. "You do not want this." With his member throbbing, he was now in agony, and he knelt down on the floor, pulling her with him. After shoving her on her back, he pushed her nightgown over her hips and knelt over her while he opened his breeches and then entered her immediately, and he had never felt more like a beast than he did at that moment.

Darcy was sure he was hurting his wife, but instead of whimpers, he heard soft moans and felt her pelvis thrust against his. Her movements sent a charge through his body, and he went from agony to ecstasy in a moment, and as he lifted his chest off of hers, he felt the full force of his release. Now, completely spent, he collapsed on top of her. Ashamed at his performance, he tried to withdraw, but he felt her tightening around his member, holding him inside her. "Please, don't go yet," she whispered and ran her hands up and down his back, and only when she felt his muscles completely relax did she unwrap her legs and free him.

Darcy rolled off of her and stared at the ceiling, refusing to look at her, and after seeing the tears in his eyes, she kissed him and told him how much she loved him.

"But I hurt you," he said, the tears spilling over onto his cheeks.

"No, you did not hurt me. I swear to you that you did not."

"You should not have come, Elizabeth," he said, choking on his words. "I understand why you did, but you should have waited for me in your room as I asked you to do."

"But I wanted to see your scar."

Darcy rolled on his side and looked at her. "What?"

"Your scar. From when you were bitten."

"But you have seen it a number of times now," he said confused.

"No, I haven't. I always look straight ahead—never down."

Darcy nodded his head in understanding at what she was trying to do, and he started to laugh. "Well, then I must have been with someone else on the night of December 24th because that lady definitely looked at me."

"All right. I confess. I did look at you—in all your majesty," she said, smiling. Darcy, overwhelmed by the power of her love, pulled her onto his chest and held her against his heart.

❧

After pouring himself a whisky, Darcy went and sat next to Elizabeth on the sofa. "Are you sure you don't want anything?"

"No," she answered, as she rested her head on his shoulder. "I have everything I want right here."

"You must promise me never to..." Before he could finish, she was shaking her head. "Elizabeth, you are my wife and have taken a vow of obedience to your husband." Lizzy kept shaking her head. "Why?" he asked in an exasperated voice.

"Although I must accept that I cannot be with you when you are a wolf, I refuse to be kept from you when you are not."

"You do not understand the process."

"Oh, I do. You explained it all to me. Your mind is slower to transform than your body, but if you think about it, I believe my being here accelerated that process. When we started to make love, you were more wolf than man. By the time we had finished, you were more man than wolf."

"You call that lovemaking? I was brutal to you."

Lizzy assured him with her smile that he had not been a brute, and he could tell from her scent and the light in her eyes that she was telling the truth. After standing up, he took her hand and walked with her to the fur rug in front of the fireplace.

"You look lovely," he said as he helped her out of her robe, and he whispered, "I love you" as she stepped out of her nightgown. He knelt down on the rug, gently pulling her to the floor, and after tasting and touching every inch of her, he entered her, and in her mind, he was fully human.

CHAPTER 37

AFTER MAKING LOVE, LIZZY and Darcy fell into a deep sleep, and it was only a dying fire and a chilly room that awakened the exhausted pair. There was also the matter of a not quite eighteen-year-old Georgiana. Since she did not know they were in the study, she must be wondering why the newlyweds were still abed at noon, especially since she was teased unmercifully by her brother about her habit of sleeping so late into the day. So instead of crawling into a warm bed, both scooted up the backstairs, got dressed, and joined Georgiana in the sitting room, finding her dressed for another day of playing in the snow.

Darcy needed little encouragement, and both returned to their rooms to change into something more appropriate for an outing. Georgiana was eager to show her brother the snowman they had created the previous day, but when they stepped out onto the portico, they could see that their creation was now a mound of snow with Darcy's top hat embedded in the pile.

After studying the blob before him, Darcy offered his opinion: "Except for that perfectly good top hat, I must say that I am unimpressed with your efforts."

Georgiana sputtered an explanation for the use of what she thought was an old top hat. She was about to point out the obvious, that yesterday's warm temperatures had caused the snowman to melt, when Lizzy hit him in the back with a snowball. Thus began a blizzard of white missiles flying through the air, with no quarter given by either sex. Victory was declared when Darcy dropped to his knees and covered his head with his hands, indicating defeat.

After they stopped laughing, all agreed that they needed to go into the woods and make another snowman, one that would not fall victim to the rays of the sun. Darcy retrieved the hat and after dusting it off said, "Obviously, that fellow did not appreciate the quality or cost of this hat, so we shall give it to the new snowman, who will, hopefully, take better care of it."

With David and Goliath at their master's heels, they marched off to the woods, and while Lizzy and Georgiana gathered branches, twigs, and rocks for the arms and face, Darcy worked alone in crafting, in his opinion, the perfect snowman, and to show that he was not displeased with his wife and sister for using his apparel to clothe their frozen creation, he took the scarf from around his neck and placed it on the snowman.

When the ladies suggested that he join them in making snow angels, he declined. Although he had been willing to have a snowball fight and to build a snowman, he had to draw the line somewhere. He held firm until the ladies knocked him down.

As they ventured farther into the woods, Darcy pointed out the cave in which he transformed each nightfall. It was an ideal location and perfectly concealed within a copse of trees and thickets. To further put her mind at ease, Darcy explained to Lizzy how the cave was connected to the house through a tunnel that only Mercer and Jackson knew about.

Lizzy commented that it was a well-chosen site and in-dicated that she could rest easy now that she knew how he returned to the house at daybreak. But in her mind, she could picture her husband and his black coat contrasted against the blazing white snow, but because this was now her life, she remained silent.

❧

"Will, so much has happened in such a short time, I almost forgot. It is New Year's Eve," Georgiana reminded her brother.

"So it is. Between the wedding and nightfall, Christmas came and went unobserved, and here we are on the cusp of a new year. Personally, I found 1811 to be the best year of my life," William said, smiling at Lizzy, "but I predict that 1812 will be even better for everyone. Hopefully, Napoleon will be stopped and peace will return to Europe."

"I shall pray for peace in Europe," Georgiana quickly replied. "But, Will, this is also the year I shall come out into society."

"Of course, my apologies for the oversight. Your debut is much more important than something as insignificant as putting an end to two decades of misery caused by that Corsican corporal."

"Your brother is teasing you," Lizzy said, giving him a look to let him know that Georgiana's debut was as important to her as their wedding had been to them. "So what do the Darcys do to usher in the new year?"

"The family and the senior servants gather in the upstairs sitting room," Georgiana explained, "and we bid farewell to the old and welcome in the new with a toast in which we wish everyone health and happiness."

"That is it?" Lizzy asked. "All you do is stare at the clock until it strikes midnight and drink a toast? What about opening the back door to let out the old year?"

"Superstitious nonsense," Darcy grumbled, "practiced by the ignorant and those from the provinces. The custom is especially prevalent in Hertfordshire."

"Well, then, what about the symbols of the new year: coal to ensure the home will always be warm?" Lizzy asked, ignoring his comments.

"No worries there. We have timber enough for a lifetime, and unlike Antony, I pay my coal bills."

"Salt and money to ensure the household will be prosperous?"

"We are not doing too badly financially."

"Bread to ensure that the occupants will be well fed?"

"If you want some bread, I shall ring for a servant."

"Greenery to ensure long life and good luck?" Lizzy said, pretending to be desperate.

"Well, it is true that we did not string garland over the mantel of the drawing room, and there was no wreath upon the door. So with my permission, you may go out tomorrow and cut some holly, which I know you know how to do, and we shall use it as a centerpiece for our New Year's Day dinner," Darcy said, smiling graciously.

"Oh, Elizabeth, he is only teasing," Georgiana said, in case Lizzy did not appreciate her brother's sense of humor. "Do you have any more New Year's customs?"

"Yes, the first dark-haired male stranger is invited into the house, that is, if he comes bearing one of the gifts I mentioned. No matter how humble his station in life, he is invited to take dinner with the family."

"Dark haired?" Darcy asked. "So what you are saying is that if Charles Bingley or Colonel Fitzwilliam were strangers to us, they would not benefit from our hospitality because they have red and blond hair?"

"That is correct, as those with dark hair tend to brood

and scowl more than their fair-haired brethren, making them much more intriguing."

"Oh, Will, Elizabeth is only teasing," Georgiana again piped in, but Lizzy looked away from her husband, refusing to confirm that she truly was in jest.

◦✦◦

Along with the three Darcys, Mr. Jackson, Mrs. Bradshaw, Mrs. Reynolds, Mrs. Brotherton, and Mercer waited for the arrival of 1812 in the upstairs sitting room. Mrs. Bradshaw used the opportunity to "suggest" that a Christmas dinner be served on Twelfth Night with a goose and all the trimmings.

"Of course we must also have a Christmas pudding, and Cassie, the stillroom maid, makes an excellent wassail. It is a Darcy tradition to have a complete Christmas dinner served in the servants' hall as well," Mrs. Bradshaw added, and before Lizzy could say yes or no, the cook had detailed everything that would be on the menu, but she did allow her mistress to decide if the family wished to exchange Christmas gifts.

Mrs. Bradshaw and Mrs. Reynolds, who were believers in early to bed and early to rise, chose to depart two hours before the clock struck midnight. But before returning to her kitchen, Mrs. Bradshaw whispered to Elizabeth, "I have known Mr. Darcy since he was five years old, and I have seen him grow from a sweet boy into a fine man. With all that he suffers, he deserves to be happy, and now that he has you as his wife, he will be." Lizzy, caught completely unawares, was speechless and nodded her thanks.

Minutes before the new year, Darcy asked Mr. Jackson to pour whisky for the men and a Madeira for the ladies, and when the clock tolled the midnight hour, all raised their glasses and wished each other all the best in the new year, and when Georgiana mentioned again that this was the year she would come out into society, everyone laughed.

CHAPTER 38

LIZZY, DARCY, AND GEORGIANA were still at breakfast when Mr. Jackson announced that Teddy had
returned to Pemberley and wished to speak to the master at
his convenience.

"Thank you, Jackson. Tell Teddy that he should visit
with his mother first, and then we shall talk in the library."

As soon as Mr. Jackson mentioned Teddy's name,
Georgiana's face lit up. Lizzy had suspected that she had a romantic interest in the son of her lady's maid and that look had
confirmed it. But there was nothing wrong with a young girl
admiring a handsome young man, especially one who was
her brother's hunting partner and companion. Of course,
Georgiana did not know that Teddy would be leaving for
North America in the spring, and Lizzy knew that she would
be unhappy when she learned of it. But once she had made
her debut, this beautiful girl with her dazzling smile would
have the young gents flying to her like moths to a flame.

While Darcy was meeting with Teddy, Elizabeth received
a note from Lady Helen asking if she could call the next
morning. Of course, it was impossible to deny the request,
and so she wrote a response, her first on the Pemberley statio-
nery. After signing her name as Mrs. Fitzwilliam Darcy, she
handed it to Lord Granyard's groom. When Darcy emerged
from the study, she showed him Nell's letter.

"Well, you may receive her, but I am still annoyed and have no wish to see her until next nightfall. So I shall go riding tomorrow morning."

"Coward."

"Sticks and stones," Darcy said, laughing. "Besides, she asked to visit with you, not me."

"Speaking of visits. What news from Teddy?"

Darcy gestured for Lizzy to follow him into the study because, with all the Darcys in residence, the junior servants were everywhere.

"Apparently, there is a war going on in Herefordshire. There are three groups of Frenchmen: the elite, the bourgeois, and a group of farmers and herders from the Pyrenees. It seems that the first two have been lording it over the other members of the pack, and there has been a peasant revolt. The farmers have elected to emigrate en masse to French-speaking North America, so that will bring the population down to a manageable size. The males will join Teddy and Rupert in the spring, and once they are established in Quebec, they will send for their wives and children. That should be interesting because there are no she wolves in the French delegation, so these men will have to cook and clean and do everything by themselves."

"As you did," Lizzy added.

"Yes, as I did, and I have no doubt of their eventual success as these are rough mountain men, but they are as quarrelsome a group as I have ever met."

"This does not affect the two candidates for my lady's maid, does it?"

"Well, we are down to only one candidate as the other has accepted a marriage proposal from one of the emigrating Frenchmen and will join him once the group is established in their new quarters."

"The thought of working in your household scared off one of the women, did it?"

"It was not me who scared her off. Teddy told her frightful tales about the razor tongue of the mistress of the manor, displays of impertinence to your husband, and…" That was all he could get out before Lizzy punched him in the arm.

"I suspected you had violent tendencies, so I shall have to tame you." He lay down on top of her on the sofa, and she made no objection.

✑

Unsure of what Nell might say, Lizzy had secured Darcy's permission to meet with Lady Helen in his study. Her purpose in coming was twofold. First, she wanted to know if Alpha was annoyed with her as he had given her that impression at daybreak and, second, had he met with her prospective groom?

"Both of those matters are pack business, and I have nothing to do with that. You will have to speak to Mr. Darcy."

"I believe he is upset with me because of what I said to you here at Pemberley. I did not mean to give offense, but you can imagine my surprise when I learned that he was interested in you, and not just because of your lack of rank. You see, I was bitten while Mr. Darcy was away in North America, and fearing risk of discovery, my family insisted that I live in this dreadful, damp convent in Ireland. But when Mr. Darcy returned to England and learned of my fate, he came to Ireland and brought me home. How would you interpret such a generous gesture?" she asked Lizzy, but did not wait for an answer.

"And we get along so well in the wild. We never argue, and Alpha is so attentive to all my needs. He loves to groom me, you know. I merely have to look at him with what he describes as 'eyes the color of a summer sky,' and he comes and rakes his claws through my luxurious fur. I think it is his favorite thing to do."

"I can form no opinion of his intentions as I never witnessed these kindnesses," Lizzy said, trying not to roll her eyes. If Mr. Darcy was so taken in by her beautiful coat and summer sky eyes, then why was she Mrs. Darcy and not Nell? The woman was as dense as an iron skillet. "All that is in the past, so let us leave it there. We are neighbors, and we should be friends."

"But will I continue to be your neighbor? What does Mr. Darcy say about Monsieur Reynard? I fear he has a pointy nose. All Frenchmen have pointy noses. I cannot abide a pointy nose."

Lizzy could not help but laugh. An entire nation with the same physical characteristic? "You will have to ask Mr. Darcy for Monsieur Reynard's physical description, but to say that all Frenchmen have pointy noses is like saying that all Englishmen are short with big bellies. They are both caricatures used in the press to ridicule."

"Will you please ask Mr. Darcy for a detailed description about monsieur and write to me as soon as you do?"

"Of course. But I do know one thing about the Reynard family. They are all gourmands, and when they fled France, their chef came with them."

"Really? Gourmands, you say? With their own chef? The Devonshires have a French chef, and we frequently dine with them. I am very fond of beef in *sauce bourguignon*, *foie gras* with truffles, *confit de canard*, *cassoulet*…"

When Nell finally brought her litany of French dishes to a conclusion, Lizzy could see that Lady Helen was in a much better humor, and she hinted to Lizzy that she might have had a culinary close call. If she had become Mrs. Darcy, she would have been subjected to Mrs. Bradshaw's cooking, and although she was a perfectly good cook, capable of producing roasts and stews, she was not, by any stretch of the imagination, a chef.

❧

"William, how would you describe my eyes," Lizzy asked as her husband brushed her hair, a task he performed each night with great pleasure.

"Dark brown."

"How would you describe my hair?"

"Dark brown and curly."

Lizzy grabbed the brush out of his hand. "So Lady Helen has golden hair and eyes as blue as a summer sky while I have dark brown eyes, the color of bark, and curly dark hair?"

"I would not use the word 'bark.'" Darcy successfully ducked a flying brush. "Are you in need of compliments, my dear?"

"This morning, Nell happened to mention how your favorite thing to do in the whole world is to run your claws through her luxurious coat and to compliment her on her seasonal eye color."

"My favorite thing to do is to run my hands over your luxurious body and to gaze into your dark eyes, which are pieces of onyx carved out of the night sky."

"Ahhh," she said. "That was a good answer."

"As I told you before, Nell is a beautiful woman on the outside, but because she is also selfish and conceited, little beauty shines from within. Since you are beautiful inside and out, there is no comparison to be made. As for running my claws through her coat, when Teddy is not there, I do it so that I might have some peace but also because it makes her drowsy. It is the same as telling children a story so that they will finally fall off to sleep. On the other hand, I hope to keep you awake for most of the night."

"Ahhh, that is another good answer."

After they had made love, Darcy asked Lizzy what she thought would happen in their first year together.

"You and I shall have so much fun getting to know each other better, and I shall learn how to be the mistress of this great estate. Georgiana will come out and will have a brilliant debut, but she will not marry, as she is too young, and I do so want her to marry for love. You and I shall become an uncle and aunt, twice over, with Lydia and Jane, and Anne and Lady Catherine will be frequent visitors to Pemberley. We shall have puppies, all black, running all over the estate, all named Wolfie. I shall succeed in getting Mr. Jackson to smile at least once a month with you present to witness it, and Mrs. Bradshaw will be open to suggestions from me regarding the menus. And by the end of the year, we shall discuss starting our own family."

"All right, my turn," Darcy said. "In the coming year, Nell will marry Monsieur Reynard, and the couple will eat their way to wedded bliss. David and Goliath will finally accept you, or at least stop grumbling when you walk by. As you said, Georgiana will make a brilliant debut, and I agree that she should marry only if she is in love. I shall not deny her what I have. I shall see you grow into your role as mistress of Pemberley, and I shall endeavor to be the best husband I can be. I could tell you that I will be more in love with you next year than I am at this moment, but that is an impossibility as I am filled to overflowing."

As they lay in each other's arms, they continued to talk well into the night about their future together, but neither thought to say anything about the other incarnation of Mr. Darcy.

CHAPTER 39

W ILLIAM AND LIZZY'S FIRST year of marriage could
only be described as blissful. The sole rough spot was
Lizzy's cool reception by the ton, but after six weeks spent in
the company of women who were immoral and unkind and
delighted in ridiculing those whom they considered to be beneath them, she decided it was a compliment to her character
that she did not fit in.

It was during their second year that the couple had their
first disagreement. Darcy steadfastly refused to come to his
wife when she was fertile, and Lizzy knew his reasons. In addition to his fear of losing her in childbirth, he believed that
his children would reject him once they learned of his other
nature. She decided to take the matter into her own hands.
With potpourri sachets scattered about her bedchamber, a
nightgown covered with scented powder, and a body bathed
in perfumed water, her husband's ability to determine where
she was in her cycle faltered, and Lizzy became pregnant.

Although Lizzy's labor was hard and long, there were
no complications. Darcy was so delighted by the birth of
his son, David, that he agreed to father a second child, and
Fitzwilliam Jr. arrived two years later. Darcy was relieved
that both of his children were boys. It would be easier for
lads to understand that their father was a werewolf. His sons
would see their Papa's transformation as something to be

marveled at and not repelled by. But what would a daughter think? He was soon to find out that a little girl would think that her father had hung the moon.

⌒≫

Over Lizzy and Darcy's objections, Georgiana, in her twentieth year, married the widowed Viscount Wilston, the heir to Granyard Hall, and became a mother to his three children. Although Georgiana liked her husband very much, she did not love him, and Lizzy was convinced that she had married into the Granyard family for the protection it afforded her brother and because she loved another. After ten years of marriage, her husband, now the Earl of Granyard, died of a fever, and the Dowager Countess and Mrs. Brotherton returned to Pemberley. It was shortly after Granyard's death that a handsome, dark-haired stranger, Thomas Benson, bought a farmhouse near Lambton. Although an Englishman, the gentleman had gone to America when he was a young man and had made his fortune in steamships, plying the waters of the St. Lawrence River in Canada. After selling his business, he decided to return to his home country to live the life of a gentleman farmer.

Mr. Benson chose New Year's Eve to introduce himself to his neighbors at Pemberley. He had learned that the Darcys celebrated a new year's tradition of welcoming a dark-haired stranger into their home, and so the gentleman came bearing a gift of a pine wreath to ensure long life and good luck and was invited to stay for supper. Despite the lapse of more than a dozen years, Georgiana knew Teddy Brotherton as soon as she saw him. As she had told Lizzy long ago, everything about a werewolf changes, except the eyes, and Georgiana knew those eyes.

Their marriage raised eyebrows among the elite of London society, but Georgiana had tired of their company and was perfectly content to remain in the country with her husband and their two children. Mr. Benson proved to be a stellar citizen and eventually served as the mayor of Lambton. Many people remarked on how well Mr. Darcy and Mr. Benson got on and how much they had in common, especially their need to always be on the move and their love of large black dogs.

~⚬~

From their earliest years, the Darcy children heard stories about wolves who became men during a full moon and who fought evil in both their incarnations. These stories were the favorite of all three, and when it came time for Darcy to tell his children of their Papa's other life, the boys thought it was the most wonderful thing in the world and were thrilled to be let in on his secret. But Annie immediately understood that there were people out in the wider world who would hurt her father if they knew that he was a werewolf, and because of this, Annie told her parents that she would never marry.

Darcy and Lizzy understood their daughter's reasons for making such an offer, but they encouraged her to find a partner with whom she could enjoy a marriage as wonderful as that of her parents. Even though she attracted the attention of many fine gentlemen, she gave them no encouragement. Unlike her mother, who had grown more comfortable with each succeeding nightfall, Annie became more anxious with each full moon. Every time her father went out, she feared that something awful would happen to her beloved Papa. With each passing year, her worries increased, and she would plead with him not to go out when the weather was anything less than ideal. By the time Darcy entered his sixth decade, Lizzy had her own concerns and mentioned them to her husband. As expected, she was rebuffed.

"We have this argument every single nightfall," Darcy said in a harsh tone of voice, which did nothing to deter Lizzy.

"Untrue. We have only had this argument for the last three years—since you turned sixty. You are not as young as you used to be. You have arthritis in your hind legs and shoulders and a sore back. When you come through that panel after nightfall, you are practically creaking."

"If it bothers you, then stop sleeping on the sofa while I am gone."

"Never!" She went over and put her arms around his neck and kissed the top of his head. "If you ever come through that door, and I am not here, you will know that I have gone to meet my maker."

"Elizabeth, do not say that. You know I hate when you say things like that."

"Then show me how much you love me by sleeping in the hidden room."

"No."

And so it went, month after month, until a particularly nasty ice storm barreled in from the north, and with every tree and bush encased in ice and icicles hanging from every eave, Lizzy pleaded with him not to go out in such weather. After uttering a few mild oaths, he stormed off and passed his daughter in the hall without saying a word to her.

"Mama, Papa has a raspiness in his chest. I am sure he has pneumonia," Annie said with tears in her eyes. "There is no way he can hunt tonight, so I do not understand why he must go out. With Uncle Teddy gone, if something happens to him while he is out there," she said, pointing to the window and beyond, "we will not know it. And by the time we find him, he will be dead."

"Yes, yes, I know," Lizzy said. The same thoughts had occurred to her, but having it said aloud was more than she could bear. "I agree and I intend to do something about it, so go to bed. Everything is under control." Lizzy immediately went to her husband's room.

"While you are out there tonight, you might wish to visit me on the terrace because if you insist on going out in this awful weather that is where I shall be. I can be as stubborn as you are."

Darcy sat down on the bed and nodded his head in acknowledgment that she had won. He actually had not intended to go any farther than the cave, but he had said nothing to Lizzy or Annie, knowing that if he readily agreed to their scheme, the pair of them would be after him to remain in the house every nightfall, and he hated being cooped up.

"I am henpecked and chickpecked by the two women in my life, and if I am to have any peace, I must do as they ask."

"Thank you," she said and hugged him, but he refused to put his arms around her waist, and so she put them there herself. "I shall go and get your water bowl. Do you want any meat?"

"Yes, and a bone as well. Since I will not be hunting for the next two days, I shall have to find ways to kill time. Now won't I?"

"You know Annie and I will visit you." Before leaving, she blew him a kiss.

Although she had succeeded in keeping him indoors on this particular nightfall, the time for a permanent solution had come, and so tonight she would implement a plan that she had been thinking about for the last few years. After the entire house was asleep, Lizzy went down to the study. After putting her ear to the hidden door and determining that Will was asleep, she slid back the panel.

"So you snore as badly when a wolf as you do when a man. I suspected as much," Lizzy said to her sleeping husband. "Look at you. You are dead to the world, but you were going to go out on such a night. What a mule you are." She spread out a blanket and sat down next to him. After running her hand along the length of his coat, she could hear the change in his breathing as he responded to her touch, and she whispered to him, "'Entreat me not to leave thee or return from following after thee; for wither thou goest, I shall go.' I love you, Fitzwilliam Darcy." She put her finger into his mouth and pressed it against his tooth. After squeezing her finger to make sure that there was blood, she lay down on the blanket and backed into him. As he did when he was in his human form, he rested his front paw on her arm, and they spooned, or as much as a wolf and future wolf are capable of spooning.

FINAL NOTE

During the Darcys' lifetime, the werewolf population in Great Britain dropped significantly. With the arrival of the Industrial Age, forests and woodlands were being denuded, and there were few safe places for a werewolf to hide. Most chose to emigrate to British North America or to the sparsely populated areas of the upper American Midwest. As a result, incidences of contact between werewolves and humans dropped dramatically in England as well as in Western Europe, and none was recorded in Britain after 1832.

The final entry in the records of the Council was the death in 1856 of the last surviving werewolf living in England. The Council was disbanded the following year, and the Underhill property was deeded over to the National Trust of Scotland, and thus an era where wolves—and werewolves—had roamed the British Isles came to an end.

Acknowledgments

Without the support of my editor at Sourcebooks, Deb Werksman, my third Austen reimagining would not have become a reality. I would also like to acknowledge my readers on Jane Austen fan fiction sites—where a much rougher version of this story, titled *Mr. Darcy and the Eve of All Saints' Day*, first appeared—as well as Tony Grant of the United Kingdom for helping me with the Scottish dialogue. There is also a great group of ladies and one gentleman at www.austenauthors.com who provide support for writers who cannot seem to get enough of Jane Austen.

ABOUT THE AUTHOR

Mary Lydon Simonsen, the author of *Searching for Pemberley*, *The Perfect Bride for Mr. Darcy, Anne Elliot, A New Beginning*, and *The Second Date, Love Italian-American Style*, has combined her love of history and the novels of Jane Austen in her third story inspired by *Pride and Prejudice*. The author lives in Arizona. For more information, please visit http://marysimonsenfanfiction.blogspot.com.

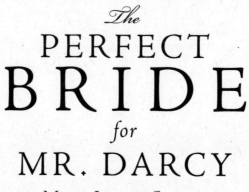

The
PERFECT
BRIDE
for
MR. DARCY
by Mary Lydon Simonsen

If the two of them weren't so stubborn...

It's obvious to Georgiana Darcy that the lovely Elizabeth Bennet is her brother's perfect match, but Darcy's pigheadedness and Elizabeth's wounded pride are going to keep them both from the loves of their lives.

Georgiana can't let that happen, so she readily agrees to help her accommodating cousin, Anne de Bourgh, do everything within their power to assure her beloved brother's happiness.

But the path of matchmaking never runs smoothly...

Praise for *Searching for Pemberley*
"A precious jewel of a novel with a strong love story and page-turning mystery. Absorbing, amusing, and very cleverly written."
— *The Searcher*, Newsletter of NEPA Genealogy Society

978-1-4022-4025-6 • $14.99 U.S./£9.99 UK

SEARCHING *for* PEMBERLEY

BY MARY LYDON SIMONSEN

Maggie went in search of a love story, but she never expected to find her own…

Desperate to escape her life in a small Pennsylvania mining town, Maggie Joyce accepts a job in post-World War II London, hoping to find adventure. While touring Derbyshire, she stumbles upon the stately Montclair, rumored by locals to be the inspiration for Pemberley, the centerpiece of Jane Austen's beloved *Pride and Prejudice*. Determined to discover the truth behind the rumors, Maggie embarks on a journey through the letters and journals of Montclair's former owners, the Lacey family, searching for signs of Darcy and Elizabeth.

But when the search introduces her to both a dashing American pilot and a handsome descendant of the "Darcy" line, Maggie must decide how her own love story will end…

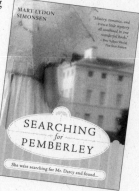

Praise for *Searching for Pemberley*

"A shining addition to the world of historical fiction."
– CURLED UP WITH A GOOD BOOK

"A resounding success on all levels."
– ROUNDTABLE REVIEWS

978-1-4022-2439-3 • $14.99 U.S./£7.99 UK

Mr. Darcy, Vampyre
Pride and Prejudice continues...
Amanda Grange

"A seductively gothic tale..." —Romance Buy the Book

A test of love that will take them to hell and back...

My dearest Jane,

My hand is trembling as I write this letter. My nerves are in tatters and I am so altered that I believe you would not recognise me. The past two months have been a nightmarish whirl of strange and disturbing circumstances, and the future...

Jane, I am afraid.

It was all so different a few short months ago. When I awoke on my wedding morning, I thought myself the happiest woman alive...

978-1-4022-3697-6
$14.99 US/$18.99 CAN/£7.99 UK

"Amanda Grange has crafted a clever homage to the Gothic novels that Jane Austen so enjoyed." —*AustenBlog*

"Compelling, heartbreaking, and triumphant all at once."
—*Bloody Bad Books*

"The romance and mystery in this story melded together perfectly... a real page-turner." —*Night Owl Romance*

"Mr. Darcy makes an inordinately attractive vampire.... *Mr. Darcy, Vampyre* delights lovers of Jane Austen that are looking for more." —*Armchair Interviews*